CITRON
PRESS

RICHARD **JENKINS**

Richard Jenkins grew up in Northern Ireland and spent many years living in Swansea: the only two places he has ever really called home. After working as a musician, in an engineering factory, and as a youth worker, he trained in social anthropology, and has carried out research in Belfast, the West Midlands, south Wales and western Denmark. The father of two grown-up sons, he currently lives and teaches in Sheffield. Although he has written a number of anthropology and sociology books, this is his first published novel.

CITRON
PRESS

Fresh ideas from

NEW AUTHORS
CO-OPERATIVE

Published by Citron Press
Connors Corp. Ltd., Suite 155, Business Design Centre,
52 Upper Street, Islington Green, London N1 0QH, Great Britain
www.citronpress.co.uk

ISBN 0754400182

Printed and bound in Great Britain by Esparto Digital Ltd., Slack Lane, Derby.

Walter de la Mare's *Silver* is quoted by permission of the Literary Trustees of Walter de la Mare, and the Society of Authors, as their representative.

A copy of this book is held at the British Library.

THE ARCHAEOLOGIST

RICHARD **JENKINS**

The archaeologist is digging up, not things, but people. Unless the bits and pieces with which he deals be alive to him, unless he have himself the common touch, he had better seek out other disciplines for his exercise... Dead archaeology is the driest dust that blows.

Sir Mortimer Wheeler

CHAPTER ONE

DEVIL'S LEAP

Gregory Alexander woke early. His travelling alarm clock was still silent. For a moment, in the strange bed with its soft mattress and heavy covers, he was not sure where he was. In the dusk of receding sleep a shy and shapeless shadow lurked, a trace perhaps of something that had just happened or was just about to happen. If he had been dreaming, he couldn't remember what about. Whatever it was, whatever it had been, the fugitive feeling didn't disturb him. Beyond the rails and spindles of the wooden bedfoot he could see thin cold sunshine, entering the room through a gap at one end of the heavy green boarding-house curtains and catching his clothes, folded tidily over the back of an armchair. The light was sharp and dustless. Under the quilt none of the air's chill reached him. A faint smell of bacon frying did. Tucking the covers more snugly round his cheeks and chin, he dozed off again. There was no rush.

As the coffin was lowered into the hole, Gregory looked up. The earlier promise of a bright, mild day had faded into a bank of plate-grey cloud which hung upon the Hill, almost seeming to touch the back wall of the graveyard as it reached up towards the rough heather, whin bushes and rock of the moor beyond. The kirk, such an enormous and imposing building to him in his childhood, seemed tiny now, almost pathetic in its refusal to acknowledge the final power of the elements that weathered its paint and penetrated its crumbling slate roof, and the damp that seeped up through its foundations and walls. It still had a congregation that saw to it that paint was applied when strictly necessary, and roofers summoned after each gale, but there was no mistaking the signs and portents of decay. Setting its strait-laced back firmly to the wilderness, the kirk put on the bravest face it could for the benefit of the village that stretched out beneath its gate.

One in the small gathering of mourners was looking at him without any pretence of doing otherwise. He knew the face well enough, Mr Muirhead from the wee shop on the corner of his mother's street. His mother had always said that Muirhead had no manners: ill-reared and it showed. Gregory turned his attention back to the box which contained her remains. His mother's street: how long now since it had been his street? Twenty years? He wasn't sure that it had ever been his street. God knows, but there'd always been somebody ready to charge him the price of belonging to it. Even now he could feel the righteous prurience of Mr Muirhead's eyes upon him. Some things probably never changed.

The minister had finished. Gregory had not been listening, so it came as an abrupt surprise to find himself shaking the thrust-out hand. Reverend Taggart was an old man now, eighty or more perhaps by the look of him. He had come out of retirement specially to bury Martha Alexander. He had come that day from a Church of Scotland retirement home near Troon, driven by a deferential young minister, a son of one of his nephews apparently. It was the same hand that had christened the infant Gregory Thompson Hume Alexander. The same hand that had pulled his ear or cuffed the back of his head over poorly memorised scripture. The same hand that had once stroked the inside of his thigh, sitting next to him on the back seat of the coach on a Sunday School outing to the holiday camp at Ayr, telling him all the while how Jesus loved little children.

'She was a good woman Gregory.' The old man still held him fast by the same hand. Despite himself Gregory was drawn into meeting the minister's washed-out gaze. The cold March wind forced tears into the pouches and wrinkles behind the thick spectacle lenses. He seemed not to notice that Gregory did not answer. 'Aye, she was that indeed. An example to us all, God rest her.'

Gregory said nothing. Held fascinated, like a rabbit by a fox, he waited for the strike. Reverend Taggart sniffed. A drop of water was forming on the end of his nose.

'I know. At a time like this there's never anything to be said.' Reverend Taggart patted Gregory's hand once, twice, once again, before releasing it. 'I'll be going now. I'll leave you to...' He gestured down into the dark earth of the grave. 'I'll be at the Manse for a wee while, with Mr Lynas.'

Gregory breathed out. He felt a racing pulse of relief in his temples and ribcage as the old man's back moved away down the gravel path towards the village, his grandnephew in attendance under his left arm. Most of the mourners fell in behind him. Those who shook Gregory's hand before they left, did so with the briefest of contact and the shortest of muttered condolences. He thanked them and tried not to smile. Mr Muirhead didn't bother.

Some people, however, remained standing at the graveside. Beyond the pile of dirt and stones under which Martha Alexander would now lie forever, the two gravediggers stood waiting. One of them - about Gregory's age but with more hair left on his head - looked familiar, but Gregory had no idea who he was. Two five-pound notes changed hands: the younger of the two, awkward with his spade in one hand, looking as if he were about to say something. Gregory turned away. He didn't much care what they thought. Grief would be held to excuse him.

Charlie Hume was there waiting for him. Best blue suit, serge and double-breasted, and a black armband. White shirt and a black tie. Younger than his sister by nearly fifteen years, Uncle Charlie's nose and cheeks had been scoured to a deep, grainy blush by a lifetime of working in the open air. He took his watch out of his waistcoat pocket. The battered silver casing caught what there was of the light. A quarter to twelve. The bar of the Glenvie Hotel would already be open and busy. Charlie smiled.

'Alright Gregory?'

'Aye Charlie, I'm fine.'

'Come away then. Let's be gettin' on before the rain.' He turned back briefly and nodded. 'Alec, Rab... Thanks a lot. We'll be off now.' The gravediggers nodded in reply, and bent their backs to the pile of soil that still had to be shifted. As much like brothers as uncle and nephew, Gregory and Charlie turned their back on the scratch of the shovel's dip, the clatter of earth and stones on varnished wood.

The stag's head which was mounted on the wall over the hotel bar had one thing in common with the Mona Lisa: no matter where you sat, the glass beads that were now its eyes followed you. So folk had always said, anyway. For as long as Gregory could remember the faded head and antlers had been there, between the antique mirror advertising Beecham's Pills, and the King's Own Scottish Borderers plaque; held together by dust and cobwebs as much as anything else. Some landlord who had the hotel before the war thought that the tourists might like it – as indeed they might have done, if there had been any. Mind you, there hadn't been any deer either.

Charlie came back over with the drinks. A pint of Gillespies for himself and a gin and tonic for his nephew. Gregory had decided that his usual scotch and ginger would provoke too much local contempt. Charlie lifted the gin to his nose and wrinkled his face.

'Dinna tell me ye actually like thon stuff? Smells more like scent than drink.' The uncle sat down, slowly, a man who was finding his legs and back stiffer with every winter. 'Folk'll be talkin' aboot ye.'

Gregory shrugged and smiled. 'Aye well... Cheers.' He liked Charlie and it was good to see him. 'Good health.'

'Aye. Same to you too.' He took a long sup at the head on the black beer. It left a thin cream moustache. 'So then young Gregory, how're ye keepin'?' The conversational niceties appropriate to the occasion: the tributes to mother and sister, as became polite and mutual hypocrisy, had been disposed of before the funeral. 'What hae ye been doing wi' yerself?'

'Not a lot. You know how it is. This and that.'

Charlie took a fresh swallow of his pint and waited for Gregory to continue. He didn't know how it was, but he didn't miss knowing either. Inasmuch as he wanted to hear news, it was news from another mysterious world, the world that his nephew inhabited. Sophistication perhaps, gossip and scandal from below the border. This and that.

'It's quiet at the moment Charlie. Things are always a bit hectic in work, we've so many students these days we don't where to put them. We had all those cuts a few years back, but things're a wee bit better now... I think we've seen the worst of it in my department. We're safe enough for the time being.'

'It must be grand, all the same... Ah, but your father'd'ae been proud of ye, may he rest in peace. To think of it...Thompson Alexander's wee boy grown up tae be a lecturer in a university...and in England too. Who ever'd've thought it?'

'Not so much of the wee boy, please. And it's Wales. Not the same thing at all.' Gregory laughed quietly. His glass was nearly empty. 'Another?'

At the bar, Gregory exchanged subdued pleasantries with the barman. Douglas looked as if he had been pulling pints there at least as long as the stag had been watching over the place. He had certainly always been there in Gregory's time. He was sorry to hear about Gregory's mother, a fine woman. Still, we all have to go sometime, don't we? And if you had to pick how to go, in your sleep like that, it could have been worse. There are worse things. A couple of men standing at the other end of the bar nodded their agreement and murmured in commiseration.

Walking back to the table, something dawned on Gregory. It had been bothering him since they had first walked through the engraved glass doors. Something a wee bit odd, but he couldn't quite place it. Now it came to him. There was not one woman to be seen at lunchtime in the bar of the Glenvie Hotel. Not one. Not behind the counter, not in front of it. Something else that obviously hadn't changed.

By the time the doors of the Glenvie closed behind them, it was after three. Gregory's head was thick with gin, although Charlie didn't seem too much the worse for five pints, chased down by two or three Cream of the Barleys. They crossed the town square, wet with the rain of the early afternoon showers. Past the Cenotaph, with Thompson Alexander's name added as a Korean War afterthought, round the corner by the police station, up the hill as it curved round towards the wee street where there now stood an empty terraced house.

Charlie cast a careful eye over his nephew as they walked along side by side, observing that Gregory could have been steadier on his feet around the corners. He couldn't remember the last time the lad had been home for anything more than a flying visit. Or the last time they had sat down together for a drink. It was just a shame that it had to wait for this. Still, maybe they'd see more of him in the future, now that the house was his. Now that his mother was... Charlie pushed the thought away, and turned back to consider the house. Mind you, now that it was his, what would he want to be doing with it...? Hard to imagine.

They were standing in front of the door. Lace curtains, polished brass, doorstep scrubbed until it shone. Martha Alexander had only been cold five days and the mist of her breath on the windows had yet to fade. Gregory dug into his pocket and brought out her keys. They hung on a clear plastic fob with a Biblical text captured within: 'But seek ye first the kingdom of God, and his righteousness.' Another verse went through his head, an echo from Sunday School. He was sure that he'd got it wrong: 'Blessed are the little children, forbid them not, for of such is the kingdom of Heaven'.

'Keys to the kingdom Charlie, eh?' He dangled them from one finger. Front door, back door, coal shed, yard. It was the first time that Gregory had possessed his own keys for the house in which he had grown up.

'Aye, well, it's yours now.' There was a silence. 'Ye'll be wantin' to sell it I suppose?'

'No...no, I don't think I'll be selling it.'

'What d'ye mean? No' sell it? What'll you want wi' a...'

'Oh, I don't want it Charlie. No. Sure I've a place of my own.' Gregory turned to face the older man. 'In fact I want nothing to do with it. Here, you have it. Here.' He placed the keys in Charlie's hand and closed his fingers on them. 'Here, go on, it's all yours. I'll get my solicitor to sort out the papers. All you need's a new key ring.'

'But Gregory, it's... I dinna...'

'Hold your wheesht now. D'you not think it's about time you had a place of your own? And anyway, it's more yours by right than it is mine...after all, it was you looked after the auld...well...it was you, not me.'

'That's no way tae talk...'

'Maybe not, but it's true. And I want to hear no more about it.' Gregory could imagine the faces behind the curtains up and down the street. The eyes and noses, peering and sniffing, watching and wondering what was going on. 'I'm going now. I'll be off home later on this afternoon. Away you on in and sort yourself out. I'll drop you a line.'

Charlie looked at Gregory and looked at the keys and looked at Gregory again. He said nothing, but put out his right hand and took his nephew's arm with his left. They shook hands and Gregory walked away, leaving his uncle alone on the pavement. Disinherited by a ghost before ever his foot had passed over the threshold, Gregory did not turn round for one last look. Sobering up rapidly, he retraced his steps. There were a few spots of fresh rain in the air.

At about half past seven that evening, a red Ford Escort with a Cardiff registration drove slowly out of Glenvie. The rain had stopped, but there were more clouds gathering, stealing away what little was left of the light. The motorway to the north of Carlisle was no more than two hours away, taking the drive at a steady pace. A nap in the guest house – 'Highland Vista', run by a couple who had moved from Doncaster a few years earlier – followed by an extravagant plateful of meat and potato pie, with apple crumble and custard for pudding, had restored Gregory to something approaching readiness for the trip.

Up the side of the hill ran the road, across the moor and away down the other side, coming gradually on to the gentle roll of the lowland stretching away to the eventual sea. Halfway down, the road crossed over a small glen, a precipitous wooded ravine. The bridge was a grand and substantial viaduct of five high arches, stalking through the air with the brash confidence of Victorian progress, contemptuous of the rush and rumble of the river below. In his childhood Gregory had heard stories about the Devil's Leap. When the moon was full - or was it when there was no moon? - you could hear the Devil howling from the rocks below, trapped in a cave under the waterfall below the bridge.

He parked the car at the end of the bridge, being careful to leave his sidelights on for safety's sake. On the back seat was the heavy wooden box, the one thing that he had taken from the house before the funeral. The only thing that he had wanted. It was locked. The brass key, green with disuse, was in his pocket. Inside were papers, photographs, medals, letters, certificates. His mother's hoard. Her claim on the lives of Thompson and Gregory Alexander. Gregory did not know exactly what it contained. That far he had never been trusted. He knew that he hadn't been trusted that far now.

Standing in the middle of the great stone span he lifted the box over his head. It was heavy enough to require both hands. Then it went, almost without premeditation, down into the darkness of the water and the stones. There was no sound from the Devil tonight. Gregory walked back to the car and drove away.

CHAPTER TWO

THE FRONT PAGE

'Have you seen this? Have you fucking seen this?'

Gregory did not have to lift his head from the essay he had just finished reading, or swivel his chair round, to recognise the speaker. The sudden entry without knocking. The pervasive smell of French cigarettes. The ever-so-familiar voice, awkwardly sliding up and down the register between profundity and squeaky excitement. Philip. He had every other aspect of his public presence under control, but not his voice. And it always gave the game away. Always. Philip was squeaking now.

Gregory's chair needed oiling. It squeaked too as he turned to face his visitor. The younger by perhaps five years, Philip stood waving a newspaper. The Western Gazette by the look of things.

Along nearly every dimension the contrast between the two was absolute. Gregory wore a subdued dark green crew-neck sweater, a checked shirt without a tie, brown jumbo cord jeans and tan desert boots. His thinning head of wavy brown hair was cut to no particular style or length and parted on one side. Philip's hair was definitely styled: black, dull and dyed, very short at the back and sides and then straight up into a flat top. His moustache, by contrast, was its natural mousy brown. Over a baggy T-shirt with a complex geometrical pattern of black and yellow, red braces held up wide bright blue serge trousers with turn-ups. Red lace-up boots, a green suede jacket marked with shiny patches of wear, and a pair of Ray-ban sunglasses on a string round his neck completed the outfit. A gold half moon hung from his right earlobe. As usual, Philip was dressed for anything.

'Good morning, Philip. Nice to see you too. How are you?'

Philip didn't answer. His elbow locked straight and rigid, he held the paper out to Gregory. He waggled it up and down with the urgency of a demand.

Gregory gave in quickly. 'Okay, okay, have I seen what? Let's have a look at that.'

It was The Gazette. 'The Voice of the People of South Wales' was the proud boast above the title. On the front-page the main headline read, 'GAY SCANDAL IN COUNTY SCHOOLS'. It was sub-headed, 'Councillor accuses lecturer of pervert propaganda', and underneath there was a fuzzy picture of the public representative involved. Plump and well-scrubbed, Councillor Bill Standup was elected member for the University ward. Standup, Standup for Jesus...it was an obvious local joke.

Gregory read on. What was it all about? Skimming over the page it wasn't easy to tell. Particularly with Philip fidgeting in the doorway, looking for something to occupy the animation that possessed his hands. He plucked a book from the shelves and Gregory turned his attention back to the paper.

Councillor Standup was creating a lot of fuss and press attention. He was a prospective parliamentary candidate too, Gregory remembered. There was nothing new in that. But this time he was up in arms about Philip's health education research programme into public awareness of HIV. Further down, the article said that the research team had been interviewing teenagers in local schools about their knowledge of safe sex precautions and – which seemed to be what the fuss was about – their sexual orientations and activities. According to the reporter, someone called Gaynor Preece, researchers had told the pupils 'that being gay was perfectly normal and a good thing to be.' She went on:

'The matter came to Councillor Standup's attention when a distraught parent contacted him to complain that her fifteen-year-old daughter came home in tears after being interrogated by a lesbian student. The girl told her it was normal to be homosexual and asked her if she was a lesbian too. Councillor Standup is due to raise the matter at tonight's meeting of Llanorgan Borough Council and is demanding an inquiry from the Education Department and the University.'

The piece finished with outraged reaction from a local Evangelical lay preacher, who suggested that eternal hellfire was not only too good for 'these people' but the very best they could expect on Judgement Day; and a 'no comment' from 'a University spokesman'.

Gregory folded the newspaper carefully and put it on the desk. 'I take it that this is all as daft as it sounds?' His confident tone belied growing unease: what had Philip done now?

'Of course it is. What d'you think?' Gregory did not feel much like answering that question. Philip replaced the book he had been pretending to read, P. V. Glob's *Mound People*. It remained sticking out at an awkward angle, interrupting the tidy line in which Gregory liked to keep his books. 'What the fuck d'you think I am? Completely mad?'

Gregory didn't feel like answering that question either. What he really wanted was to get back to his essay marking. It was the last week of the spring term and he had yet to put the finishing touches to the paper he was due to read to a conference at Southampton the weekend after next. And he couldn't get on with that until he had dealt with the backlog of essays, on time and late, that always accumulated at this time of year. And he didn't want to be anywhere near Philip. He didn't even want to see Philip, let alone get involved in whatever his issue of the moment was.

Philip's life was full of issues. Typically issues around things rather than about them, but issues for all that. And typically other people's. Instead of saying any of this, Gregory contented himself with a close examination of the neat fingernails on his left hand while his visitor continued.

'Of course it's not bloody true.' Philip had moved out of the open doorway now and sat down in one of the plastic chairs ranged along the back wall of the office, under the glass cabinet filled with flint tools and potsherds. 'That bastard Standup's got the pink peril on the brain. Poofters under the bed...' Philip laughed, and then began to giggle. 'He should be so lucky.'

'So, what's the problem then? Don't tell me that he's made it all up?'

'Well, no...not exactly. Not made it up.'

'So?'

'Well, it's just what it says, really...it's the research project on health education and HIV. You know, the safe sex study.'

Gregory knew something about it. He had, in fact, felt more than a nip of envy when he had read about it in *In-House*, the college newsletter, before Christmas. It was the kind of coup of which promotions are made. The Vice-Chancellor had lauded the project as an example of the kind of contemporary relevance that would enable the college to expand and build 'towards the Millennium'. A good bit more than a hundred thousand it was, from the Department of Health and the Welsh Office...a figure which went much of the way towards explaining the V-C's enthusiasm.

'...It's quite simple, really. We're interviewing fifth and sixth formers, and such sweet young things they are too, about their knowledge of...'

'But what's all this? Telling them it's good to be gay, that it's normal?'

'That's part of the warm-up for the interview, to reassure them that being gay or lesbian's not unnatural. To try and get them to feel okay about admitting if they've...come on Gregory, how the fuck can we expect them to if...all we say is that it's nothing to be ashamed of.'

'So what do you ask them? You know, whether they've ever...'

'Just if they've ever had sex with a member of the same sex. And if so, what kind of sex and whether they used precautions or not. And if so, what. That's all.'

'And you ask them about ordinary...about straight sex too?'

'Oh yes.' Philip assumed his outraged what-do-you-mean-my-dear look that Gregory used to find so funny. 'We ask them about that. Naturally.'

'And do they tell you?'

'Some of them.'

'Did the headmaster know what you were going to ask them?'

'Of course he did. Don't be stupid. And the bloody County Education Committee... we got the permission of everyone except the Prince of Wales and the rugby selectors. We sent home notes to parents explaining all about it. All the kids have the option to refuse. And some have. Nobody's making them do it, they don't have to be bloody well interviewed... For fuck's sake Greg, the Welsh Office is funding it. We've only had this one complaint.'

'Fine. So what's all the fuss about?'

'It's this bastard Standup... If he works up enough righteous indignation it'll ruin the whole project. And we're not even half-way through the interviewing yet. Po-faced-fucking-Chapel-sanctimony I can live without just at the moment.'

'So why don't you just talk to the newspaper? Explain what the research is all about.'

'What good would that do? Can't you just see it? Play right into their hands, that would. I can just see it... And anyway, why? What right do they have? Why should I have to?' Philip was back on his feet now, colour flushing into his cheeks. 'So they can twist it round to make it mean whatever they want? At least if I don't talk to them, they can't make it up... Why should I offer those bastards an opportunity on a plate for some more queer-bashing?'

'I suppose you could argue that, well, it's public money after all. People have a right to know about it.'

'Right to know! Right to know, my arse!... It's got nothing to do with a right to know... it's all about a good story. Selling papers. Fags and fairies on the front fucking page. You should hear yourself, right to know, public money... pathetic. Who believes that shit? It'll be the freedom of the press next!'

Once again, as ever with Philip, Gregory could not come to his own rescue with an appropriate reply. Philip stood over him. 'So, what're we going to do about it then?'

'What d'you mean we?' Gregory could hear the trap being set.

'I mean me, you, Michael and Anthony', who worked in the Registry, 'James', Mechanical Engineering, 'Rosemary and Claire', Drama and the Library respectively, 'and...'

'And Uncle Tom Cobbley and all, I suppose? Come on Philip, what d'you expect us to do? A torchlight procession? You're not on Christopher Street now, you know. And anyway, nothing's happened yet... It'll all blow over if you keep your head down. No point in...'

'I want you to sign a letter to Rees.' Philip sat back down. 'Asking him to publicly repudiate Standup, to underline his commitment to gay rights and civil liberties, and to reaffirm his support for academic freedom.'

'But he doesn't support academic freedom... Talk about me being naive. And as for gay rights...'

'But he won't have any choice.'

'Rubbish. D'you honestly expect me to write to the Vice-Chancellor, telling him to...'

'Asking him, asking him.'

'Asking him publicly to tell Standup where to go? That's great, just great. I don't know, he'll...'

'Are you saying you won't do it?' Philip was standing again. On his feet and on his dignity. 'I suppose I should have known better. David said you wouldn't have the nerve.'

'I don't care what David said. And I don't see why we have to bring him into it please.'

'My God, just listen to you.' Philip camped his voice into a passable lowland Scots and put one hand on his hip. 'I don't see why we have to bring him into it... I bet you don't.'

'Do we have to do this? All I'm saying is that there's no sense in stirring up a hornet's nest for nothing.' Gregory was increasingly aware of the open door, the corridor, goodness only knew who was listening. 'And let's not get heated.'

'Oh no, we couldn't get heated. We wouldn't want that would we? Don't worry. I'm going...Wouldn't want to spoil your senior lectureship chances, would we now?' Before Gregory could rise to this, Philip was gone. Seconds later, a slammed door indicated that he had gone down the stairs round the corner.

Gregory looked at the wall for a minute and stood up. He shook his head and looked out of the window. The ad hocery of the University College of South Wales spread out in front of him, an inglorious jumble of old and new, stone and cement, venerable horse chestnuts and arriviste willows leaning over ornamental, but now fishless, fishponds. Beyond the buildings were the windswept playing fields. Beyond them, there was the abrupt line of the cliff which isolated the town of Llanorgan from the beach, with its fossils and pavement rock formations, and the Bristol Channel. From this angle the town - the Promenade, the Pier, the ranks of Edwardian guest houses - was out of vision, but off to the left Gregory could see the lighthouses, old and new, and the eroded remains of Caer Isaf, an iron age promontory fort.

Leaning out towards the glass, Gregory could look down into the broad courtyard formed by the wings of the Humanities Building. As he watched, Philip emerged from the main entrance. A young man with bleached-blonde spiky hair and a leather jacket, who had been sitting under one of the flowering cherry trees, rose to meet him. He touched Philip on the arm in an unaffected gesture of recognition and they walked together towards Management and Social Sciences, a smoked glass stack looming gracelessly over the classical revivalist lines of the Library.

Gregory turned away and sat at his desk again. He picked up the essay: 'Discuss the impact upon our understanding of European prehistory of calibrated radiocarbon dating.' It was terrible. He wrote in the mark, forty per cent. Delyth Dunwoody, despite the fact that he'd just given her first-year group a tutorial on it, hadn't even read, let alone understood, Colin Renfrew. Firming up his grip on the red pen he began to write his comments in a precise and tidy hand.

CHAPTER THREE

THE PARTY

Ellie Sollenheimer's party was on its way to secure establishment as an annual institution in the busy and somewhat self-absorbed social life of Llanorgan West. By a mysterious process of unspoken election, the last Friday of the university's spring term seemed by now to have been allocated as its slot in the calendar.

Although Ellie had only been in the department for five years, three years less than Gregory – had it really been that long since old Witherspoon had had his stroke? – it probably seemed like forty to some of their colleagues. Forty years and a plague of locusts. He did not share their distaste for her American informality, or her businesslike approach. What really galled them, he was sure, was not that she was good, respectably published and relatively young – or at least not only that – but that she was a woman. The first in the department's history. Not bad looking, either, as Adrian had slyly observed the day she'd been interviewed for the job. And she was well liked by the students. Her third book, an introduction to practical archaeology for local historians and amateur enthusiasts, was due out in the autumn. Not least because it might actually sell a few copies, it could only make the pomposity – her description of most of her colleagues – even more condescending, even more dismissive, and even more threatened. They'd never admit to being threatened, of course, but none of them dared miss her parties. Ellie was a breath of fresh air, and the closest thing to a friend that Gregory had along the corridor.

At this Gregory began to detect the stirring of a germ of something approximating to tepid enthusiasm. He hated parties. Never knew what to do at them. It was hard enough to make small talk with people he knew, let along mingle with complete strangers. Mingle...the very word suggested something amorphous and shapeless, the social equivalent of an amoeba, neither proper conversation nor polite inattention. And that was before you even began to consider the people who went to parties...Gregory remembered something that Oscar Wilde was supposed to have said...about not wanting to go to any party he was invited to. That wasn't quite the exact quote though...

Still, it was Ellie's party, and he'd only stay for an hour or so. At the most. Just long enough to pass himself...that had been one of his mother's favourite expressions, as she dinned the virtues of respectability and the importance of what other folk might think into her son's head. Even if it had not been Ellie's party, the weight of his sense of social obligation, the terror of what might be said about him if he didn't go, would probably have pushed his reluctant feet towards the festivities.

It was ten past ten. Gregory had only just made it to the off-licence in time. Working late on his conference paper, he had finally agreed a title with himself: 'Social Theory, Conceit and the Limits of Interpretation: A Critique of the New Archaeology'. That should give them something to think about at Southampton. He shuddered, clutched the litre bottle of Bulgarian Merlot to ward off the demons waiting on the other side of the door, and rang the bell. It was a three-storied terraced house in a narrow street just off the Promenade, and the ground-level bay window was open. A hubbub of loud music and louder voices was only inefficiently muffled by the partly drawn curtains. Gregory had to press the button three times before anybody came.

'Greg...I thought you weren't coming. You shoulda just come on in, the door's open.' Ellie grabbed him, smacking a big kiss on his cheek as she dragged him into the hall. Tonight it was difficult to distinguish her everyday fizz from the sparkle of boozy exuberance. Looking at the bloom on her cheekbones, Gregory was inclined to go for the latter...that or heavy make-up. 'Come on through. On you go, to the kitchen. Where've you been, anyway? The party's been going for hours.' Make-up or no, Ellie had long since sought asylum across the borders of insobriety.

'Sorry...I was working on a few things and I didn't notice the time.' Even he was ready to admit that tonight he had been at it too long. His back ached and his eyes were prickling from too much VDU time.

'It's that goddamn paper, isn't it?' Ellie was from New York, but that didn't allow Gregory to like it any better when she swore. 'Always the bloody same...all work and no play, you know,' she took his jacket and under his disapproving eyes slung it on top of the heap which was obstructing the bottom of the stairs, 'makes Greg a very dull boy.' In the same sweeping movement she took charge of the bottle. 'On your own?'

'Now Ellie, of course I'm on my own. As you very well know... Who would I bring anyway?'

'It's about time you found yourself a nice man. Still, none of my business, I suppose. Philip's in there, by the way,' she nodded in the direction of a door as they passed by, 'just so you know. With what's his name. Funny young man. Come on, let's get you a drink.'

Pushing through a thicket of people towards the back of the hall who were arguing rowdily about something called normalisation, they reached the kitchen. It was busy in there too: lots of people, mainly men, standing round in fours and fives. Neat sweaters – a couple with Pringle logos – tidy slacks and well-ironed denims, spotless trainers and casual slip-on shoes. Friends of Art's from Llanorgan Rugby Club.

Ellie's husband – although since crossing the Atlantic he had become, publicly at least, her partner – was Art Mirsky, a manager with an American electronics firm in Bridgend. Art had embraced rugby with evangelical fervour, as a substitute for American football. Not that the one stopped him watching the other on Channel Four as well. Nor talking about installing a satellite dish so that he could watch more of it. A couple of the men were vaguely familiar faces from college, registry probably, but nobody that Gregory knew.

Ellie handed him a plastic cup of red wine. A quick squeeze of his arm and she was off again.

'Must get back to Art. Last time I looked, Adrian had him pinned down in a corner...telling him all about mediaeval trade tokens. The cavalry had better ride to the rescue before there's a massacre.'

Abandoned, Gregory retreated to the safety of a kitchen unit upon which to lean and take stock. Art had just finished rebuilding the entire kitchen single-handed – Ellie had been broadcasting situation reports since before Christmas – and the new work surfaces gleamed a heavy brown against the lighter varnished wood of the doors and bases, and the stainless steel of the plumbing and the kitchen equipment. Even the toaster was stainless steel. Always keen to restore to himself the necessities of his native Long Island, Art had, at great expense, installed a garbage guzzler under the sink. Gregory understood from Ellie that it had become something of a six-day wonder among the neighbours. All round, it was a good job.

Glasses, bottles – some open, some not – a couple of wine boxes, big plastic bottles of spring water, cartons of fruit juice, all stood waiting on the draining board by the new sink unit. At the other end of the room a huge and heavy white wood table, which might have looked less out of place in an old-fashioned butcher's shop, was covered in food. From where he was standing, Gregory surveyed quiches and pizzas of many varieties, the vegetarian ones clearly labelled; wooden and plastic bowls filled with salads, green and otherwise; garlic bread in baskets lined with gaudy tissue paper; brown rice, yellow rice, and white rice; pâtés and a multilayered and multicoloured vegetable terrine; baked potatoes; cottage cheese; bread sticks and assorted dips; a large bowl of green and black grapes; an enormous slab of what looked like proper cheddar; many smaller chunks of more exotic cheeses; a varied selection of fresh and dried fruit; small bowls of different nuts in the spaces between the large offerings; and other goodies which Gregory couldn't see for people who were busy helping themselves. Not a cocktail sausage, not a cheese-and-pineapple-on-a-stick, not an individual pork pie to be seen. Paper plates and napkins. plastic spoons and forks. Just as he would have expected of Ellie: maybe a wee bit over the top, but a good spread and well organised. Already the floor under and around the table was thick with debris. Still, Art's newly laid quarry tiles would be easy to clean in the morning.

Looking at the food, Gregory was suddenly hungry. He realised that he had eaten nothing since lunchtime, and that had only been a bought sandwich. Just as he was about to rouse himself to investigate the possibilities, a familiar voice popped gently in his left ear, followed by an equally gentle kiss on the cheek.

'Gotcha.' Faye put an arm around Gregory's waist. 'Hiya gorgeous. How long've you been lurking in here?'

'Just got here...feels like hours already.'

'Balls. Standing eyeing up the talent, more like.'

'Shh...' He whispered. 'Don't be so loud. You're outrageous...wicked woman.'

And Faye looked every inch a wicked woman: black knitted silk jumper, sleeves pulled up above her elbows, a neckline that descended an unrespectable distance, even if it didn't quite plunge; black skirt well above the knee; black silk stockings sparkling with silver speckles, slim legs all the way down to silver leather pumps. Her face and arms looked just a little too brown for the local sunshine. Plain rods of silver dangling from her ears and dancing in and out of her hair. More than one man in the kitchen sneaked a greedy look at her and an envious one at Gregory. She removed her arm and waved an empty wineglass.

'Another drink? That's what I want right now.'

'No thanks, I'm alright, I still have this. And I'm driving...'

'Driving? Don't be so bloody daft. You only live two streets away, for God's sake. And if you're worried about the bogeyman, I'll walk you home. Keep you nice and safe. So drink up and let's have another one.' She walked over and lifted an open bottle of red. 'It's only Bulgarian, and I know you're used to better, but it'll do nicely. Come on. Down the hatch... I don't know, you'll never grow up to be a big strong boy.'

'And you're pissed.' He watched her pour the wine. A couple of drops splashed onto his hand. 'Careful now.'

'Jesus but you're a boring old fart.' An affectionate squeeze accompanied this judgement. Faye's head, hair the colour of a well-oiled chestnut, thick and shining, flecked through with silver glitter - it was, after all, a party - flopped onto his shoulder. 'And you've got big lipstick lips on your cheek. Faithless jade.'

'That was Ellie.'

'Oh I know it was Ellie...who else wears rhesus positive lipstick?'

'Miaow...' Gregory mimed a cat extending its claws. 'Ellie's alright.'

'If you like that sort of thing.'

They were silent for a while, Gregory sipping his wine, Faye humming along with Dire Straits - money for nothing and your kicks for free... - which was coming through from the front of the house. He put his arm around her shoulder.

'So, how were our transatlantic cousins? Have a good time?'

'It was alright. Bloody hard work.' Faye lifted her head for a mouthful of wine. 'Tell you what, they don't hand out travel grants for nothing. Five universities in less than three weeks. Poughkeepsie to Spokane. Completely mad...I must've left bits behind in three different time zones.'

'Any interesting bits?'

'Wouldn't you like to know? Nosey bugger...if you're very good you might eventually find out.'

'Can't wait. When d'you get back anyway?'

'Lunchtime Wednesday. But I didn't get back here 'til today. Had to go and see my mother for a couple of days.'

'How is she?'

'Oh, you know her. I'm beginning to think she's going to go on for ever...she's such a difficult old crow, I don't think they want her over the other side...neither of them.'

They were distracted by a burst of hooting and guffawing from the other end of the kitchen, over by the food. A short fat man in a red pullover adorned with the three white feathers of Wales on the left breast was bent over as far as his size and shape permitted, choking loudly and theatrically. One of his companions, a thin man who had adopted the comb-the-last-few-strands-across-the-top-from-the-ear strategy for drawing attention to his baldness, was determinedly banging him on the back with both clenched fists. The offending obstruction shot out suddenly in a spray of spittle and spattered against one leg of the table. It was still just about recognisable as a chunk of quiche: its size suggested of its eater more greedy optimism than sense. There were further uproarious trumpets of laughter. A quick slug from a can of Felinfoel appeared to restore the casualty's equilibrium. When he finally found it again, his voice was as loud as his laugh and as coarse as his bite.

'That's a good 'un, it is. Great, great...and then there was this other one. Oh it's great it is, mun. Heard it in work. About this bloke, bloody poofter he was, see, he was going in for a sex change. And anyway, he came to the point and he backed out at the last minute. Trouble was, trouble was see, he couldn't face having his brain shrunk and his mouth enlarged all at the same time...'

The end of the joke was submerged under a further swell of honking and backslapping. More beer was necessary before the comic could straighten up again. By this time his mate's hair had finally come adrift from its moorings and was drooping across one eye. Nobody seemed to notice.

The doorbell rang. Four times the doorbell rang. More people crushed into the kitchen. An increasing area of quarry tiles vanished under legs and feet and droppings from the buffet. More bottles of wine appeared, and beer in six-packs and plastic take-away cartons. Faye snuggled in closer to Gregory. He looked at his watch: twenty to eleven. Things would only get worse once the pubs kicked out.

For the time of year in south Wales, it was a mild and a pleasant night. High cloud obscured the stars, but helped to hold close to the earth what there was of the day's warmth lingering on in the air. Since early morning, it had been a reasonably dry day too. The grass and the earth were just damp enough for their smell to mingle with that of the honeysuckle that straggled along the back wall. Art and Ellie's garden was lit at one end by the kitchen windows and at the other by a lurid orange street lamp in the back lane that ran between the terraces. The two-seated swing, a relic from a time when children had lived in the house, groaned and its rusty fittings squeaked under Faye's weight. Gregory sat on a white plastic chair he had discovered near the dustbins. On his knee balanced a paper plate piled with quiche, pâté, terrine, and garlic bread. In one hand he held a double slice of pizza. With his other hand he picked out the olives and threw them into the bushes. Faye protested.

'Wait...don't throw those away. Here, I'll have them...'

'Sorry, too late. That was the last one. Why don't they put green olives on pizzas? Why is it always black ones with stones?'

'What a picky bloody eater.' A newly opened bottle of red wine in one hand, their glasses in the other, Faye watched him eat. She belched quietly. 'You are going to get fat.' She belched again. 'Very fat.'

'And you, my dear, if you are not already, are going to get drunk. Very drunk.'

'Anyway, what've you got there?' She leaned across, the swing squealing its outrage, and poked around on Gregory's plate. 'This'll do.' With the bottle secured firmly between her knees, she took an end of garlic bread. 'Wonderful.' Two bites, several licks of her fingers, and it was gone.

'Do you mind? I thought you'd already had something yourself...there's a kitchen full of food in there. Away in and get some yourself...'

'Don't be so bloody anal...you can be a pain in the butt sometimes. And who's calling who greedy? There's enough there to sink the sodding Titanic.' She poured a full glass of wine. 'Here you are.' And another for herself. 'Cheers. Here's to icebergs.'

For a moment, perhaps two, they did not talk. Gregory moved onto the quiche, then the pâté and the bread. He had changed his mind about the terrine. The jelly reminded him of the amoebas he had been thinking about earlier... Faye watched the goings-on inside the kitchen without any apparent interest. She spoke first.

'I heard about your mother. I'm really sorry.'

'Aye.' He paused before replying. In the half-dark and deep shadows of the garden it was difficult to see whether this was simply to empty his mouth before speaking, or some other kind of hesitation.

'Ellie told me.'

'Uh huh.'

'How d'you feel? Are you alright?'

'Couldn't be better...I mean, it wasn't as if we were exactly close or anything.' He had turned his head a little to one side. Faye could not see much of his face now at all. 'God knows, we couldn't really have been much further apart.'

'How was the funeral?'

'How's any funeral? It wasn't too bad.'

'Poor you, eh? And having to sort it all out on your own.'

'Nothing to it...'

'No, I mean it. All that to sort out and...'

'The solicitor did all that...And Charlie. Her brother.'

'And the house?'

'That's going to Charlie. God knows he deserves it. He was more good to her than I ever was. Poor auld Charlie. I think she made his life a misery right up to the end.'

'What happened?'

'What d'you mean?'

'What happened... How did she...'

'Oh, right. Died in her sleep apparently. Right as rain one day, gone the next. Charlie found her when he called in to see if she wanted any shopping. "Called to God peacefully", as the death notice put it.'

'There's worse ways.'

'Aye.'

They each took another drink, and again it was Faye who spoke first.

'So, is that it then?'

'What? Is that what? I'm not with you.'

'You always said that when your mother died you'd be finished with the place...what's it called again?'

'Glenvie.'

'That's right. You always said you'd never go back once she was dead. And now she is.'

'Aye, now she is. Dead and buried.' He raised his plastic cup. 'God rest her soul.' He drank a small mouthful. 'And the Devil take Glenvie.' Another drink, a full swallow this time. 'I'll drink to that.'

It was quiet again in the garden. Not much in the way of the hubbub inside the house found its way out past the new UPVC double-glazing. Faye leaned across and stroked Gregory's knee, absent-mindedly, almost like smoothing a cat, an old and familiar cat. She looked up.

'Philip's in good form tonight.'

Gregory looked at her for an explanation. She nodded towards the kitchen. With the light at his back, Philip was visible in half silhouette. He was leaning on someone else's shoulder – David? It was difficult to tell; whoever it was stood largely out of sight – head back, mouth wide open, arm up, wrist bent, shaking. The picture of merriment. Gregory looked away.

'So I see.'

'Oh come on now. Philip's not the world's worst ' She poured him some more wine.

'Bloody drama queen... Honest to God, I mean, would you look at him.'

'That's as maybe. But you can bet he's giving those bloody rugby club prats something to think about. Give him his due, he doesn't walk around apologising for himself.'

'The English art of understatement...No, he certainly doesn't, but does he have to prance around rubbing everybody's noses in it? I mean it's not...'

Another silence.

'Not what?' Her hand stayed on his knee. 'Not nice? Not...'

'No...no.' It was an emphatic interruption. Gregory rarely interrupted anyone. His mother's punishment for interruption had been to forbid him to speak until the next meal. Not even, when he was very small, to ask for the toilet. He had wet himself once, sitting on the top of the stairs. That had meant another slapping. 'No, it's not...,' his wine shook in the cup, 'not...necessary. That's it. It's just not called for. There's no need. No need at all.'

'Well maybe there is no need, but what the fuck – excuse me – what d'you think those arseholes in there are doing? They're not rubbing everybody's faces in their sexuality? What d'you think that's all about in there?... Alright, alright, I'll shut up.' Her hand was stroking his knee again. Squeezing reassurance out of the night air between them. 'Never mind.'

Faye shook her head in the darkness. Gregory sat with his head down over his plate. Not for the first time, Faye thought of what she might have to say if she ever came face to face with the woman who had done this to him.

Only now it was too late for that.

CHAPTER FOUR

THE MORNING AFTER

Gregory's kitchen was small. There was a place for everything and everything was in its place. There were lots of things for which places had to be found. Different varieties, colours, and shapes of pasta in matching glass containers with sparkling ground glass stoppers. Likewise rice, dried beans, and lentils. Herbs and spices in neatly hand-labelled pottery jars, arranged in alphabetical order in a two-tiered wooden rack mounted on the wall. Olive oil, corn oil, and sesame oil. Cutting and chopping boards. Six matching stoneware mugs hanging tidily on a wooden tree. A small stock of wine, New World reds in the main, in a wooden rack next to the brown and cream bread crock. Bright stainless steel utensils at rest on their hooks, above matching pans in a pyramidal storage rack. Sugar and flour and other baking ingredients in one cupboard, sauces and pickles and savoury cooking ingredients in another. Clean towels and drying cloths on pegs by the sink. An anthropologist's dream of classificatory order.

This morning, however, the boundary had been breached. Chaos, in the shape and person of Faye Watson, was inside the gates. Milk and sugar oozed together and stuck on the work surfaces where she had helped herself to muesli. The passage of the latter from cupboard to bowl was marked by an intermittent trail of assorted whole grains and dried fruit. A carton of orange juice, roughly torn at one corner where she had taken her teeth to it in frustration, stood among the debris. Now she was grinding coffee beans. As she turned the machine off and spooned coffee into the cafetière, flecks of aromatic brown contributed to the spreading pollution.

Gregory stood in the doorway.

'Thought I heard you up.' His short dressing gown revealed hairy legs and pink feet. He yawned. According to the wall clock it was coming up to eight forty-five. 'Is it not just a wee bit early for activity?'

'I needed a pee. All the drink from last night.' Faye rubbed her head and frowned. 'Then

I saw the time and there wasn't much point in going back to bed.' She had spent the night in the bed settee in the living room. 'I'm making some coffee.'

'So I see.' Gregory took a cloth from behind the taps and began to wipe up the space around the juice carton. He dried off its bottom and stowed it safely away inside the fridge door. 'There was one already open. It's nice and cold too.' That was the one he took out now and placed on the table.

'Sorry... You know what a slob I am. Just leave it, I'll tidy it all up afterwards.' She looked him up and down. 'Um...not bad. You're looking good these days. Very fit. Trim even. Been going to the gym?'

'Aye, that'll be the day...if you don't mind, I think I'll just do a bit now, while I'm at it.' He began to round up the coffee grounds and muesli. 'Anyway, you're not looking so bad yourself. Have you been working out?' Faye had borrowed one of his long T-shirts to sleep in, plain grey apart from the Fruit of the Loom logo. The soft rise and curve of her breasts was highlighted by her nipples, erect in the cold of the morning. As she turned away towards the table, Gregory was granted a glimpse of pubic hair sneaking out past the elastic of the black knickers that peeped out from underneath.

'Not in the gym, my dear, not in the gym. Not bad for an old woman of 37, eh?' Faye sashayed across the room with an exaggerated twist of her hips. 'Life in the old bones yet.'

'Thirty-eight in July, as I recall.'

'How d'you do that? Memory like a bloody elephant. And what of it anyway...? You're no spring chicken yourself.'

'Ain't that the truth ma'am.' Gregory's attempt at a down-home Southern accent owed more to Ronald McDonald than it did to Colonel Sanders. He sat down opposite her. She was staring down into her muesli. 'Penny for 'em.'

'Not worth it.' She began to shunt the cereal and fruit around with her spoon. 'Just a bit of nonsense.'

'Come on...tell your Uncle Gregory. What is it?'

'It's just. I mean...' He had never seen Faye blush before. The morning light was behind her, and her face was still touched by the warmth of sleep, so he wasn't sure he was seeing it now. 'I was thinking last night, have you ever wondered... It's an obvious question, really, so obvious it's stupid. What would happen if, you know, if you weren't gay? You and me. Have you ever thought about it?'

Gregory paused for a moment.

'But I am...inasmuch as I'm anything, that is. Gay is what I am.' He squeezed her hand. 'Not that I'm particularly expert at it, mind you. And no, I haven't thought about it.' Not quite the truth, that, but close enough and convincing enough.

'It's only a daft thought anyway.' She grinned, stood up and moved over to where the mugs were. 'And how would you ever put up with me? You'd spend half your life running round cleaning up after me, and the other half wanting some peace and quiet. One of us'd swing for the other. To change the subject, where d'you keep the paracetamol...you do have paracetamol? That red wine's taking its revenge on my poor old head.'

Faye busied herself with the coffee while Gregory fetched the painkillers from the bathroom cabinet.

Outside in the garden a thrush won its struggle with an earthworm, only to drop it in hasty flight from the black-and-white tomcat that lived two doors down. The house next to where the cat lived had recently been converted into a private residential care home, and one of the residents, a young man with Down's Syndrome wearing an ill-fitting orange wig and heavy horn-rimmed glasses, was sitting on the still-fresh black paint of the recently installed fire escape steps, humming quietly to himself. Thousands of feet above his head, the blue sky of a fresh day was broken by the vapour trail of a jumbo jet, inward bound from the other side of the Atlantic. A different world.

CHAPTER FIVE

LOVE AND PORTHCAWL

On top of the photocopier three green lights in the shape of a triangle were flashing erratically. A sequence of yellow LCD numbers was repeating itself in the window marked 'number of copies': 99-44-12-99-44...and so on. An illuminated image of a little man in overalls clutching a spanner as big as himself glared a petulant red from the left-hand side of the panel, just by the on-off switch. Gregory was sure he could smell burning. The machine shuddered and a rustling and ripping sound came from behind the paper-sorting racks.

'Going to be long?' Adrian Wallbutton's heavily eyebrowed face appeared around the door of the photocopying room.

'Forever and a day, by the look of things.' Gregory hit the top of the photocopier with the palm of his hand. 'It's on the blink again.' He gathered up a folder full of papers from the side table. 'And I've got better things to do than stand around here waiting for a miracle.'

'Does Pauline know?' Adrian was inside the door now, clutching a copy of the New Mexico Journal of Mediaeval and Renaissance Studies to his amply upholstered breast. Behind the mustard waistcoat was a duck-egg blue shirt and what looked like a regimental tie. 'She'd better call the repair chappie in.'

'Pauline's off sick... Anyway, you tell her.' High-handed sod. Since his promotion Adrian had become even more unbearable than usual. Readerships were still being handed out as long-service medals...and for licking the right boots in the complex dominance hierarchies of the Senior Common Room. That was an uncharitable thought... It was like water off a gannet's back anyway, Adrian never took a blind bit of notice of anything that was said to him.

'How did it go?' Adrian was now bent over the plate glass on the copier's top, fiddling with something out of sight at the back. There was a series of loud clicks and the machine shuddered again. 'Let's have a look at this gadget.'

'What? How did what go?'

'The conference. Your paper...I wonder if this...'

'Oh, aye. Well enough. You know what these things are like.' Gregory knew that Adrian did not. 'Ten minutes to present it, ten minutes of questions. Wham-bam and thank you ma'am. People coming from all over the world and all most of them do is go shopping... Still, no-one threw anything.'

'Are they going to publish it?' He leaned further over behind the machine. 'Come on you little rascal.'

'They'll be letting us know in a few weeks.' The chances of that were remote, however, allowing for the pack of self-serving, back-scratching toadies on the conference committee. 'I'm not sure that it's quite ready yet, anyway.' Gregory was positive that he could smell burning. It was definitely burning.

'Well, if you want someone to read it. A fresh eye and all that. A few useful comments. AAAH!' Adrian's hand appeared at high speed from the shadows behind the photocopier and went straight into his mouth.

'Hot?'

'Mmm...' The hand came out and he shook it vigorously. 'Bloody electric shock...' Back in the mouth.

'Well, if I were you, I'd turn it off and leave well enough alone until someone can come out to fix it.'

'Gregory? Ah, there you are.' It was Ellie's head round the door this time. 'Your 'phone was ringing, so I answered it. It's Faye.'

'Okay, coming now... Switch it off man, you'll do yourself a damage.'

Adrian did not reply. He bent back over the machine. Hand still in mouth, the Reader in Medieval Archaeology was investigating the possibility of doing himself some really serious harm by operating further on the photocopier's dark heart and innards. Gregory shrugged and followed Ellie round to his office on the other side of the building.

Dr Watson of the American Studies Centre - Faye to most people - was late. She was generally late, and generally Gregory tolerated it. This was not a tolerance that he extended to many other people. He was well known for expecting his colleagues to be where they had said they were going to be, when they had said they were going to be there. And his students to be where he said they were going to be and when. He was equally well known for his occasional petulance if they weren't. At grammar school his German teacher, Mr Donald, used to lecture his pupils on punctuality being the politeness of princes, an attitude that had obviously rubbed off on at least one of his pupils.

Gregory and Faye had first met nearly nine years ago, at a beginning of term reception held by the Vice-Chancellor in his official residence overlooking the sea at Nag's Point. A large bungalow with sweeping striped lawns, it looked like an illustration from a gardener's seed catalogue, set in grounds that would have been big enough for a modest housing development. They had both just been appointed to their respective 'new blood' lectureships. By the end of the reception Gregory had felt like rolling up his sleeve and offering to open a vein for anyone who was in need of a top-up: 'Ah, Vice-Chancellor, have you met our new blood yet?'...'So you're one of these new blood people, then?'...'Nice to meet you. We're expecting great things, of course, with this new blood scheme and what have you'...and so on. Nobody had been interested in what he was called, or what he did.

The new blood was thinner now and flowed more slowly, even though Registry persisted in identifying him in official correspondence as 'New Blood Lecturer'. But he still thought that nobody in Llanorgan was interested in him or what he did. Not unless there was some gossip potential in it.

After the reception he had, with some reluctance, accepted this woman Faye's suggestion that they go for a drink. Desperation drove him to do so, for if truth be told he was very lonely. He knew no-one and in the six weeks he had lived in Llanorgan, he had ventured no further than his office, the bed-sit he had rented five minutes' walk away, and the local shops. The off-licence in particular. Faye, however, seemed quite settled in: she already knew her way round the local pubs, if nothing else.

The Pipe Organ was down by the harbour, where the new marina development was at that time still only beginning to take its first concrete form and shape. Then, it was a crazy place, run by an outrageous queen called Anthony who spotted Gregory the moment he had gone up to the bar: 'And what'll it be for you my lovely boy?' The booths were hung like four-poster beds with tasselled curtains – it was impossible to say what colour they were, between the gloom and the grime – which made it seem more like an opium den or a movie brothel than a pub. From time to time, other things and goings-on added to each of these resemblances. The denizens – in the Pipe Organ, customers never seemed quite the right word – only added to the effect. Everyone from the winos waiting for the night shelter round the corner to open its doors, to Anthony's camp followers, with an assortment of innocent bystanders thrown in. And a few that were not so innocent. That night, when they first walked in the door, Gregory actually asked Faye whether it was the sort of place that was suitable. She laughed at him. That was nine years ago and she had been laughing at him ever since, although now she tried harder not to offend him, and he was a little thicker-skinned. He was certainly no longer the pompous pillock she accused him of being as he first peered into the dark interior of the Pipe Organ.

The pub was a very different establishment these days. Anthony did a bunk with the takings one Easter weekend after the national sailing championships – there must have been thousands upon thousands in the till – and had last been heard of running a leather bar in Ibiza. The brewery closed the place for a while after that. Suitably done out – themed as a waterside tavern – the new Spyglass Inn now catered largely to the boat and flat owners of the marina. Gregory had not been in since it opened. The night shelter was long since gone as well. God knows what had happened to the winos.

'Wakey, wakey.' Faye was standing by his elbow. Against the drab magnolia paint and heavy stained wood of the Senior Common Room her hair was almost framed by its own halo. She sat down, smiling the smile that was her face's greatest glory. 'Cat got your tongue? You were miles away.'

'No...not miles. Years. For some reason I was thinking back to that first night we went down the old Pipe Organ. After that do at the V-C's.'

'And you were scared to go in... I think there were fewer villains in that pub than there were at the party.' She laughed quietly. 'God...d'you remember? I felt like the blushing bride at the wedding feast. Mr and Mrs New Blood!' She started to giggle and put her hand up to her mouth. 'One pint or two?...Dracula's bride!'

'It's funny, it doesn't seem like nine years. It is nine isn't it? Yes, must be.'

'Well...they say that time flies when you're having fun.'

'Oh aye, absolutely, this place is a barrel of laughs.'

'Never mind, beggars can't be choosers. There's nowhere else to go, so it's no good moaning about it. Anyway it's the same everywhere these days. And it could be worse, you could be at Cardiff...or even Swansea.'

'Heaven forbid! Swansea. What is it they call it? The graveyard of ambition? Still, what's this place? All graveyard and no ambition...anyway, let's talk about something cheerful...what about the land of wide-open spaces and opportunity for all? You still haven't told me all about it. No chance of anything over there then?'

'The States?...I don't think so. No opportunities for someone like me. The funny thing about American Studies is that the only place you can teach it is everywhere but America. Now it'd be different for you...'

'Not really. What do I know about Mississippi burial mounds or Clovis points?'

'Obviously a great deal more than I do.' Faye's eyebrows arched. 'Stop showing off... God, that night in the Pipe. It seems like such a long time ago...I had such plans for you. Thought you were quite fanciable...I was going to lure you back to my place and do wicked things to you. Mind you, I was so bloody hard up I'm not sure it was a compliment. And I'd had a few. Quite a few as I recall. Free wine, it'll do it every time.' Gregory put down his half-pint of bitter and looked out of the window, shaking his head. Faye continued. 'And then there was that bloody barman...what was his name? Tony?'

'Anthony.'

'Yes. He gave your game away.'

'Just like you'll be doing if you don't keep your voice down.'

'Sorry. Anyway, I've told you before, it's not as if it's a secret, is it? Not that anyone's ever said anything to me, you understand, and of course they wouldn't, but getting involved with Philip wasn't exactly discreet now, was it? Not exactly staying in the closet with the door closed...' She subsided into whispered theatricality. 'Stuffy old bastards. Look at them all.'

She nodded towards the assorted colleagues with whom they were sharing the SCR Lounge. 'Bet most of them haven't had it up in years...Too busy with wine tastings, wet dreams and wittering. You can see it in the way their eyes follow a pretty young arse up the stairs. Even a female arse... And some of the young ones are the worst. Busy thinking about what it was they were missing when they had their head stuck inside a book instead of between a pair of nice warm thighs.'

'Don't you think that you might just be guilty of projecting your own enthusiasms onto other people?'

Faye stuck her tongue out. It was a long tongue and she could curl it over on itself in the middle. Gregory's nose wrinkled.

'You're surely not going to put that back in your mouth now, are you?' He sipped his beer. 'If they're all so disgusting, why do we have to have lunch here?'

'Good for your reputation, my boy, keep them guessing... Anyway, to get back to that night in the Pipe – why have we never talked about this before? – You should have seen your face. Wonderful.'

'Well I wasn't to know, was I?'

'What? Know what?'

'That you wouldn't just...that it wouldn't matter.'

Faye's face softened, turning the few tiny crow's feet around her eyes to full advantage. 'No. I'm sorry, that's enough for one lunchtime. I shouldn't tease you. I'm full of shit today, I'm afraid. You'll just have to put up with me.'

'Oh good, I look forward to this. And why, pray tell, is the lady so full of...so full of nonsense?'

'I'll come to that in a minute. Right now I'm starving, let's get something to eat. Another drink?'

By the time they returned to the small round table in the corner by the sea-facing windows, the lounge was filling up. They bought rolls, fruit, a Diet Coke for Faye and another half of bitter for Gregory. One o'clock had just struck in Founder's Tower and lunchtime business in the Senior Common Room was beginning in earnest. Here and there throughout the room unofficial chairmen – emphatically not chairpersons – were calling to order unofficial committees. Here it was that opinion was sounded, unofficially of course; that standing and repute were constructed or demolished, unofficially of course; that consensus was shaped and channelled before ever it might be arrived at, just as unofficially, of course. Here too the distinction between academic and administrator vanished in membership of the College's select – and completely unofficial, of course – Supper Club, its initiates quietly pursuing their hidden agendas in undetected orchestration. Rumour had it that Adrian was a new recruit to their company. Thus it was that the University College was governed and many of its affairs transacted. For the moment, however, Faye and Gregory's business was strictly alimentary.

'It's not exactly the place for a chat, is it?' Gregory's mouth was full of wholemeal bap, tinned salmon and mayonnaise. He saved a crumb from falling with the back of his hand.

'No. Not really.' Faye washed down a munch of beef roll – hers was white bread – with her Coke. 'My mistake. Just goes to show how often I bother with my colleagues.' She returned a wave from a woman at the other side of the room. At least ten years Faye's senior, the other woman's most noticeable feature from this distance was a very large backside inside very tight mauve cord jeans. Her hair was frizzy-permed and an odd shade of orange. The frames of her huge round spectacles had obviously been chosen with an eye – or even both eyes, perhaps – to the colour co-ordination of the rest of the ensemble. They were vivid lime green.

'Who is that? I keep seeing her around.'

'Antonia Grimaldi. New social work lecturer...works with Philip. Same floor.' Faye bit another large hole in her roll. She chewed for a few seconds. 'Specialist in child abuse.'

'And just about looks the part too. Cruella de Ville gone to seed. Thank God she's not teaching interior decorating.'

'Don't be catty now. Her trousers are too tight for her bum.' Another mouthful and the roll was gone. 'That's all. She's in the College women's group.'

'I thought you'd given up on them. What about the group down in town? You told me you couldn't stand this lot anymore.'

'I know...I still go to the College group sometimes. It's not like the bloody Boy Scouts, you know. You don't have to join.'

'Point taken...and anyway, don't you mean the Girl Guides?'

'Smart arse.' She stuck out her tongue again. The effect was less coquettish this time: a lump of spit and half-chewed beef decorated its tip.

'As I said before, you're not going to put that back in your mouth are you?'

'Where else would you like me to put it? Eh big boy?'

'Behave. You're in public.'

'Far too bloody public, if you ask me. C'mon, let's finish up and go for a walk...quick, before la belle Grimaldi decides to come across and say hello.'

The path leading round the College's Educational Gardens – the sign, in Welsh and English, said open to the public by prior arrangement with the Department of Botany – was greasy, following the showers of the previous few days. Gregory and Faye held hands in the most slippery places, where the clay was shiny and dangerous and the grass too long to allow for a relatively dry-shod diversion. Beyond the Gardens' stone boundary wall a beech hedge extended off towards the expensive villas, holiday chalets and caravan parks of Nag's Head and Grimslade. It was the furthest edge of the College precinct. Just ahead the path went straight towards the ivory tower's defensive thicket, passing through a gap made by more than seventy years of students heading towards Town Point for an afternoon's drinking or an evening's canoodling. More than seventy years of gardeners had tried to hold the pass – chicken wire, wooden stakes and the head of an old bedstead lurked overgrown in the hedge bottom, relics of former campaigns – but the route remained open. This year's obstacle, a decorator's trestle with one leg missing, lay base over apex beside the path, less use than a Dutch boy's finger to a dyke.

Beyond the hedge the turf was suddenly dry and springy and the path petered out, gradually dissipating itself in a hundred different directions. Tiny yellow flowers shone among the coarse tufted grass. Immediately in front of them was the dip and rise, dip and rise, of Caer Isaf fort and beyond that again were the lighthouses: one disused Victorian stump on the pine end of a row of keepers' cottages, and the present operational tower (open on Sundays during the summer by arrangement with the keepers). Off to the right a public footpath, fenced and tarmacked a few years earlier by workers on a Community Programme scheme, led along the edge of the cliff from town to Point. On the landward side of Caer Isaf's ramparts was a row of benches – another product of the Community Programme – and sooner than slide up and down the ditches, Faye and Gregory sat and took in the intermittent sunshine and onshore wind of the Bristol Channel coast in the first week of May.

'So then, there was something you wanted to tell me.' Gregory hunched his hands deep into the pockets of his imitation Barbour jacket. 'What was it that couldn't wait?'

'Well...' Faye turned towards him, twisting round on the bench to do so, her elbow on the backrest. 'There is, but...don't know where to start really. What would you say if I told you I was in love?' The wind blew her hair back from her face, her cheeks pink with the weather and flushed with excitement. She leaned forward, her eyes on his.

Gregory laughed. And again. 'What would I say? I'd have to say, so what else is new? Who is it this time?'

'Don't be mean.' The shadow of a cloud passed over her eyes. 'That's not fair and you know it. I fancy people, all the time...But I've never ever told you I'm in love before. Never ever. And I never have been. And you don't know him.' She moved along the bench, away from Gregory's laughter. Her surprise, her great moment of revelation had been spoilt.

'Okay, I'm sorry...you're quite right. So who is this lucky chap?' He rested a hand gently on her arm.

'I met him, oh, it must be a fortnight ago. While you were away at that conference, or maybe it was just before you went. He's from Porthcawl, of all places.'

'Porthcawl? My dear...that's a bit, well, end-of-the-pier isn't it?' Faye could feel herself relaxing again. Gregory's camp routine was a familiar flag of truce. 'What does he do, this wonderful item? Look after the dodgem cars? A candy floss concession? A donkey man perhaps? Where did you meet him? Selling tickets for the Ghost Train?'

'Will you be serious?' Gregory accepted a playful slap on the back of his hand with an exaggerated good grace. 'I met him on the train... I mean, can you believe it? Coming back from London, I'd been down to an opening, with Suzie, you remember Suzie...'

Gregory would have found it more difficult to forget Suzie than to remember her. She'd come down for a weekend with Faye about eighteen months earlier – they'd been at Girton together as postgrads – and Gregory had been drafted in as the entertainment for Sunday. After a walk along the cliff path during which she had complained about everything from the wind to the state of her shoes to her love life, Suzie had thrown up all over Gregory's lap in the seafood restaurant down by the old harbour. And it wasn't the langoustine that had been the problem, it was the Muscadet.

'Anyway, the train was crowded and he sat down next to me. All the way from Paddington, talking non-stop... When we both got out at Bridgend, he suggested a drink, and that was it. One thing led to another...'

'And another, and another...I wondered why I hadn't heard from you. I should have guessed.' The role of confidante and father-confessor rolled into one was well rehearsed. It suited Gregory perfectly, listening rather than talking; her life rather than his. 'So what does he do?'

'He's an accountant...not an accountant like that.' She had registered Gregory's wrinkled nose. 'Works for the County Council. Under-Assistant Chief Finance Officer or something... He's about the same age as you. Going a bit thin on top too...and he drives an Escort. Could almost be you. Only his is an XR3. A classic car, so he tells me.'

Gregory was happy enough to be teased. 'So you've been locked in rapture for the last ten days or so?'

'Well that's what...that's the funny thing. No.' She rummaged around in her bag and brought out a packet of Marlboro Lights. The wind kept blowing the match out and in the end she had to turn her back to Gregory to light one of the four or five cigarettes she allowed herself a day. 'I've seen him. Nearly every day in fact. Lunch, out for dinner, in for dinner – he cooks like an angel, you'd approve – walks. We were at the opera in Cardiff last night. But, as I say, that's the funny thing, nothing else. Not even come close. I can't wait to shag him – God knows I can't wait to shag him – '

'Such a delicate turn of phrase.'

'But it just hasn't happened. It feels like being sixteen again.' She broke the matchstick between her fingers and tossed it into the wind.

'So why the sudden outbreak of propriety?'

'Don't ask me... It's not me, that's for sure.'

'No...I suppose not. Be a bit out of character. Perhaps he's just an old-fashioned gentleman.'

'Perhaps. But it's just... oh Greg, I don't know, it's all so...so wonderful when I'm with him. Brilliant. That's a funny word to use, isn't it? I can hardly think of anything else. Just him. I sit in the office and daydream about him. I even gave the house a proper clean when he came round first. And I cooked him a meal...I mean, me, cooking.'

'Did he survive?'

'Cheeky swine.' She punched him gently on the upper arm. 'Anyway, I cooked a meal for you once.'

'You made me a salad, with tinned tuna... And there was no mayonnaise, only salad cream. What did you make him, anyway?'

'Goulash. Out of a recipe book.'

'Where d'you find that?'

'What?'

'The cook book.'

'Ha bloody ha, very droll. If you must know, I went out and bought it.'

'I'm impressed...and? How was it?'

'It was fine, although I think the dumplings were a mistake. Bit on the dense side. Didn't float too well, not like in the picture anyway...'

'What did he think of it?'

'Wiped his plate clean. Literally. Asked for a slice of bread to mop up the gravy.'

'So...what about the way to a man's heart being through his belly? Or doesn't this particular army march on its stomach?'

'I don't know. Like I said, it just never seems to happen. We get so far, and then it's time to go. He's got a meeting in the morning, or there's something on the telly...'

'The telly? Really?'

'Really. Night before last, some Channel Four programme. About jazz. Some bloody trumpet player who killed himself...not very flattering is it?'

'Come on now, it's early days yet. Maybe he's just not one for leaping into things.'

'Like me, you mean?'

'Well you do tend to...you know, it's not...'

'I leap into bed with people?'

'That's not what I'm...'

'No. But maybe you're right. But dammit, a fortnight's not leaping into bed...' She turned her head round to face Gregory, her nose only inches from his. 'I want him Greg. I want him. Not having him hurts. You know how it feels...'

The last sentence was barely out, but already she could have bitten off her tongue. It was treacherous territory. She squeezed his arm gently. Gregory's eyes would not meet hers. He looked straight ahead, focusing far beyond the lighthouses and the end of the point, on the distant hills of the north Devon coast. There were white caps on the waves and the seagulls rose and fell in the wind against the cliffs. Finally he answered.

'Aye, but that's the trouble, isn't it? I'm not sure I do know. Not really. Why you ever talk to me about this stuff I'll never know. Might as well ask a deaf man what he thinks about Mozart.' Now it was his turn to regret his words, to repent their transparent hurt, Faye's to look away. She slackened her hold on his arm, then let go altogether. Her hand dropped to her lap, to join its fellow in the comfort of interlocking fingers, the security of thumb over thumb.

The silence between them lasted for several minutes. A siren sounded – an ambulance probably – coming and going, somewhere off and away in the town beneath them. The gulls called to each other in the eddies and currents of their element. Way, way off to the west the dark line of a ship, long and low in the water, moved slowly towards Port Talbot, its belly full of South American iron ore.

'Sorry.' Gregory took one of her hands, gently prising it away from the other, squeezed it. She let him. 'I don't mean to be so touchy...It's just not something I've ever been very good at. You know...either talking about it or doing it.'

'And I'm afraid I can't stop doing either. What a pair, eh?'

'And maybe that's your answer.' Faye turned her head, an unspoken question in the tightening of her eyebrows, the barely perceptible purse of her lips. Gregory continued. 'Ask him. Talk to him about it. It's not something you have to be shy about. I mean, the worst thing that'll happen is that you'll get nowhere...and you're doing that already.'

'Tell me about it.' She looked at her watch. 'Shit. Got to go. Bloody staff meeting.' They stood up, Faye stretching as wide and as high as the tips of her toes would let her, shaking her head and her hair in the wind as she relaxed her limbs again. 'I am getting old. Old, fat and stiff. Back to aerobics and yoga for me, I think.'

'You could always try eating less lunch. And cutting down on the dumplings.'

'Pig.' She linked her arm in his. 'Anyway, look who's talking.'

'What's this man's name, anyway?' They started back towards the hedge.

'Ioan...very Welsh he is, see. Valleys boy.' Her southern Welsh accent was no more and no less than the parody she intended. 'Plays rugby too. I've promised to go and watch next Saturday.'

'My dear, I just can't wait to meet him.'

'You should be so lucky.' They were back at the gap now.

'No. You should.' Gregory took hold of Faye's shoulders. 'If it really means all you say, you talk to him. Otherwise, in six months time you'll be back where you started, wondering what was wrong. Ask him.'

'I will...' She shrugged away, towards College. 'I will.'

Gregory followed, back to the gardens of education and culture. Behind them, the seagulls continued their crying in Eden.

CHAPTER SIX

STAND UP

The light escaping from the open fridge fell on a wedge of vinyl-covered floor. On the top shelf, Gregory found the half bottle of Brown Brothers Muscat and Orange Flora that he was looking for. Leaving the door to swing to behind him, he walked across the gloom of the kitchen, lit only by the window, which overlooked the back garden, to the work top on the left wall. The corkscrew was in the drawer, a glass in the wall cupboard immediately above. Quickly, with an efficiency that was almost forensic, he opened the wine and poured himself a drink. Taking a plastic stopper from the same drawer, he re-sealed the bottle and replaced it where he had found it. He turned round and chose a ripe nectarine from the fruit bowl.

A small luxury to wash down dinner, he said to himself. On the smoked glass table in the living room, his plate bore the few remains of cauliflower cheese and a veal cutlet, both home cooked. Sitting down on the wicker rocking chair, he belched quietly, picked up the remote control and switched on the television for the Channel Four News. It was after seven o'clock and they were already well into the programme: at the moment it was a report on the Balkan war crimes tribunal. The presenter, and the Junior Minister from the Foreign Office who he was interviewing, seemed to think that nothing more could be done to apprehend the wanted men without making the situation worse, and endangering an already fragile situation. A Serbian spokesman was talking about 'ethnic cleansing' as if it were a public health measure; it certainly had nothing to do with them. The French spokeswoman from the International Court of Justice just sounded as if she was pissed off and didn't care who knew it. She probably was, and she probably didn't.

Gregory, however, did not pay the news much attention. On and off all afternoon he had been rehashing his conversation with Faye on the Point at lunchtime. Ever since saying cheerio to her, he had been aware of a sense of discontent that niggled but would never quite come out into the open. And that in itself bred its own further preoccupation... Why should Faye's news fill him with so little pleasure? Nor was it that simple either, there was more to it. But what? What did he feel? Unhappiness? That wasn't it. He had nothing to be unhappy about, after all. Faye was just a wee bit miserable, he'd seen her worse...and no, not even that, she was thwarted...couldn't get her own way, for a change. Probably more frustrated than anything else. So was this...Was this, Ioan she'd said his name was, was he not good enough for Faye? The very idea diverted him with a moment's awkward amusement. What was he thinking of? Pompous ass. Who was he, to be concerned about that? He had a brief glimpse of himself as others might see him. It wasn't comfortable. And anyway, he didn't even know the man.

What was he thinking of? He dodged around the question for a moment. The only answer that he could come up with made no sense at all. Jealousy was not really believable. The green-eyed God? No, he couldn't believe it. It was ridiculous. He'd heard too much in the past, sat through too many confessions for that to bother him. No...it couldn't be that...

The doorbell rang.

Gregory's eyes refocused on the still-full glass of wine on the table. His palms were clammy, a pulse pounded between his temples. The nectarine was in his hand, with only one bite out of it. With the back of one hand he wiped the sweat from his forehead.

The bell rang again.

Gregory stood up, put the fruit down on the table, walked across the room behind the sofa, into the hall, out of his front door and into the communal hallway. He stopped for a minute in front of the mirror above the bare hall table. Then he opened the door onto the street.

A man in a dark blue pin-stripe suit stood on the step, a blue rosette in his left lapel, a clutch of leaflets in his left hand, good humour and comradeship in his outstretched and open right hand. Before Gregory had time to say anything, his own hand was being vigorously shaken.

'Good evening...Mr, er...' The man consulted some notes which he also held in his left hand. 'Mr Alexander, ground-floor flat?'

Now Gregory was paying attention. The ruddy open face was somehow familiar. His accent was definitely local. What Gregory's mother would have call 'well spoken'. What he imagined would be 'very tidy, very respectable' in Llanorgan.

'I'm Bill Standup, your local Conservative councillor. Delighted to meet you.' So that was who it was. No wonder the face was familiar, it was never out of the local paper. 'Standing for re-election I am. Just knocking on doors, to remind you that I'm here and always at your service. I hope I can rely on your vote...?' Gregory never voted. 'I'm afraid we don't have a huge party organisation, not like the other lot. Just me and a few hard workers in the ward, we do it all.' He gestured down the street. Two other people were busy in doorways. A third, a middle-aged woman with black hair that was obviously dyed, wearing an elaborately tooled and ornamented leather coat with padded shoulders, stood behind her leader at the foot of the steps leading up to Gregory's door. 'But we do our best, we try to serve everyone. I'm not a great believer in too many posh leaflets, waste of money I say.' He handed Gregory a piece of paper, folded. 'Much better the personal touch, don't you think? Not like the Labour Party, eh? Forever wasting ratepayers' money on this and that bit of nonsense.' Although his shirt was blue, his collar was white. Gregory found this rather curious. 'We're the party whose mission it is not to waste money. Our money, Mr...', the candidate looked quickly at his notes again, 'Alexander. Our money it is, and it's not to be wasted...so, may I ask you if we can depend on your vote on Polling Day?'

Gregory tried to speak. Nothing more than a grunt came out. His head moved. A nod? It was like a dream, a dream in which he could stand to one side and observe himself. He looked up and down the street. Was anyone he knew watching this fiasco? Not that he really knew anybody in the street for them to see.

'Excellent, that's excellent.' Councillor Standup took a pen out of his jacket pocket, a cheap Bic, and made a mark on his notes. 'It's so refreshing to meet one of the, yes, one of the younger generation, who still has respect for traditional values and right thinking.' He moved forward, one foot up on the doorstep, half inside the doorway now. Gregory found himself gradually retreating. 'And you know, it's not just wasting money we've got to be vigilant about. Oh no, it's time to stand up and be counted. Moral laxity, perversion, it's everywhere, see. We must fight the good fight as the hymn book says. That's why we started our campaign about homosexuality.'

Go on, say something, tell him, pack him off. Are you a man or a mouse, sleekit, cow'rin' and tim'rous? Say something. Nailed down by panic, Gregory could not move. A grunt, another nod. Uh huh.

'Don't get me wrong, mind. It's none of our business what these people get up to in private. We mightn't like it, mightn't want it next door, so to speak, but that's a different matter all together. But there's far too much of it. And in public, see. The parks aren't safe for children to play in any more, you daren't use a...,' Councillor Standup's voice dropped, 'public convenience these days... Spreading AIDS, molesting youngsters. And in the schools too, it is, now... Only last month it was, did you read about it in The Gazette, those people from the University?' His face reddened. It was impossible to tell which outraged him more, the researchers or the institution itself. His eyes narrowed behind their glasses. 'Well, the people in the University ward, the ordinary Llanorgan people, are sending me a very strong message. They won't stand for it. We won't stand for it.' He reached behind with one arm as he spoke. The woman waiting patiently on the pavement climbed one step and handed him a clipboard. 'This is the petition we've got up.' He thrust it towards Gregory, another Bic dangling from a bit of string. 'Against the activities of the College and demanding that these...activities...,' he spat out the word, 'cease forthwith.' He smiled again, abruptly smoothing over the hard lines of righteousness on his face. 'I hope we can have your support too?'

It was Gregory's last chance. He could see it coming and he watched it go. Another nod. A hand that held a pen, that scrawled a signature, that wrote an address. And what if the signature was unrecognisable? It was still there in front of him.

As quickly as it took to turn round, Councillor Standup was gone, waving his thanks. In his hand Gregory found a printed card: Bill Standup, Conservative, Standing for Honesty, Decency and Integrity, followed by an address and a phone number. The address was over Nag's Head way. Regardless of how he felt about the ratepayers', Bill Standup obviously knew how to make and spend his own money...and better than to do it in the University ward.

For another minute or so Gregory stared at the card, witless with confusion and shame. A couple of times he turned it over as if there might be some secret alternative message to be found on the other side. There was none. Then he looked down the street. Another conversation was already going on next door, and the woman in leather was once again in waiting with the clipboard and the pen. Briefly her eyes met Gregory's. A sharp inspection and then away. She did look to be so easily fooled. He wanted to call her back so that he could cross out the impostor's signature, explain that there had been a mistake, but he did not. He retreated instead.

Inside the hall, Gregory closed the door behind him. Was it the stable door, now that the horse had bolted? Or the closet? More like the trapdoor, at the gallow's foot. St Peter came in to his mind, in Jerusalem the night before Golgotha... Three times he had denied himself. Good enough for a Muslim divorce. Gregory listened for the cock's crow. Slowly he went back into the flat.

The bedroom was dark. Gregory sat up with a start. His bedclothes were half on, half off the bed. His knees were tucked up under his chin, firmly clasped by his arms in front of him. He was naked and dripping with sweat. His mouth and tongue tasted dry and foul from the red wine he had put himself to sleep with, and his head was bursting. He needed to pee.

His mother had been here, in the room with him. Standing over by the door, walking slowly towards him. Not a frail or elderly woman, but the sturdy mother of his childhood. He had seen her.

She had been here. And she knew. Gregory was certain that she knew. Like the woman on the pavement, she was not so easily fooled. Now she knew. At last. Gregory rested his head on his knees and wept.

CHAPTER SEVEN

THE GAIETY

Gregory replaced the telephone on its rest. Faye wasn't there. Again. Apart from two chance and very hurried meetings in College House last week, he hadn't seen her since she'd told him about her new love. And on both of those occasions she had been distracted and preoccupied. Three weeks it had been now. Perhaps twenty times he'd rung her at home, perhaps more. Either she was never there or she'd unplugged the phone.

And more than twenty times he had tried to banish from his mind the grotesque gargoyle which was haunting him; Faye and the faceless Ioan wound together in a Sheelagh-na-Gig of horrendous proportions. The rugby player. Gregory could still remember the rugby players at grammar school. One in particular, Finlay McClintoch, had bullied him all the way from primary school to the sixth form. When Gregory had last heard of him he was a branch manager for the Royal Bank of Scotland. Finlay, Ioan, it was all the same. The image, and its grossness, pursued him along corridors, up and down lifts, along supermarket aisles, between the lights of his car on the wet road home. He, who had never been much interested in sex, now could think of nothing else but theirs. If they were having any.

And while Faye had the day shift, his mother had the night. Darkness came and he found himself waiting for the dream. Was it out there, watching in the wings, waiting for its cue, or was it his own anticipation that called it into being? Sometimes he wasn't sure any more that it was a dream. Four times, perhaps five, it was impossible to be completely certain, at least four, he had woken up in the room where his mother had just been. Each time it seemed to Gregory that she had moved a little closer to the bed before he woke. The last time he had deliberately willed himself awake before she could get too close. He was afraid of her. He had always been afraid of her, but now it was worse, now that she knew.

He was drinking in order to sleep at all, a full bottle of wine and more some nights. In work he was walking around like a zombie. More than once he'd gone in unshaven. It was so bad that Pauline had come into his office, closed the door and asked him if he was alright:

was there anything he wanted to talk about? But Faye's sudden absence from his world meant that he had nobody he could talk to about what was happening to him. Not that he would have told Faye very much if she'd been there. Wasn't that half the problem? All he really wanted from her was her presence. But that wasn't enough. He couldn't offer her what Ioan could. Slowly, minute by minute, hour by hour, day by day, soon it would be week by week, he was being forced to recognise the solitary emptiness of his life, the isolation. How over-dependent on Faye he had become. He had always been secure in the thought that she needed him as much as he did her. Only now she didn't seem to.

Gregory was ashamed in his selfishness: miserable, lonely, confused and pursued by his own impotence... He wasn't even sure what it was he couldn't do. His head span, trapped on a merry-go-round of possibilities and plausibilities, each one supplanting its predecessor as it came in to view, only to be overtaken in turn by the doubts that rode in its wake. Each one too fast to catch and too far away to reach.

He had considered going to the doctor, but she'd only tell him he was a bit depressed because of his mother's death. She might give him some sleeping pills. That was no good. Worse than the drink.

But he had to talk to somebody. Dreams like this could drive you mad...was that what was happening to him? Or were the dreams a symptom of madness? Once again he wondered whether it actually was a dream. He could not be sure any more. In the loneliness of after midnight, disbelief and scepticism became steadily more vulnerable to a half-forgotten twilight world of childhood. A world that was filled with the thunder of Old Testament prophecy and the creak and swing of dead men hanged at the crossroads by the Redcoats, that was inhabited by great black dogs that stalked the woods, and witches, sent by the Devil to steal your soul before you woke. And now by his mother.

In the daylight, under the sun, Gregory wondered had he ever stop believing in ghosts, whether science, the rationalism in and by which he had been educated, might not be just one more absurdity among many. He had even managed a brief and circumlocutory conversation about the matter with Grenville Evans from Philosophy, one lunchtime in the Senior Common Room bar. About the nature of reality and science. By then, Grenville had already downed his customary lunchtime second bottle of Diät Pils. All he could offer was a suggestion that Gregory read somebody called Winch, and the opinion – punctuated by a large and unexcuse-me'd burp – that, 'At the end of the day, it doesn't matter a fuck anyway. It's a non-issue and it always was...water doesn't flow uphill.'

But sometimes at night, even though he had taken to leaving the light on in the hall, and even though the water in the taps continued to obey the law of gravity, Gregory stopped wondering and the uncertain terror of belief without faith filled his heart.

He lifted the phone the moment that it rang.

'Hello?'

'Gregory?'

'Yes...'

'It's Trev.'

Gregory had to think. His head was full of cobwebs. Trev..? Trevor Thomas. Oh no...

'Oh...Trevor. Hello. How are things?'

'Fine, fine, you know how it is dear boy. Just phoning to say I heard about your mother. I've been away. I was very sorry to hear...is everything okay? Bearing up?'

Trevor was older than Gregory. About fifty, give or take a few years. Hard to tell except in an unkind light. He had tried it on several times, at parties, the club. Never awkward though.

'Gregory? Are you still there?'

'What? Sorry. I was miles away when the phone rang. How're you?'

'How am I? I was asking you...anyway, I'm fine. Why I rang was, I was wondering, why don't you come out this evening?'

Gregory took a few seconds to answer. Was Trevor on the make, or was he just being friendly?

'Where?'

'Nowhere special. It's only Thursday night. How about taking a run down the club, just a few drinks? Come on man, get you out of yourself it will.'

Out of my head, more like. Gregory looked at his watch. Just gone eight thirty.

'Well I don't know really... It's a wee bit late, I wasn't planning on...'

'Nonsense, the night is yet young.' Trevor was never one to be imaginative if a well-worn cliché was ready to hand. 'I won't take no for an answer. Still in the same flat, is it? I'll be round in two shakes of a horse's wotsit. Half an hour. See you later. Tara...'

'Well...'

Gregory was prevaricating to the dialling tone. Trevor had hung up.

An hour and a half later, Gregory was leaning over the balcony of the Gaiety Club, absent-mindedly scanning the dance floor below. It was early yet and the place was less than half full. The disco was pushing out a lot of bass under an old favourite, Gloria Gaynor's 'I Will Survive'.

The club's name was more straightforward than it seemed. No joke was necessarily intended. The building had once been The Gaiety Theatre, a small Edwardian music hall, a relic from a time when gaiety had been innocently available to all. Marie Lloyd was reputed to have trodden the boards where the deejay's console now stood, a pulpit wound around with a tracery of multicoloured flashing lights in plastic tubes. On either side stood large speaker stacks. Other speakers were more or less visible at different points around the room. Behind the record decks, the faded scarlet and gold of velvet curtains was nearly invisible in the gloom and the glare.

Other famous names usually linked to the place's past glories were George Formby and

Laurel and Hardy. They would have been hard pushed to recognise much of the interior these days. The dance floor had been constructed over the orchestra pit and the slope of the stalls. Nearly level with the original front of the stage, it was laid out in black and white squares. All along the wall opposite Gregory, a series of continuous mirrors extended from floor to just above head height. A young man in a crumpled business suit, the lights reflecting every now and then on his gelled blonde hair, was dancing with his own reflection, moving forward every now and then to rub up against his alter ego. In and out, pelvis to pelvis, lips to lips, crotch to crotch.

Gregory shook his head. What a place. The balcony was quieter, downstairs was more where the scene was. If you could call it that. He looked at his dark blue Wrangler cords, at his brogues - Hush Puppies - at his plain navy blue sweatshirt. Definitely non-scene. Every time he came down to the club it was the same. Within half an hour of coming through the tacky front doors he found himself asking what he was doing there. Usually it didn't even take that long, one look at the bouncers was enough.

'Here you are.' Trevor reappeared at his elbow, bringing their third round of drinks from the upstairs bar.

'I thought you were driving?' Gregory nodded at the Bacardi and Coke in Trevor's hand as he walked the few feet from the circle rail to their table.

'Well yes...but I thought, you're only young once.' He grinned, a Just-William grin, straight off the front of library books that Gregory could remember... Or was it Jennings? 'If need be I'll leave the car here and we can fetch a taxi.'

Gregory could see either a long night stretching before him if Trevor settled into drinking, or an immediate exit. He took a mouthful of whisky and ginger. At least the club didn't serve their drinks decorated with bloody silly paper parasols.

And, to be honest, he didn't actually want to go yet. That, of course, was the other thing about the club, a bit of a contradiction really. He didn't have to pretend he was anything he wasn't. Not one way or the other. Nothing was what he could be, and no-one seemed to mind. Nor even be interested, in fact. For that, if nothing else, it was worth putting up with the place.

Down in the disco, Gloria Gaynor continued to survive. A revolving glass ball high in the roof, where the remains of a splendid gold and red stucco ceiling lingered, bounced random shafts of light around the top of the club. Over to their right, at the far end of the balcony, two women were kissing with a passion that was quite theatrical and clearly not intended solely for their own consumption. The one with her back to Gregory, a slim woman with long black hair, was wearing a short red dress that had worked its way above her stocking tops. She appeared to have a small tattoo on the top of her thigh, but he couldn't work out what it was. The only other tables occupied upstairs were over by the bar. It would be quiet up here until about midnight. After that it would be busier than the dance floor.

'You're very quiet.' Trevor laid his hand on Gregory's.

'No...no.' Gregory lifted his drink. To do that he had first to lift his hand out from under his companion's. 'No, not really. It's this place. It's just not me, I suppose.'

'Gerraway with you...it's the most fun you can have in this bloody town with your clothes on.' Trevor arched an eyebrow and laughed. His non-verbals were always more expressive than his use of English. 'We'll get you another one of those in a minute.' He patted Gregory's hand and pointed to his now-empty glass. 'You'll be the life and soul of the party before you know where you are. Paint the old town red tonight, eh?'

Three minutes later, four at most, Gregory's turn to go the bar came round as Trevor's rum vanished 'down the hatch'. From the bar he had an uninterrupted view of the staircase which led down in a grand curving sweep to the foyer. At least Gloria Gaynor had stopped. Gregory didn't recognise the record that was now on. It sounded like the Chipmunks singing over a fast and very heavy beat: something about Betty Boob? It was hard to make out and not really worth the effort of trying. As he turned to carry the drinks back, he did recognise Philip's head and shoulders as they appeared at the top of the stairs. And David with him. Gregory carried on turning and walked back to Trevor.

'Look what the cat's dragged in.' Trevor nodded his head over Gregory's shoulder.

'Aye, I saw him.' Gregory sat down. 'You were saying, about where you were on holiday.'

'Sitges, yes. Just south of Barcelona. Thought I fancied a bit of a change from Ibiza. Lovely it was.'

'What sort of place is it? Very commercialised? Lots of package tours?'

'No. Not at all. It's beautiful, absolutely fabulous. Unspoilt, see...and the men. My dear, the fleet was in every night.' Trevor looked up. 'Speaking of which, I spy a sail on the port bow.'

Gregory looked round. Philip was standing at his elbow, David just behind him. Philip put a hand on the table, leaning towards Gregory and over him. His breath smelled sweet and stale of alcohol and tobacco, and there was a glass of red wine tipping at an angle in his right hand.

'Well, look who's here. It's Greg. Hello Greg, how's things? How're the promotion stakes coming on? Staying out of trouble? Getting enough of the right sort of shit up your nose?'

For a moment they just looked at each other, Gregory and Philip, caught in the public awkwardness of extinct intimacies. When Gregory finally spoke, it was with elaborate knowing patience and obvious long-suffering.

'What's the matter now? This little tableau...' Gregory shifted in his seat and waved his hand to include David. 'What's it all in aid of then?'

'I'll tell you what it's all in aid of, you patronising little prick, I'll tell you what it's in fucking aid of.' Philip wasn't very steady, his voice was dipping and sliding now, up and down the range. Some of the wine sloshed over the rim of his glass on to the table. It narrowly missed Trevor's chinos. The women at the end of the balcony had shifted their attention from each other to the more interesting possibility of a scene. Even a fight perhaps. Black Hair adjusted her dress. Philip brought his face closer to Gregory's. 'My fucking research project. Cancelled by the holier-than-thou-Sunday-go-to-meeting-fucking-Welsh-Office. And no-one...no-one in the College lifted a finger, not a fucking finger, to stop it. Not my Department, not the good-for-nothing bloody union, not bloody Rees, nobody. Look at you, sitting here, really out of the fucking closet aren't we? Why don't you go and drink somewhere you belong, because you don't fucking belong here.'

'Excuse me.' Trevor was standing up. He was taller than Philip. 'I don't think we've been introduced. Philip isn't it?' Trevor extended his shaking hand. Philip, social graces on the autopilot, put down his glass and took it. 'Trevor the name is. Now, let's not have a fuss, eh?' Philip was starting to blink. The bones in his hand were being efficiently ground together. 'I tell you what, why don't you just toddle back downstairs, there's a good lad.' He drew Philip towards him and Philip didn't have much choice but to follow his hand. 'And let's all have a nice evening, eh?'

'Let go...let go.' Tears shone in the corners of Philip's eyes. 'Tell your gorilla to let go Greg. If he doesn't...'

'If I don't, what? Eh? What?' Philip said nothing. He was on his tiptoes, as Trevor gradually lifted his hand higher. By now the barman had been polishing the same glass for a good two minutes, keeping an eye on them. 'Well now I'll tell you what. If you don't get the fuck down those stairs,' Trevor's tone was quiet, almost soothing, 'I'll break your elbow as well as your hand. And I'll stuff your poodle's head,' he nodded towards David, who had taken several steps back, 'up your pretty little arse to follow. And then, then, I'll stuff my dick so far down your throat, he can give me a nice long gobble...That clear?' Philip nodded as best he could. 'Good. Nice meeting you. Enjoy your evening.' He patted Philip on the upper arm as he released his hand.

By the time Trevor was back in his seat, genteely sipping his Bacardi, he and Gregory were alone again. Gregory played with his half-empty glass, moving it from hand to hand as if it were a potato he had just raked out of the bottom of a bonfire.

'There there dear boy. You don't think I meant it do you?' Trevor smiled, it was almost bashful embarrassment. 'That was just a little speech I learned when I was at sea. Off a stoker called Maureen. Big Mo.' He laughed at his own joke. 'Don't let that twat get to you. Come on, smile and the world smiles with you...that's better. Now then, another drink? My shout it is.'

Trevor stood up, rummaging in his pockets for change. A new record was on: Shirley Bassey's 'Big Spender'. A request. The barman had lost interest in their table and was serving someone. The couple at the end of the balcony were trying to freshen their make-up in the half-darkness. A crowd of men spilled over the top of the stairs and clattered towards the bar. Gregory finished his scotch and waited for the next one.

CHAPTER EIGHT

PROMOTIONS

'The Western seaboard of Europe provided rich pickings and easy access for the shallow vessels of the Norsemen. At first they started by going away on pirate expeditions. As time went on these became settlements...'

Siân Morris, of Friday morning's second-year tutorial group, had just begun her presentation on archaeological evidence for the centrality of Scandinavian migration to the revitalisation of Europe at the end of the Dark Ages. She was bent over her notes, long thin brown hair, neatly parted in the middle, hanging down around large wire-framed glasses. Gregory picked up a pencil off his desk: Siân probably knew as much as he did about the bloody Vikings, and cared more. She certainly seemed to care more at this minute than most of the others in the group. He shifted slightly in his chair, looking for a better view of them.

Diana Stone, sitting next to Siân and the epicentre of the smell of patchouli that would linger in the small room for the rest of the day, focused her gaze somewhere in the cosmic infinity that lay beyond the filing cabinets. Cosmic was her word, not Gregory's. She persisted in patronising Gregory - Doctor Alexander, as she insisted on calling him - by attending tutorials, but her studious inattention was his punishment for failing her first essay of the year. And perhaps he had been a little too sharp in his comments: 'Ley lines and water-divining may impress your hippy friends, Diana, but they will not see you through your mid-sessional examinations.' Today she was sporting a ragged black T-shirt with 'Legalise It' in fading letters over her very obvious nipples. Far out, indeed.

Alun Prosser, mid-thirties and balding, union badge in his denim jacket and a full bag of chips on his shoulder, sat with his legs apart, T-shirted belly bulging over the belt of his jeans, and his head back, listening, with his mouth half open. A Britannia Airways shoulder bag was tucked neatly under his chair. Thinking up something to say at the end. With any luck it might be to the point this week. Gregory wasn't sure why he was doing Archaeology; he seemed more the type for Politics or Sociology. But he was a hard worker, and not stupid.

His written work had improved beyond recognition since the beginning of the year, although he still said things that might often have been better left unsaid. When he called the Britons' Rome 'the working class', for example. Still, it was nothing worse than a mild case of tunnel vision, with a job in teaching or County Hall at the end of it. If he was lucky. And who could blame him? There was nothing left for him in coal mining any more.

'...it was about this time that the sea-rovers, or Normans as we now know them, began to challenge the supremacy of the Franks...'

'Hold on Siân. What's the matter with what Siân just said? Anybody?'

If they knew, they weren't saying. And Gregory knew, from a wealth of past experience, that waiting for these particular watched pots to boil was futile.

'Well Siân, do you think that at this time...what period is it that you're talking about here?'

'Um...'She looked down at the papers in her hands. 'Ninth century?' She smiled as she lifted her face.

'Well...do you think they were called Normans in the ninth century?'

Her smile faltered.

'No...that's right. You must beware of anachronism in your writing. Still, it's an easy mistake to make.' Gregory smiled at her. 'Carry on then.' Gregory drifted back to his consideration of the others. Gwyneth Williams, the other mature student, older and much too aware of what she saw as her weaknesses, was busily taking notes in a shorthand notebook. Before having her three children, she had been a secretary. If only she could pluck up the nerve to talk in tutorials with the same determination which she applied to her note-taking. He would try and have another wee chat with her afterwards.

And, finally, there was Michael Shannon, an attractive, fresh-faced nineteen-year old. Nice young lad. A boy. Difficult to know what else to call him, really. All tousled hair, freckles and torn jeans. Gregory found it hard to believe what he had read somewhere, that you could actually buy them like that, already torn. More expensive than brand new ones. He wondered whether Michael had ripped them himself. They must be mad.

The phone rang.

'Hold on Siân, sorry about this. Hello, Gregory Alexander.'

'Greg, it's Trev here. Sorry to ring you at work.'

'Yes.'

'Still speaking to me? Are you there?'

'I am.'

'Can't talk is it? Is that what it is?'

'That's right.'

'Okay, I'll be quick then. I just wanted to apologise...for last night. One over the nine, dear boy. You know how it is...still, no harm done, eh? Greg? Still there?'

'Yes.'

'So, no offence taken? Nothing ventured, eh?'

'No problem.'

'Maybe better luck next time? Never know your luck.'

'We'll have to see. Don't worry about it.'

'Well that's alright then. All's well that ends...'

'I'd better go now.'

'Right. Yes. I'll ring you. See you...'

'Cheerio then.'

Gregory put the phone down. The man was unspeakable. It was all he could do not to shudder at the thought of Trevor Thomas. He returned his attention to the tutorial. 'Sorry about that. There's always something, isn't there? So then Siân, where were we?'

Gwyneth Williams closed the door behind her with a quiet delicacy that might have been appropriate on leaving a room where a poorly child had finally gone off to sleep. In the middle of a busy university day it was merely theatrically timid. Gregory shook his head. Yes, she had said, I'm sure you're right, but I'm quite happy the way I am, I get lots out of tutorials. I take lots of notes, and they're very useful. Full of information... No, on reflection, whatever Gwyneth was she wasn't timid.

The phone rang. Gregory stood up, replaced his tutorial file in the second draw of the grey metal filing cabinet nearest to his desk, restacked the moulded plastic chairs, put them back in their place in the corner and returned to his desk.

'Gregory Alexander.' If it was bloody Trevor again...

'Greg...It's Adrian here. Have you got a minute?'

'Sure.'

'Do you want to just pop down the corridor then?'

Gregory replaced the phone. There had been a hesitancy in Adrian's voice. What was it now? Had he taken two A4 pads from the stationery cupboard at the same time? Was Adrian going to query his photocopying usage? His telephone bill? God knows. The sooner they got a proper Head of Department, the better. The sooner Adrian's trivial enthusiasms could be put back into proper perspective; although Gregory tried not to think about who the obvious candidate for the job actually was... Adrian had effortlessly filled the vacuum created by Bill Bellamy's retirement with a blizzard of memos and an avalanche of staff meeting resolutions – the one about the need to economise on A4 pads was one such – out of which he had created himself as a snowman tyrant. Gregory laughed at the thought... He could almost see Adrian melting. They just had to hope that College wouldn't be too long filling the chair.

He walked along to where the door of the word-processing room stood open. Pauline was busy with the automatic hopper feed of the printer. She looked up and smiled.

'And how are we today?' There was a soft undulation to her voice. West Wales. She was originally from just outside Carmarthen.

'Bearing up. Just been summoned to the presence.'

'Ooh...' She raised an eyebrow. 'What've you been up to then? Naughty boy.'

'Just what I was thinking. Exactly.'

'Go on then, or you'll never find out.' She winked, her face covering all the ground from maternal concern, to lascivious longing, to wide-eyed - what me? - innocence, all in the time it took to replace the printer's acoustic hood. 'Let's just hope he's not in a caning mood today... Oh, and I've done those references for you. They're in your tray.'

'I should be so lucky...thanks.'

Five steps further along the corridor, Gregory knocked on the door marked 'Mr Adrian Wallbutton M.A.'. He interpreted a muffled noise from the other side as an invitation to enter.

All that was visible of the man whose name was on the door was his backside, only just contained within the polished Terylene of a pair of trousers that had probably come from British Home Stores. Adrian had once confided to Gregory - standing with a urinal between them in the Gents at the time - that really, well, Marks and Sparks was a little up-market. A desk, nearly bare apart from a blotter, some pens and a phone stood between Gregory and Adrian. Behind Adrian and to one side was a large table which more than compensated for the Spartan minimalism of his desk: papers in untidy and promiscuous heaps jostled for space with paperbacks, rolled-up maps, ancient leather-bound tomes, old newspapers, box-files and half-empty jars of instant coffee, dried milk and sugar. The latter came complete with some mugs and spoons that looked as though they hadn't seen soap and water since the last Deluge, and a chromed kettle that obviously needed a new flex. Rustling paper was the only sound in the office. Adrian was rooting around in the bin. His face appeared over the edge of the desk, eyebrows awry and his glasses slipping ever further down his nose.

'Ah, Greg, there you are. Sit...sit.' He manoeuvred, breathless, into the high-backed swivel chair and tried to look serious. Gregory folded himself down onto the pine and cloth armchair that stood by the bookshelves. He was about eighteen inches below Adrian's eye level, but the only alternative was one of the plastic chairs behind the door. Adrian gestured towards the bin, now out of Gregory's sight. 'I've lost a memo. Thought perhaps it had found its way into the bin by mistake.'

Gregory smiled a small smile, thin and economical. 'I'm sure it'll turn up somewhere.'

Adrian was still looking at the bin. He shook his head.

'Yes, yes. Somewhere...now, what was it? Oh yes, it's good news. Well,' he laughed with half his mouth, 'good news for some. As of the first of next month, I got the letter this morning, as of next month I shall be officially Head of Department.' His cheeks shone and his eyes twinkled behind their horn-rimmed glasses. Gregory half-expected to see him take them off and polish them on his tie. Adrian always wore a tie. He had a selection which ranged from Gonville and Caius to Royal Porthcawl Golf Club.

'Well done. Meg must be very pleased.'

What might have been a small cloud passed over Adrian's smooth face. 'She doesn't know yet. Off shopping...in Cardiff.' Meg Wallbutton was fifteen years Adrian's junior. An ex-graduate student, she was the Dr Wallbutton whose name was on their joint bank account. 'Anyway, the point is, you see, the point is, one of the first things I've got to deal with, well, it's your SL. Appointments and Staffing meets in,' Adrian looked at his watch, 'four weeks. I'll have to do the Departmental Head's report. Just wanted you to know, to reassure you. Nothing to worry about, I'm sure, do all I can for you. Of course. Another Senior Lecturer...just what we need.' He laughed and looked anxiously at the bin again. 'Before we know where we are.'

'Yes. I'm sure...have to wait and see, eh?' Gregory shifted in the chair, making ready to stand up and leave. There was a silence. Adrian was still fretting over the lost memo. 'Was there anything else?'

'No, no... Where could I have put the wretched thing?'

'Maybe Pauline has it.' Gregory was on his feet.

'Yes...that's probably it.'

'Shall I send her in?' Gregory's hand was reaching for the door.

'No, I'll...wait a moment. There was something else.' Adrian was blushing, his neck and forehead as red as his cheeks. 'Sorry, I'm a bit distracted this morning.' He moved over to the window and stood with his back to the room. Beyond him, beyond the venetian blinds, Gregory could see the sea.

Gregory waited.

Adrian put both his hands in his pockets before he finally spoke.

'Have you heard about Braithwaite? You know...Philip Braithwaite. His research grant.'

'Uh huh. I have heard something.'

'Well...I'm sure it doesn't take me to emphasise what a...what an unfortunate business it is.'

Adrian waited, as if he was expecting an answer. There was none, so he turned to face his junior colleague.

'Yes, very unfortunate. Not least of all for College... Grants of that size aren't to be had every day. No. Still, let's hope that Braithwaite doesn't make a song and dance about it. No point in making things worse.' This time he very clearly was expecting an answer. He nearly looked Gregory in the eye as he waited.

'No...no point at all.' Gregory opened the door.

'Absolutely. Nothing to be gained by a lot of fuss and bother.'

Adrian turned back to his view of the Bristol Channel.

Gregory closed the door.

Pauline watched his back as he walked round the corner to his office without saying a word.

CHAPTER NINE

FRIDAY AFTERNOON

American Studies was located in a new red-brick building next door to the South Wales Venture Park on the town side of the campus. A white satellite dish on the roof stood next to a flagpole on which a grimy stars-and-stripes hung. Although it was a warm day, with little or no breeze to animate the listless flag, the light overcast did not allow enough sun through to create definite shadows. In a different setting the light might have called the Impressionists to mind; as it was, it was simply flat and thin.

Half an hour after his interview with Adrian, Gregory turned round the building's corner towards the front entrance. Two years after moving in, the Maintenance Department were still getting around to fitting a departmental name plate. Instead, a piece of yellow card with the name in Welsh and English in large, but by now somewhat faded, felt-tip letters was sellotaped in one of the windows. Faye's Metro – more or less the same yellow as the sign – was in the car park.

Her office was at the end of the central corridor. On the brick wall beside her door – grey bricks inside the building – was a full-length black-and-white photograph of Marilyn Monroe with her skirt billowing up in the air. Gregory could never remember which film it was from. On the wall opposite, next to the Ladies' toilet, was another photograph of the same size: John F. Kennedy on his Inauguration Day, standing with his right hand raised to God. Their face-to-face juxtaposition in the corridor had been Faye's idea. Somebody else had given JFK a toothbrush moustache in pencil. A number of attempts to rub it out had simply produced a grey smudge in the middle of his face.

Faye's door was open. There were no voices coming from within.

'Hello there.' Gregory poked his head inside.

Faye turned in her chair, then the chair turned on its castors with the movement of her body.

'Greg.' It was not her usual smile. It wasn't much of a smile at all.

'Can I come in?'

'Don't be silly.' She waved him over to the room's one armchair. As she did so, her other hand slid under her seat and moved the lever, which lowered it to the same level as her visitor. This was a standard courtesy on Faye's part, she did it without thinking. 'And to what do I owe this pleasure?'

'Nothing really...nothing special. I've been trying to get you for weeks. Must've phoned the house about twenty times. More in fact.' Faye lived miles away, at the top end of one of the small valleys on the other side of the motorway. 'Isn't it about time you bought yourself an answering machine?'

'You could've rung me here.'

'How many times have you told me you don't like people calling you at work? Anyway, I did. Two or three times. So in the end I decided I'd better come over and see where you were hiding yourself.'

'Well, as you can see, I'm not hiding myself. Was there anything else you wanted?'

'I'm not sure if there was. Not if you're in this kind of mood.' Faye opened her mouth to reply. She thought better of it. Gregory continued. 'I was wondering if you were free over the weekend. I know it's a wee bit short notice, today being Friday and things, you know, but maybe tomorrow...for a meal maybe...if you're not too busy with Ioan.'

'And what does that mean? And no, I am not too busy with fucking Ioan.' Faye turned away and stared at the year planner pinned on the notice-board above her desk. It shared the space with a colour poster of an elephant's backside in close-up, underneath which, in large pink letters, it said: 'Go On, Try And Make Me'.

There was also a postcard of St Mark's Square... Gregory recognised it as the one he had sent her on his last trip to Venice, nine, ten months ago. Nearly a year. The last time he had spent with Philip.

'Nothing... It doesn't mean anything. What's going on? For God's sake, I thought I was the one who needed cheering up...'

'I don't need cheering up...'

'Well, is everything alright then?' What a stupid question...

'No it bloody isn't. Does it look like everything's alright?' There were tears on the brink of trickling down on to her cheeks. She banged one of her fists, white to the knuckle, on the chair arm. 'What a bloody state to get into. And over what? Over a man?' She turned back to look at Gregory.

'D'you want to talk about it?' Locked away inside him, Gregory was sure that there was a lame script for a lame movie – a TV movie, by the sound of things, maybe even an Australian soap – just waiting for an appreciative audience in order to reveal itself. He couldn't believe he was saying this stuff.

'No...not now anyway.' Faye pulled a handful of tissues from a box on the floor at her feet and wiped her eyes. She blew her nose and threw the crumpled paper in the bin. It missed. Gregory picked it up and placed it carefully among the discarded junk mail, orange peel and dried-out tea bags. There were some other tissues in there already. Faye laughed, nearly. 'You'll make somebody a lovely wife one day.' She sniffed and wiped her nose on the back of her hand.

Gregory did not acknowledge the joke. She'd cracked it several times before. It hadn't been funny the first time and it didn't improve with repetition.

'Maybe I'd better just go and leave you in peace?'

'No, no...' Faye's mascara was smudged on both eyes and her hair looked as if it hadn't been combed that morning. 'Jesus, what am I doing...? Greg, I'm sorry. There's no excuse for treating you like a prat...fucking daft, isn't it? Sorry, I know you don't like swearing. And d'you know? If it was that...If it was Ioan sitting in that chair, I'd be behaving myself. Nice as bloody pie.'

A bird sang outside the open window. A blackbird. Faye's office looked out onto the back of the new College Sports Centre, the water-purifying plant for the swimming pool. It was one of her stock jokes for visitors that the pipe work had been assembled according to a more coherent set of aesthetic values and principles than some of the sculpture that cropped up here and there around campus. And, as she was only too ready to admit, the main thing wrong with that joke was that it was probably true... The blackbird stopped. She took a cigarette from the packet on the desk and lit it.

'Do you know how many of these I'm smoking a day? It's ridiculous. Sitting here daydreaming...like Rapunzel in her bloody tower. Up a gum tree, more like.'

'So what have you been doing?'

'Not a lot...believe me, not a lot.'

'And...'

'Don't ask.'

'So what about doing something then? Tonight?'

'Well I'm not doing anything.'

'So?'

'Okay...No, I'll tell you what. Come up to my place. I'll cook.'

Gregory pulled a face: 'Tuna salad?'

'If you don't shut up, you'll end up with dumplings... I've been practising. Madhur Jaffrey eat your heart out. Curry alright?'

'I'll bring the Setlers.'

'No need. I've got a king-size box of Kwells left over from America.'

'What're you doing this afternoon?'

'Working...' Her desk was piled with essays. 'And then I'd better go to Tesco's... I've got this divine man coming to dinner, and if I don't do something the cupboard will most definitely be bare when he arrives...and we couldn't have that now, could we? Anyway, speaking of work,' Faye stood up and looked at her watch, 'I've got to get on. These have all got to be marked this afternoon.'

'Alright, alright. No need to push me out the door.'

'I didn't go on that assertiveness course for nothing...'

'What did you go for?'

Faye aimed a cuff at his ear as he rose to his feet. The hand hooked around his neck instead and pulled him towards her. It was a very tight hug and Gregory hugged her back. For a minute or so they stood there. Faye patted him on the back and tousled his hair.

'Thanks...for coming to see me.'

'Get away.'

They stood close together for another moment. Faye kissed him on the cheek.

'There. Off you go now.'

'Aye.' Gregory could feel his eyes moistening now.

'I'll see you later.'

'About what time d'you want me?'

'Sevenish?'

'Fine.'

'We'll talk then. Tell you all about it. 'She patted him on the arm. 'I'll get lots of wine. I could do with getting completely rat-arsed.'

'That makes two of us.'

CHAPTER TEN

SATURDAY MORNING (AND FRIDAY NIGHT)

Faye lived in a modern bungalow with whitewashed walls and a grey tile roof. It had been christened 'High Chaparral' by the people who had sold it to her, and since she had done nothing about the poker-work wooden name-board hanging on its wrought-iron frame by the gate, that was its name still.

The house stood on the western side of the valley, just where it elbowed and narrowed on its slow trail down from the upland plateau beyond, turning at this point into a long, crooked gulch, reaching southwards towards the flatlands of the Bristol Channel shore. Although only a small valley, it had been home to half a dozen or so pits in the years before the Great War. Now there were none. Not a heritage park or an open-air museum was left. The last cage had been wound up and the last pit-head cut up for scrap more than fifteen years ago. Today there was only the great desolate scab of the open-cast on the top of the hill to the west, the sawmill, and a Japanese factory assembling circuitry for television remote-control units. And adult male unemployment well into double figures.

Various attempts at reclaiming and landscaping the debris of more than a century's mining had wreaked their own tidy havoc upon the cwm. There was too much plain green open space, and it was all much too regular, much too smooth. Although it pleased the Development Agency planners, and might even have been some kind of improvement on the spoil tips and rusting sidings that the grass now covered, there was now a hygienic look to the place that didn't quite fit. Even after all that expensive attention, the eye still fell everywhere and anywhere upon brick-built megaliths and cast-iron alignments, monuments to the recent Industrial Age. And where once there had been thousands of people, only a few hundred remained, many either old or ageing - grey-haired and black-lunged - faster than they had ever feared they would.

Many times Faye had been asked, why? Why choose to live in a place like this? What followed depended on who was doing the asking. Why not live closer to College? In a smaller house? By the sea? Closer to Cardiff? – that was her personal favourite, that one. Or somewhere with more people that she knew? Which usually translated as more people that the questioner knew. Somewhere more scenic? Or, for heaven's sake, somewhere with a little more character? And there were variations on these themes. Wouldn't it be difficult to sell? Wasn't it gloomy? Boring? Or so far away from any decent shops? Weren't the valleys people very close-knit communities, unfriendly to strangers? And don't most of them speak Welsh when you get that far up? They wouldn't be likely to welcome an English woman, living on her own. And so on, and so on...

Her answer was always the same. Where else could you walk a mile up the road, stand on the top of the valley, and see the Black Mountains to the east, the Brecon Beacons to the north-west, and the sea to the south? Where else did you only see friends who'd bothered to come up and see you – and therefore presumably wanted to see you – and where else could you go away for a few weeks, leave the key with a neighbour and know the house would be looked after until you got back? And all for under fifty thousand? You couldn't find a cubby-hole for that price anywhere near College.

Not that finding it had been easy. Faye had spent months hunting. Up and down the valleys, in and out at every other bend in the road, always knowing more-or-less what she was looking for. Modern – that way it would be easier and cheaper to maintain – not too big, and on a western valley side. She'd rather look at the sun rising than face it setting...although on a good summer evening that didn't stop her walking to the top of the road, or driving the three or four miles up to the standing stone at the head of the valley, to catch the sun's final curtain call, off to the west.

And this morning the sun had risen. Which is not to suggest that it didn't always, but, the weather in those parts being what it is, sunrise wasn't always a visible event. Today the sky was a lovely thin blue, apart from a few clouds assembling slowly over the Beacons, and the sun shone full in through the window of Faye's bedroom, past the open curtains and on to the crumpled pillows and duvet of a broad double bed.

She stood in the light, stretching and feeling the soft hair on the back of her neck ruffle as she moved, this way and that as the sinews of her still sleeping muscles tightened. Her breasts rose and fell as she leant over, first backwards and then forwards. She touched her toes and stayed down, grasping her ankles to maintain the pressure in the back of her calves.

There was a noise in the doorway behind her. Without standing up Faye caught an upside-down glimpse of movement.

'Sorry...' The doorway was empty again.

Gregory! That was a view-and-a-half to greet him first thing. She straightened, moved over to the wardrobe and slipped on the dressing gown that hung on the door handle.

In the kitchen, cups and glasses rattled and cupboard doors banged open and shut. Gregory was making coffee. He was also cleaning away the flotsam of last night's meal and making a start on the washing up. He didn't look up from the sink as Faye came in. She stood behind him. Close enough but not too close.

'Sorry about that...didn't know you were up.'

'No, no...my fault. You don't just wander around somebody else's house and...'

"Fraid you do when you're a guest here...anyway, I hope it wasn't too shocking a sight.' She wanted to reach out, to touch perhaps just an elbow. A shoulder even. Her hands stayed in the dressing gown pockets. She craved a cigarette. Where were they?

'Not at all...no.' Was he embarrassed, or what? She couldn't tell. His voice didn't give anything away. 'Shocking? No, no...you see worse any day of the week on the beach in Spain.' He took his hands out of the soapy water and began to towel them dry. Still he did not turn around.

'Don't you mean you'd see better?' She took her hands out of the safety of their pockets and put one on each of Gregory's shoulders. 'Come here.' She turned him round. 'You lovely, silly man.' Now she was hugging him. 'It's not important...Oh, Greg.' He hugged her back. 'What's a bare bum between friends?' Faye started to laugh. Slowly, his head tucked in between her ear and her shoulder, Gregory joined in.

'I don't think it was actually the bum that was the problem...' Faye tapped him sharply, twice, on the back of his head with the flat of her hand. 'Anyway, since you're the lady of the house, how about making some coffee while I tidy this mess up?' Gently, Gregory disengaged himself and turned back to the sink.

But I don't even know whether I like porridge!' Faye looked down at the steaming bowl in front of her and then up at Gregory. Her nose wrinkled.

'Then what's a packet of Quaker Oats doing in the cupboard? Anyway, it's good for you.'

Gregory had set the table with napkins, cutlery, place-mats, and milk and sugar.

'But they must be ages old. Probably came with the place...and lots of things are good for me. Doesn't mean to say I have to have them for breakfast.'

He stood up and walked over to the cupboards as he replied. 'Get it down you...all it needs is a wee bit of salt.'

'Ugh...no thank you very much...where's the honey?' Now it was her turn to stand. The honey was in the fridge. 'Salt indeed.'

'Here. Try a bit.' He sat down and offered her a spoonful. 'It's the only way to take it. Honest. Go on...' He dipped the offered spoon a few times towards her. 'Taste it, it's lovely.'

'I feel as if I should be in a high chair.' She tried a little bit, leaning forward to do so, taking it off the spoon with her top front teeth and the tip of her tongue. 'It's dull. Hardly tastes of anything. I think I'll stick with milk and honey.'

'Suit yourself...you'll never grow up to be big and strong.'

Ten minutes later they were on to toast – Gregory had even located a toast-rack – and strawberry jam. The marmalade jar had been discovered to be empty apart from some spectacular blue mould.

'How's your head?' Gregory didn't pause in buttering his toast to ask the question. He reached over for the jam.

'So so...not too bad considering how much of that wine I put away last night. Pass that over when you're finished. And yours?'

'I don't think I drank as much as you did. Here.'

'Self-righteous bugger.'

'Famous for it...what time did you get to your bed at?'

'God knows...some time after four.'

'You must be tired...sorry I kept you...'

'Forget it, don't be so daft...I'm fine.'

They were silent again, crunching toast with the enthusiasm that only a mild hangover can inspire. Faye made some more coffee.

'How did you sleep?'

'Fine...great. It's a very comfy bed.'

'No dream?'

'No.' He opened a fresh carton and poured some milk into his cup. 'No...maybe she doesn't dare trespass on another woman's territory.' The milk was on the turn and small off-white globules of cream floated on top of the coffee.

'Don't joke.' Faye shivered.

'I'm not.' Slowly, he stirred the mixture.

Faye sniffed the milk. 'Sorry about that...must've forgotten to put it in the fridge yesterday.' She pushed her plate to one side, piled high with nibbled toast crusts. 'I'll pop down to the shop and get some more.'

'Don't be daft. It'll do fine...if I stop stirring it... I'm sitting here like a zombie... Appropriate enough metaphor, eh?'

'Listen...' She picked up a crust and passed it from one set of fingers to the other and back again. Backwards and forwards. 'You know last night? Well, I don't know how you feel about it...but I think it was really important. To me, I mean...special. Know what I mean?'

Faye, in the end, had not cooked. They ate well. A take-away from the Bombay Balti Bistro, Bridgend's finest, warmed up in the microwave: lamb and spinach, various bhajis, tandoori chicken and fish – the latter not on the public menu, but Faye was a valued, and very regular, customer – rotis, keema nan, Bombay duck, channa dhall and pilau rice. Small portions of the main courses. With Thayer's chocolate ice-cream to follow there was more than enough.

Gregory was an avid reader of the wine columns in the Observer and the Independent on Sunday. His contribution was two bottles of a recent discovery, Boolagong River, an

Australian Cabernet Sauvignon; 1989 was apparently an exciting vintage. It certainly wasn't cheap. To these Faye added two Tesco's wine boxes – a red and a dry white – and a few big bottles of fizzy water. They ate the food hot and then they ate it cold, in shifts and nibbles, starting at about nine.

By eleven, they were drunk enough and sufficiently full of food to talk properly. They had, by this stage, ridiculed Adrian and the internal politics of the Archaeology Department, speculated about the rights and wrongs of an affair which one of Faye's colleagues was rumoured to be conducting with an American junior-year-abroad student, reviewed the ins-and-outs of Faye's trip to the States – and the ups-and-downs – this time with the photographs, and laughed at the most recent of her mother's tactics in nursing home terrorism.

Which eventually brought them onto Faye and Ioan. And tears and indignation. A log fire was dying down in the ranch-house style brick fireplace in the front room, the one with the picture window looking down over the valley. Faye lay on the rug, clutching a pillow under her chin, intermittently trying to drink without either having to raise her chin too much, or spill the wine.

'But do you know what it was really hurt?' On her cheeks, tear tracks had dried streaky in the heat from the embers. 'I said to him, I said, okay...' She inhaled deeply on a cigarette and flicked the butt into the fire. 'Okay, I'll go and have the test if you will. We can go together. And d'you know what he said, the bastard? He said: But I don't need to. How do you know, I said, how do you know? How do I know that you don't need to? But he just looked at me and said that he hadn't been promiscuous and that's why he didn't need to.'

She lit another cigarette. Gregory sat quietly, the last glass of Australian red in his hand reflecting the reading lamp and the glow of burning wood. Faye was talking like a stream in flood, a meltwater of words tumbling head over heels over the rocks and stones towards some unseen end.

'Promiscuous! How many fucking men does he think I have a night? But it wasn't just that, it was, I don't know, bizarre. I've never met anyone like that before...It was as if the whole world was filled with this thing, this threat that was out to get him. As if AIDS was specially aimed just at him. He wouldn't use public toilets, not even on the train. If he was really caught short he might just allow himself to have a pee, but not at a urinal, you know where they all stand together. Said you never knew if any of them were queers...queers, he said. But, and this is even funnier, that wasn't the word he used most often...and I've never heard anyone talk about it as much... There were two words really, homosexuals and perverts. He used to pronounce them so politely. Like he was in an elocution class. Ho-mo-seks-yoo-als. Purr-verts. Christ. Talk about protesting too fucking much.'

Faye was still holding the toast crust, each end balanced on a pair of fingertips. She looked under the arch that was thus formed at Gregory. Waiting for an answer. In the silence that was shaping its hood around them, filling the space in between and spilling over to the rest of the kitchen, Gregory stood up and took his breakfast dishes across to the sink.

'So what is it you see in this man? There must be something...'

'Saw, you mean. Saw. Past tense.'

'Alright, don't bite my head off. What is it you saw then?'

'Buggered if I know now, bloody stupid... No, no, that's not true. Not fair either.' Faye wiped her nose on the back of her hand and took another lungful of smoke. She leaned over, took some more wood from the side of the grate and put it on the fire. 'There was something. Difficult to say really. Isn't it always? Probably his eyes at first. Such blue eyes, deep, deep blue. Really, like a...I don't what like. Amazing. Like Paul Newman, but with warmth in them, more colour. And he could listen. In the beginning anyway...God knows, what did he see in me is maybe a better question. Did he see anything?' She wiped her nose again and stared into the fire. Flames were starting to flicker round the edges of the new logs.

Gregory remained silent, standing over the sink. The only noise in the kitchen was the tinkle and clatter of the washing up. Faye went looking for her cigarettes.

And one silence is quite different from another. Faye had cried some more. She banged her knuckles against the fireplace bricks hard enough to skin one, a swollen bruise that throbbed all through the next day. Twice she let out full-throated howls of anger and dismay. Eventually she was quiet.

They lay in the warmth and flicker of the fire. Faye had curled up, her head on Gregory's lap. For more than an hour she lay there, half dozing. She might have been asleep, although asleep she would probably have made more noise and movement than she did. Fitfully, Gregory stroked her hair as it covered her ear and cheek. For more than an hour not a word was spoken.

'Look, I'm not making a big deal out of it...Gregory, will you at least turn round and look at me?'

For a moment he did not move. Then he lifted the plate out of the bowl of soapy water, placed it carefully in the draining rack, next to last night's wineglasses which he had washed earlier, dried his hands and stood looking at her.

'What do you want me to say?' He put his hands up, palms out. 'I know, I know, it's me...I'm just not very good at this kind of thing.'

'What kind of thing?' She knew, but she wanted to hear him say it. She wanted to hear him say anything.

'About...about what you feel. About what I feel.' He sat down opposite her again, his eyes on the tablecloth with its crumbs and grains of salt. 'Oh I don't know.'

'But what do you feel?' This was a rash move, and Faye knew it. 'Wasn't it special?'

Getting no more of an answer than a movement of his finger as it traced a pattern in some spilled sugar, she pressed on. 'That's what was special, you bloody twit. You. You talking about your feelings...'

The brass carriage clock on the mantelpiece, a moving-in present from Faye's widowed aunt in St Leonard's-on-Sea, had just struck one o'clock. Faye lifted her head, then sat up, cross-legged, facing the remains of the fire. She was beginning to feel a little chilly. Rubbing her shoulders with her hands first, she set to work rebuilding the flames with more logs from the remains of the pile beside the grate. It was only a matter of minutes before she had to retreat in the face of the heat, shuffling along the floor on her bottom, back to where Gregory sat with his back to the humbug-striped sofa.

That was one of the first things which the new visitor to Faye's house noticed and had to adjust to. Nothing matched, or at least nothing matched in any conventional sense. A combination of some furniture that had come with the house, her own idiosyncratic sense of style and interior decoration, a reasonably high threshold of unconcern about her surroundings, and a low-budget, opportunistic acquisitions policy - which relied heavily on sales, special offers and second-hand shops - produced an effect that was somewhere between Ramsay Street and the Old Curiosity Shop.

The sofa shared the room with two brown cord and natural wood chairs, a floral patterned carpet, an elegant matt black TV and a similar midi system - both by Hitachi, an unusual piece of co-ordination for Faye - an old and battered sideboard in some kind of dark wood and a row of mock pine quick-assembly bookcases crammed with a higgledy-piggledy selection of airport paperbacks, academic texts and old hardback novels. Every time Gregory was in the house he noticed it all over again. Once, he had commented on the colours. Never mind, she laughed, you don't have to live here. She stuck her tongue out at him: There, she said, my manners are worse than my taste.

Faye settled down with her knees under her chin and her arms clasped round her shins.

'Did you ever stare at the fire, when you were a child? I can remember volcanoes and eruptions, great lava flows. And dragons. And the little blue flames that used to shoot out of the coal. All of a sudden, off at an angle. Like the stories you used to read about going to Mars...I read all those things in the *Eagle*. I'd steal my brother's old annuals; there was a big box full of them in the cupboard up in his bedroom. I loved Dan Dare...and that woman scientist, what was she called? God, I don't know.'

'Professor Peabody.'

'What?'

'That's what she was called. Professor Peabody.'

'That's right! Yes...Jocelyn Peabody, if memory serves. Something like that anyway.' Faye lit a cigarette and stared back into the fire, smoke curling up into the glow. They sat in silence for a moment again.

'I can remember,' Gregory shifted his position in search of comfort, 'I can remember thinking that that was what Hell must be like...only you'd burn and burn and keep burning. Never burn away. Never ever.'

Faye said nothing. The fire popped and hissed and settled in the grate. She reached out for the red wine box and filled both of their glasses. She felt that she needed to do something, anything, rather than address the silence which threatened from the shadows. For good measure she moved back over to the fire and put on one more log. Now the room was very warm. She would have given a lot to be able to take her top off. Sweat was trickling between her bra-less breasts, down into the folds of her stomach as she sat, on her hunkers now. She had eaten too much. She wanted to fart.

'I'd get the Devil from my mother and ghosts from my Uncle Charlie.' Gregory drank some wine. 'Hellfire and eternal damnation on the one hand, ghosties and ghoulies on the other. D'you know, I used to go to bed afraid of dying in the night. My mother always used to make me say my prayers at night...made me feel worse, not better.'

'That's a long time ago now.' Faye reached out for his hand.

'Aye...but is it?'

Faye's attention had wandered back to the spitting and leaping spirits of the fire. She only caught the end of Gregory's quiet question to himself.

'What? Is it what?'

'A long time ago.'

'Sorry, don't know what you're on about.'

After another mouthful of wine, Gregory moved his head to look at her.

'Do you dream much?'

'Dream? A bit, sometimes. Same as everybody I suppose...some of them are quite good.' This was accompanied by a quiet laugh as she turned back to the fire again. 'Why?'

'D'you ever have the same dream?'

'Over and over you mean?'

'Aye, something like that.'

'No...no. Though, one or two I wouldn't mind.'

'I'm not being funny.'

Gregory's voice and its emphasis were sobering. She looked at him again. His face was grey and empty, a screen waiting for a projectionist.

'What's this about? What're you getting at?'

'It's my mother. I'm dreaming about her. I think it's a dream...sometimes I'm not so sure, though, whether it's a dream or whether...something else. A ghost, I suppose. I don't know. In my room, I wake up and she's been there.'

'How many times have you dreamt this?'

'Four, five times. Hard to tell.'

'And you see her? Your mother? In your bedroom?'

'No...not exactly. Maybe I just don't remember it. I wake up and I know she's been there. I just know. She gets closer every time. To the bed.'

'It's only a dream. Just a daft dream.' Faye touched his hand again, stroked the back of it with her flat palm. 'It'll pass.'

'And she knows now. About me.'

'Knows?'

'Knows...about me.'

'Oh, right. Yes.'

'That wine's dulled your wits.'

'Perhaps you could try being a bit more direct. With yourself, even if nobody else. Try saying what you mean.'

'I was...saying what I mean.'

'Fair enough... No, I mean it...look at you. Half out of the bloody closet and half in. Everyone else knows...except you. You're the only one that doesn't know. It's you that you're fooling. No-one else.'

When he didn't reply, she carried on, staring at the fire through a cock-eyed lens of glass and wine.

'I mean, everybody knows. Greg, I don't mean to be hard on you, but sometimes...'

'Everybody doesn't know. My mother never knew... And I still don't...I don't know anything just at the moment.'

Hours later, Faye gently eased out from under the duvet of the bed in the guest room. Gregory lay with his back to her, breathing gently and very softly. It had taken a long time for his hurt to subside into rest. She had thought his head would never leave the resting-place it had finally found between her breasts, or the one hand move from its chosen spot between skin and T-shirt. Hot, stiff, uncomfortable and bored, Faye watched and waited in the dark as long as she was needed. Now he was sleeping. Standing up, she looked down where he lay, softly smoothed the covers and walked on quiet, gentle feet to her own empty bedroom.

CHAPTER ELEVEN

A SURPRISE

The first thing Gregory noticed when he stepped into the hall from the street was the small parcel on the table. He took his key from the lock and gently closed the door. There was no other post. Just brown paper and lots of sellotape. Some of the stamps were Scottish, but the postmarks were badly smudged. There was no sender's name either, nothing written in big square black felt-tip capitals other than his own name and address. It didn't look official, nor as if it was from the solicitors in Dumfries who'd been in touch on Uncle Charlie's behalf. Charlie had just made a will, and Gregory was to get the house back when he died. Curiosity tugged gently at his coat-tails as he let himself into the flat.

In the kitchen he set the package down and began to make a pot of tea. Gregory always had to think about which kind he wanted. Growing up in his mother's house there had only ever been Typhoo, there was never a decision to make. After a moment's eeny-meeny-minying he opened the lid of the English Breakfast tin. Something good and strong. He boiled the kettle, warmed the pot, wet the tea, and turned back to the table. Sometimes he enjoyed the anticipation of not opening letters or parcels at once. Now, however, today, there was nothing else to be done. He went to the drawer where the scissors lay neatly beside the tin opener, the garlic press, the cheese grater...

The phone rang.

It was Ellie.

'Gregory? Is that you?'

'And who else would it be? The Giant Pumpkin?'

'What?'

'Nothing. Just a joke...an American joke. The Giant Pumpkin? Charlie Brown on Hallowe'en? Never mind. What can I do for you?'

'What's got into you? Did somebody get out the wrong side of your bed or what?'

'Sorry...bit of a hangover.' Which wasn't true. All things considered he felt fine. Now.

After all, it was nearly half past three in the afternoon. He didn't feel too bad at all.

'So you don't feel like drinks tonight?'

'Er...where?'

'Round here, where else? Just a few people. We thought we'd celebrate Adrian's elevation...'

'Is he coming?'

'God no. I was joking this time.'

'Right.'

'We are celebrating something though...'

'Oh...what?'

'You gotta come to find out...any time after eight. Okay? Anyway...okay honey, coming right now... Look, gotta go now.'

'Right.'

'So we'll see you later then. Bye.'

'Bye then.'

He wandered back into the kitchen. What could Ellie have to celebrate?..Something to do with her book? He stopped. Ellie had mentioned Adrian. Promotion. Maybe that was it... Shit. He poured himself a cup of tea. Milk, no sugar. Absent-mindedly he closed the door. Shit!

Gregory was the last person to arrive. Late. It was nearly nine thirty. After a shower and something to eat - old chilli from the freezer and stale French bread - he had dozed off in front of the television. The last thing he could remember was *Blind Date*... Saturday night programmes were rubbish, but it was at least stupid enough to laugh at. That's what he told himself, anyway. Sandra from Darlington and Andy from Catford (or was it Andrea from Darlington and Sandy from Catford?) had been to Copenhagen. Or was it Amsterdam? Together on tape. Talking about each other...that was the last thing he heard.

The night before had exhausted his body and buffeted his mind to the point where time could no longer be passed awake. Before he knew it had happened, the LCD display on the video was reading ten to nine.

Another shower completed the recuperation which sleep had begun. A bowl full of Greek yoghurt and a banana helped too, and the walk round to Ellie and Art's. The evening was mild and sunny. A gentle on-shore breeze blew up the terraced streets and the smell of the sea raised a flare in his nostrils.

Art opened the front door. In terms of height he wasn't a big man, perhaps five four, five five. He made up for this by always wearing shoes with heels, and never looking up to anyone. At his time of life - roughly the early forties - his paunch had probably settled in for good. A thick black beard was precisely trimmed around the outside edge of his jaw, and the aviator spectacles resting on a nose that seemed too thin and sharp for the rest of his round-cheeked face were tinted, so it was never easy to properly read the expression in his deep-set, restless eyes. Even though he was indoors he wore a baseball cap...underneath, the still black hair was starting to thin. Art had a glass of white wine in his hand: fizzy white. Gregory had brought a bottle of Australian dry white. Hardy Brothers. Perhaps he should have dug out that bottle of Cava from the cupboard instead.

'Gregory. Come in, come in...bringing up the rear, eh?' Art allowed himself a sly half-chuckle.

'Sorry I'm late Art. Fell asleep...'

'Never mind. Antonia's just arrived too. Academics, all the same.'

Antonia? The name meant nothing to Gregory. There were eight or nine people in the long main room which stretched from the bay window to French doors at the back. Over the dark wood and bright tiles of the newly restored fireplace hung a framed poster for a Grant Wood exhibition. Was *American Gothic* the only bloody thing he'd ever painted? Ellie came over to greet the new arrival. She was wearing a voluminous sun dress, gathered in under her small bust. It made her look pregnant.

'Greg...where've you been? Never mind, let's get you a drink. Gimme that.'

She took the bottle that Gregory was still holding and steered him across to a trolley on which was assembled a miniature Manhattan of bottles of various shapes, sizes and colours. It looked as if she was drinking orange juice.

'What can I get you?'

'Um...is there any of that fizzy?' Gregory gestured towards where Art was standing by the window. He was talking to a woman in a blue dress, about forty but working hard at looking younger, and a bald man with the remains of his hair combed over the top of his head. He was vaguely familiar, but Gregory couldn't place him.

'I'll go and see.'

Ellie vanished into the back of the house. Gregory looked around, hoping to appear relaxed. Pauline and her husband, Eddie, were standing on their own on the other side of the fireplace. She smiled at Gregory, thinly and nervously. Eddie nodded. Eddie sold central heating. Another couple sat on the sofa, uncomfortable on its overstuffed upholstery. They were probably friends of Art. A young woman, a girl really, no more, perched beside them on one of the arms, busily chattering to the woman. The man, he looked like her husband, looked bored too.

'Here.'

Gregory turned around. The hand that offered him the glass was not Ellie's. On one of its fingers was a huge silver ring with a dark blue stone set in it. On the other end of its arm was a large woman with an enormous Afro of red hair. Brown eyes, wide open with permanent amazement at the world, unblinkingly met his from behind huge round glasses with green frames. From her ears hung heavy silver globes.

'Ellie asked me to bring it into you. You're Gregory Alexander, aren't you?' She held out her hand and Gregory had to shift the glass into his left hand to respond. It was a firm handshake. A man's handshake, thought Gregory. 'I'm Antonia Grimaldi. I've seen you in College.'

Gregory tipped his head slightly, to one side, a question.

'I work in Social Studies. With Philip...Braithwaite.'

'Ah...Philip.'

'You're a friend of his I gather...?'

The answer took a moment to come. Gregory straightened his head and looked right at the middle of her forehead.

'Yes. I know Philip.'

Antonia Grimaldi, to her credit, blushed.

'I'm sorry. You're quite right. That wasn't very direct, was it?'

'Oh...I don't know.' Gregory sipped his wine. It could have done with being colder. And drier. He looked around the room again.

'That's my daughter.' She nodded towards the young woman by the sofa. 'Marietta. She's home from University. For the weekend.'

'Where is she?'

'Aston...doing ophthalmology... I must have had more to drink than I thought.' She looked into her near-empty glass. 'I can't usually get my tongue round that...not sober.'

Gregory did not even smile. 'Very sensible, ophthalmology... Tell me,' he had been listening to her accent, 'are you a local?'

'Close. Cwmbran. It's near Newport.'

'Yes, I know. Great shopping centre.' Now he laughed, quietly. 'We don't all live in a wee University bubble, you know. But where does the name Grimaldi come from? Doesn't exactly sound Welsh.'

'Oh, it's mine. My ex was called Jackson. That's Marietta Jackson.' She indicated her daughter again. 'No, my great-grandfather came over at the turn of the century. From northern Italy. Savoy. My dad has a chip shop, his dad was in ice-cream.'

The gap that would probably have followed this last remark was forestalled by Ellie's reappearance in the doorway. She had a bottle in her hand.

'Is everyone's glass full?'

Gregory looked down at his. It would do. There were mutterings of assent and interrupted conversation.

Art's voice drew the attention which Ellie had commanded with her entrance to him.

'Are you going to tell them or shall I? Me?'

Ellie nodded. A straight return to Art over the net.

'Okay. I guess I'll have to...well folks, we asked you here today as our closest, dearest friends in Llanorgan' – he tried hard to get the double 'l' right, and it was a reasonable effort – 'to share with us some important news... No, not to share it, to celebrate it!' There was a pause. Art was an old pro. He might have been addressing a group of middle managers. Gregory felt queasy. Get on with it man. 'We...no, not we. Ellie's gonna have a baby...'

Smiles and 'oohs' and 'brilliants' – that was probably Marietta – and even a 'well done' – that was the bald man – mingled in with what Art was saying. Gregory said nothing. Insofar as she could while holding a glass of wine, Antonia clapped her hands together.

'...so we'd like you all to join us in raising our glasses...to parenthood.'

Although it was not a sentiment for which Gregory had ever felt much enthusiasm, it was better than what he had been half-expecting. Half-fearing. He warmed to his hosts' good fortune.

'To parenthood.' 'Parenthood.' The toast echoed an imperfect unison, fizzling out as the women closed around Ellie, who stood blushing and glowing, apparently stage-struck by the spotlight into which Art's announcement had thrust her.

The one woman who did not move was Antonia.

'Not going to fuss over the mother-to-be?' Gregory arched his best eyebrow and tipped his head almost imperceptibly towards Ellie.

'God no. It's not all it's cracked up to be. Motherhood...anyway, she told me yesterday. We've done all that.' She waved a dismissive hand in the direction of the doorway.

Gregory had not known that Antonia and Ellie were friends at all, let alone the intimates that was thus implied.

'Have you known Ellie long?'

'No, not really. I've only been in Llanorgan since October. September really. Moved down from London when I got the job here. Marietta hates it...pops down every once in a while. Under protest. Three-line bloody whip.'

'If she's used to London...'

'Suppose so. 'Nother drink?' She took Gregory's empty glass and went across to where Art was busily dispensing more of the same. Gregory caught Ellie's eye, no more than a second, and smiled. She barely noticed. Her arm around Marietta's shoulder, she vanished in the direction of the kitchen again. With the exception of Antonia, the other women followed.

Not more than ninety minutes later Antonia and Gregory stood on the pavement. Some of the other guests had already left, they weren't the first, and Art had seen them out with a cheery wave and a slap on the back for Gregory. Marietta, having discovered that she shared a passion for Asian cooking with Ellie, was still in the kitchen, 'just helping out'. At eleven o'clock at night they were experimenting with a new and complicated recipe that involved combining fish concentrate with several different kinds of chilli, dried and ground cardamom pods, coconut milk and freshly roasted spices...and that was before they began to prepare the red snapper and tiger prawns which Ellie had bought that morning over in Swansea market.

Antonia, however, had decided that unmarked essays called – if not immediately, certainly first thing in the morning – while Gregory was feeling the need to take evasive action against a hangover which several hairs of the dog had revived.

'I really love that smell of the sea. It was one of the things I always missed about living in London.' She took a deep and theatrical breath. 'Where d'you live?'

'A couple of streets away.' He waved towards the corner around which he would soon be turning.

'I'm that way.' The other direction. Thank goodness, thought Gregory. 'Nice meeting you anyway.' She buttoned her coat, pulling its mock-fur collar up under the frizzy hair around her ears. 'I'll have to have you round for supper sometime. If you fancy it.'

'Sure, that'd be nice.'

'With Art and Ellie. I'll give you a ring. Better go now and get some shut-eye. Nice to have met you at last.'

'Aye. You too. Cheerio then.'

Each turned away from the other without another word and traced their own way home.

CHAPTER TWELVE

DONALD

Inside the parcel was a note from Uncle Charlie. His handwriting was firm and clear, the product of traditional instruction in penmanship, enforced with the strap and the ruler:

Dear Gregory,

I found these under the floorboards in the back bedroom. They must be Martha's, I thought, so you should have them. Everything here is fine. The house is coming on nicely now. You won't know it when it's finished. If I find anything else I will send it.

Yours sincerely,

your Uncle Charlie.

P.S. Don't be a stranger. You're always welcome.

The bedroom at the back of the house had been Gregory's mother's. Now that Charlie was busy installing central heating in the old house – he had some savings and had managed to get a grant – its security had been violated by claw hammers and copper piping. It was hard to imagine.

The parcel contained two small packages, each wrapped in faded blue silk or satin – Gregory never could tell silk from satin – and tied with delicate red ribbon. One was bigger than the other although neither was much more than slim. He opened the biggest first, working intently at the knot with his nails. It had been tied a long time ago and was tight with years of slow shrinking in the damp air under the floor of the old house. Finally he had it.

There were letters inside. They appeared to be in their original envelopes, some grimy and dog-eared from their passage in the mail. Each bore the same handwriting on the front, a strong and old-fashioned copper-plate flowing in even lines across the paper, and each bore the same address: Miss Martha Hume, 11 Calvert Row, Glenvie, Kirkcudbrightshire,

Scotland (Ecosse). The stamps were French. Most of the postmarks were smudged but three or four were legible...1946 and one that looked like 1947. Posted in Lille.

There was a postcard too, a black and white photograph of the Eiffel Tower by night. It was dated 30th January 1947:

Dearest Mattie,

Paris is everything I dreamed it would be. To think that we will soon be seeing it together. I can't wait until the Seventh.

Your loving Donald xxx

The same archaic and graceful script.

Gregory put the card down on the kitchen table in front of him, picture side up. Fanning the letters like a poker hand he counted, ten in all. He put them down on the table next to the card and went over to the cupboard, returning with a large Bell's and ice. He was out of ginger.

Inspecting them more closely, the letters appeared to be in chronological order. Faintly inscribed in pencil in the bottom left-hand corner of the front of each envelope was a date. The date of receipt? This writing was small and square. Even though the letter was addressed to his mother, it was a shock to Gregory to recognise it. It could, indeed, be no-one else's hand. He had in his time carried far too many pencil-written messages to the butcher's shop or Mr Muirhead's not to know it now.

Ordinarily, Gregory hated digging. Mud and rain; lunch in cold, draughty huts; hands and knees work; muddy boots and treacherous duck-boards. The hours of forced bonhomie in the hut when it was raining, but the forecast held out the slightest prospect of work resuming before the end of the day. Above all, the responsibility. At least when you were a student the buck stopped somewhere else, even though that might mean the tyranny of an anxious and paranoid dig director to endure.

Thank heaven that that was now a thing of the past. The arrival of what some of his colleagues dismissed as 'so-called theoretical archaeology' had been his honourable discharge. That and working in a department which emphasised the 'history' in 'prehistory'. And teaching it rather than doing it.

Still, there was always the fascination of the finds. At least there had always been that. To hold something in your hand immediately after its retrieval from a subterranean limbo, to establish some kind of direct bridge with the person who had lost it or thrown it away or made it, however many years before, that was quite something. Even Gregory had to admit that. He didn't even really have to admit it, it was what had brought him to archaeology in the first place. Fitting the pieces together, like a jigsaw. Sometimes quite literally like a jigsaw.

And what he had in front of him now was a find of a sort. A jigsaw. His heart pulsed gently in his ears as he lifted the first envelope, dated 8th September 1946 on the outside. Carefully, as gingerly as any conservator encountering dusty vellum or papyrus, Gregory extracted the paper inside. It was only one sheet, folded in two, with writing on both sides. Cheap paper, outclassed by the envelope. That contrast had not been wasted on the writer either:

c/o British Consulate
183 Rue Henri Mignon
Lille, FRANCE

2nd September 1946

Dearest Mattie,

How strange it is and how exciting! How exhilarating and how desperately miserable! It is only three days since we parted and already I do not think I will be able to bear another day without you. How are you my darling? Keeping well, I hope. I think of you constantly.

The writing paper and the envelope tell their own story; Lille is full of the strangest mixtures of extravagance and shortage. Hand-made envelopes are two a penny (they're actually cheaper than that. I found bundles of them stuffed into a filing cabinet) but writing paper is hardly to be had. There is very little beef, I gather, but pheasants are dirt cheap on the black market (about which, by the way, we are not supposed to speak), and so on. Nothing is as it seems. Every day is still a brand-new surprise all of its own. The city is still in a mess with bomb sites everywhere and there are still some homeless and displaced people sleeping in sheds and carts. Still, if they weren't I suppose there'd be no work for me to do, would there?

The journey down was an Odyssey in its own right. It took more than thirty hours from leaving you in Castle Douglas to arriving in Lille. And that, I'm told was very good going. No major hitches on the way but not much sleep either. Changing trains in Paris was quite an experience. Schoolboy French isn't enough. It will have to improve! C'est la vie, eh?

Anyway, my darling, I must go now. I just wanted to let you know that I had arrived safely and am thinking of you. I will write as soon as I can. God be with you.

Your loving Donald xxx

Donald? Who was this loving Donald? The next envelope had apparently arrived in Glenvie four days later. The date inside was 7th September. This time the letter was written on heavy cream paper distinguished by an elegant watermark, an 'M' intertwined with a crown. This device was repeated in royal blue and dark green in the middle of the page at the top. Underneath was printed: 'Hotel Majestique, Avenue des Marchands, Lille'. The letterhead had been crossed out with two extravagant diagonal slashes in bright blue ink.

Dearest Mattie,

As you can see, the notepaper situation has at least improved! I found this in the store-room behind the office. Among other things it contains the unclaimed effects of some missing people. Mr MacLeod was telling me that they sometimes just vanish. One day they're trying to get you to arrange papers for Canada or Australia or wherever, the next day, well there isn't a next day. They just vanish. And sometimes we're left holding some of their belongings. Anyway I don't think the paper belonged to anyone: there was a manila envelope tucked away on one of the shelves when I was shifting things around to make more space and inside there was this beautiful paper. Romantic, don't you think? There are twenty-one sheets altogether, so I shall have to be parsimonious with them.

I have been billeted in a tiny room in a building without either hot water or heating which was requisitioned about eight months ago and looks as if it's been occupied by the barbarian hordes ever since. The room next to me is empty but there is a journalist, an Australian I think, I don't know what he's doing here, down the hall. Smells of drink all the time and comes in at all hours of the night. Still, he seems like a polite enough chap. Not that I've had that much to do with him.

The work is turning out to be routine and depressing. Filing, filing and more filing. If they'd wanted an office clerk they could have told me when I volunteered. Still, the Lord does have a reputation for moving in mysterious ways, and who am I to question it? The work seems to have been allowed to mount over the last few months. The man who was here before me seems to have been a bit of a waster. He's gone to Edinburgh to study for the ministry. Heaven help the Church of Scotland is all I can say. Once I get some sort of order in the office then we'll have a better idea how many active cases we're dealing with at the moment. You'd think that things would be gradually winding down, a year after the end of the war, but DPs (Displaced Persons in the language of the bureaucracy) still keep turning up. There was a man sitting on the doorstep the third day I was here. The French police had sent him to us. Polish, a Jew I think, speaks very little English. Somebody has told him about New Zealand and that's where he wants to go. He hasn't got a chance. At times like that I'm glad I'm only doing the files. Mr MacLeod deals with that side of things.

I am missing you more with each day. Do write soon, if you can, although I know that it is not easy for you. I look forward to hearing from you. God bless and keep you.

Your loving Donald xxx

P.S. Write c/o the Consulate. Then it can't go astray.

The conundrum became deeper, wider and more opaque. Gregory could not relate the man of the letters to his mother. Not in any way. He had never heard her called Mattie by anybody. Uncle Charlie had always addressed her as Martha, and very diffidently at that, as if he were in danger of transgressing the boundaries of proper intimacy between brother and sister by doing so. To everybody else, certainly in Gregory's hearing, it had been Mrs Alexander. She had never been one to make or take friendship. 'I've enough to look out for in my own house without taking on other folk's worries' was her motto, publicly enunciated and consistently applied. The only place she ever really saw other people was the kirk. On the street there was nothing she ever had to say to her neighbours other than the briefest of good-days, just enough to pass herself and no more; she was always careful that nobody could ever accuse her of being rude. Gregory remembered very few occasions when strangers – anybody other than her brother, that is – had been admitted to the house. No, Mattie – let alone dearest Mattie – could not be his mother.

And yet he held in his hand the evidence that insisted that she certainly had been. The key was the man, Donald. But who, or what, was he? The writing, the language, the whole tone of the letters implied a world very different to the one in which his mother had been born, had lived, and of which enough had survived her death to supervise her burial according to its prayers and proprieties. The world in which Gregory had been reared and from which he remained a fugitive. Different class, different voice. Different everything. And what was this Donald doing in Lille? Nothing was clear.

Gregory stood up to pour himself another scotch. He looked at his watch: nearly half past midnight. Abruptly the previous night's excess weighed down on his shoulders like a full pack. His eyes stung as he rubbed them and his skin was tight over his cheekbones as he yawned. Another drink was not going to provide the answer to this mystery. He would read the rest tomorrow.

CHAPTER THIRTEEN

MATTIE

Rest came to Gregory immediately and completely. Exhaustion wrapped itself around him and the last fugitive thought to accompany him over the edge of sleep was something about the 'rough male kiss of sheets'. He couldn't remember where the quotation came from but not knowing didn't bother him. The fresh cotton was a cool and simple luxury. There was no lying in the dark fretting, no tossing, no turning, neither the fear of obstinate wakefulness nor the fear of sleep and its visitor. He went to bed and slept. A simple thing made remarkable by its recent elusiveness. If his mother looked in on him, he did not wake and he remembered nothing of her passing. If his mother walked in his dreams she did not walk that night, for he had no dreams.

The next morning he woke late, went down to the kitchen, made coffee and, still wearing his dressing gown – indeed, wearing nothing else – he sat down straight away at the kitchen table and began to look at the letters again.

Lille, 18th September 1946

Dearest Mattie,

How wonderful it was to receive your letter. It came yesterday. I don't think the Consul opened it first (only joking! I hope!!). He's a very nice chap, a Welshman who's married to a French woman. He used to be in business here before the war (something to do with mining machinery) and he's come back to try and start again. A grand chap by the name of Herbert. His wife is expecting their third child any day now.

Gregory put it down. A letter from his mother? The other package. It was too much to hope for. This time he went at the knot without any delicacy. Losing patience he fetched the scissors from the drawer. Inside there were indeed more letters. Smaller envelopes, smaller, square writing. Stamps with King George's head on them. Definitely his mother's, eight altogether. No, wait a minute, only seven were his mother's.

The eighth was different. Long and thin, a stiff brown envelope which had kept some of its glaze despite the passage of the intervening years. The type-written address was: Miss Martha Hume, 24 Finlay's Terrace, Glenvie, Kirkcudbrightshire. That was an address he knew well enough. It had been his, now it was Uncle Charlie's. Gregory checked back with the other letters, from Donald. Yes, they were to a different address. More mystery.

Inside there was one sheet of crisp white paper with a heading which declared it to be a communication from James Macdonald, Ll.B, 23 Hope Street, Glasgow 1. It was dated 14th April 1947:

Dear Miss Hume,

I write to you on the instructions of my client, Mrs Oliver MacKillion. Please find enclosed letters that were found among the effects of the late Mr Donald MacKillion, which I am sure you would wish to have. Please be advised, however, that my client has no wish to enter into any correspondence with you concerning her son. Nor does she wish to discuss the matter in person. It is her most fervent wish that the episode should now be regarded as closed.

Yours faithfully,

James MacDonald

The signature was an illegible scrawl above a line of type. Lawyers then were obviously much as lawyers now. That peculiar English, all of their own. They probably had to sit special papers in 'Legal English' or some such thing in their finals.

This was only the most fleeting of Gregory's thoughts on first reading the precise, cold note. Caught off guard by his emotions he read it again and again. A dozen times he must have gone over it, searching desperately for a key; something to explain what he had read, rather than thickening the confusion in which he was entangled.

He found it when he went to replace Mr James MacDonald's letter in its envelope. Inside there was something which he had missed the first time. A newspaper cutting. No date, no indication of which paper it was from, yellow with the jaundice of more than forty years. It was not easy to read. During those years it appeared to have been folded and refolded many times:

MYSTERY OF CITY MAN'S DEATH

Police in France are still investigating the death in Lille of Mr Donald MacKillion of Hillside, Mount Florida.

Only son of the late Mr Oliver MacKillion, who until his untimely demise last year was General Manager of Clydebank Milling, Mr MacKillion was working as a volunteer with the

Scottish Joint Council for the Relief of Refugees.

The British Consul in Lille, Mr William Herbert, said in a telephone conversation today that there were no suspicious circumstances surrounding Mr MacKillion's death.

Mr MacKillion was, he said, well liked and respected by all those who had worked with him.

The body will be returned home for a private family funeral within the next few days.

At the bottom of the column, below these few brief paragraphs, was an indistinct photograph of Donald MacKillion. Faded to a slow sepia, it showed a young, fresh face, framed by dark wavy hair and creased by a shy and noncommittal smile. He appeared to be wearing a dark jacket and a striped tie. No, not a jacket, a blazer. This was a late teenaged Donald, still in his school uniform. Sixth form. The first real find. At last a bridgehead.

Gregory looked at the photograph for a long time. Eventually he put it down. He raised his hand to his brow and combed it through his own hair, stretching while he did so. It didn't after all actually help much. There was no secret message in the bland expression, no code to be cracked in the curl of Donald MacKillion's hair. No, there was probably less there than met the eye. Gregory had heard that somewhere, he couldn't remember where. Maybe it had been Faye. It sounded like the kind of thing she might come off with.

So Donald was dead. Of course he would likely have been dead anyway. But he had died all that time ago. That was at least something concrete. And a revelation. Apart from that, however, Gregory had uncovered nothing new. If he wanted to find out more, there was nothing for it but some more digging. His mother's letters. They were not in any kind of order, so that was the first thing to do. Gregory went through them. The first was dated 12th September 1946, the last 21st January 1947. They were like erratic stepping stones, set at irregular intervals of two or three weeks; written in blue ink in his mother's tight, square handwriting, on what appeared to be pages torn out of an exercise book. The paper was off-white and coarse with feint blue lines, bordered by a neat but definitely ragged edge down its left hand side.

Gregory picked up the first envelope. It was made of poor brown paper, more appropriate for a butcher's bill than a billet doux. An ancient sadness threatened to overwhelm him. So poor and mean, these windows into his mother's heart, so appropriate and so miserable. It was as if her entire life had been condensed into its dreary essence, finally weighing in as little more than a few sheets of shoddy, unbleached wood pulp. He told himself that those had been times of shortage and austerity, paper was in short supply, but he did not believe it. It was too much of a piece with everything he knew.

And, after all, if he didn't know his mother, no-one did. He felt the sand shifting under his feet as the thought passed. Perhaps no-one did. There was only one place to look:

24 Finlay's Terrace
Glenvie

12th September 1946

Dear Donald,

Thank you for your letters. I received the second one today. Maggie brought it round straight away and my mother is out shopping, so I thought I would reply at once.

Your work sounds very interesting. It must be strange to be in a place where they speak a different language. I'm sure I wouldn't know where to begin. You must have felt terribly sorry for that poor Polish man. What has become of him?

There is no news here to tell you. Glenvie seems so tiny and narrow after Glasgow. The Cottage Hospital is not much bigger than one of the wards in the Infirmary. And everyone wants to know to know everyone else's business. It's like living in a shop window. My mother is the worst of all. I am glad that I arranged for your letters to go to Maggie's. I only hope that the postman doesn't notice. If she finds out, she'll go mad. I can't wait until January. I can live without the key to the door, but I don't think I can live without you.

I'd better go now. I must get this letter to the post on time and then I'm due on the ward this afternoon. I am missing you and my prayers are with you every night.

Your loving fiancée,
Mattie xxx

There she was, Mattie. And the same three kisses. Until he had seen them on the page he would not have believed it. She had never kissed him, not once that he could ever remember. Not a peck on the cheek, not so much as the distant brush of strangers holding each other at bay by the shoulders. Until he had seen them on the page he had not even marked the fact, but now it rose up in front of him, an unanswerable accusation and an unforgivable neglect. For a long held breath he considered the three betrayals, short, compact and to the point, three Xs to mark the spot. Finding nothing more in them to make him feel either better or worse he folded the paper and replaced it in its envelope.

That must have been the letter which Donald mentioned. Gregory was managing to resist the temptation to dismiss the interloper as nothing more than MacKillion. He found the sheet of fancy notepaper which he had been reading before investigating the other bundle of correspondence and began again, skipping over the bit about the Consul and his wife:

Anyway, enough of that. I hope things are bearable for you in Glenvie. Even though I've never been there, I feel as if I know the place, between all of the things you've told me about it and the fact that it's probably like lots of other wee towns. Keep up the news. One day I hope we can go to Glenvie together, Mr and Mrs MacKillion. How does that sound? Your mother will come round, I'm sure. I'm particularly looking forward to meeting your friend Maggie. She sounds like a good sort.

Meanwhile life continues here in the boring groove that I am steadily settling into. The files are slowly beginning to shape up. Mr MacLeod says that he doesn't know how they managed before I arrived. I don't know why there should have to be so many files. What's the use in keeping a record if you can do nothing for people? Sometimes I think that perhaps Mr Mac sees the futility of it all very well and produces so much paperwork simply to justify our presence here. Sometimes I feel more like a policeman than anything else. We certainly don't seem to help many people.

Oh yes, you asked about the Polish man. Well, we couldn't do much for him and the last I heard he was on his way south to Marseilles to try and find a boat to Palestine. Poor man, he used to sit in the outer office for hours on end waiting, just waiting. I suppose when your wife and children have gone to the gas chambers and you are still here, a little waiting is neither here nor there.

Some of the stories I have heard, they're enough to make one doubt the goodness of God. May God forgive me, but I have had that thought a few times since I arrived here. Between stories about the Gestapo during the occupation and the tales which the refugees and DPs have to tell, it's a far cry from home. I don't know what to make of it all.

Anyway, I'm sure that you don't want to be hearing all of this. On a more cheerful note, my French is improving dramatically. The Australian down the hall has moved on, so, apart from a couple of Army officers on the ground floor, I've got the whole building to myself. There's talk of the French authorities taking it over as accommodation for families. Better than having it stand half empty, although I don't know where they'll put me.

Still, we'll worry about that when it happens. Anyway, I'm only here until April, so it's not a desperate worry.

Must dash now. Write soon, I miss you every day and every hour and the thought of a letter on its way makes the time pass more quickly. God bless you,

Your own, loving Donald xxx

Gregory put it away. Stretching, he stood up and poured himself another cup of coffee. There was orange juice in a carton in the fridge and he made toast which he spread with Marmite. He sat down, ate his breakfast and took up the next letter in his mother's pile. Written on 24th September, it was postmarked the following day. He was about to read it, having first carefully wiped his hands on a piece of kitchen roll which he had brought over precisely for this purpose, when he decided that some system was called for. After a moment's reflection on how this was best to be done he cleared away his plate, his glass, now empty of juice, and the wrapping and ribbon from the packages. He did not throw the latter away but placed them, gently folded, on one side. Moving his coffee mug to one side he laid out the two small piles of letters side by side. Taking first from one pile, then from the other, and so on, Gregory set about establishing a chronology.

CHAPTER FOURTEEN

MOTHERS

Something over an hour later Gregory had worked his way through all of the letters. A second run through them, ignoring the trivia of long swathes of the dialogue and stopping to think about a paragraph here or a couple of sentences there, took nearly as long again. It was still a puzzle. Or, rather, now it was several puzzles.

Gregory stood up and looked out into the back garden. The day was overcast, with little or no wind to lift it out of the doldrums. Just within Gregory's line of sight, off to the left, the young man in the orange wig was standing by the stone wall of his garden stroking the cat from next door. It paced backward and forward in a tight figure-of-eight, spine arched with rapture and tail straight up in the air with only a tiny flicker at the tip, the confines of its world drawn down in that moment to a friendly hand, the wall, and the warm air in between them. Gregory turned away and back to the table.

Some things were clearer. For example, the couple had not just been engaged, but were actually about to be married. His mother had signed herself 'Your loving fiancée' in a number of the letters. And there was the remark about the key to the door. Her twenty-first birthday would have been in 1947, on February 6th; she wouldn't have been able to marry without her mother's consent until then. They were apparently planning to get married in Paris. In the last proper letter that he had written to her, on 15th January 1947, Donald had hinted at the arrangements:

I've had a word with the Embassy in Paris and there should be no problems. The Embassy Chaplain is an Anglican, but, under the circumstances that's probably all to the good. Mr MacLeod is going to travel down from Lille for the ceremony, and Mr and Mrs Herbert will accompany him if she is feeling well enough. It will be so romantic. Imagine honeymooning in Paris. Maggie said we were lucky – she's right!

Less easy to interpret, but clear enough in their own way, were a number of remarks about the couple's respective mothers. Each seemed to have been a problem. In Glenvie, for example, the subterfuge of using a friend's address to receive post from France had been necessary in order to keep the correspondence secret from Gregory's grandmother. Not that the friend's name meant anything to Gregory; he had never heard his mother speak of a Maggie. But why the secrecy? You'd have thought that a nice young man from a middle-class family would have been eminently presentable. There'd have been respectability there and, by the sound of things, money. Even without money, however, there oughtn't to have been any obstacles in Donald and Mattie's way.

Gregory had begun to think about her in the language of the letters. After all, she was Mattie on the page in front of him and the page was really all he had to be going on. It was simpler too, he could keep Mattie and his mother in separate boxes.

The problem with Donald's mother was perhaps easier to fathom, and for precisely the reason that Gregory's grandmother's disapproval was perplexing. Money and class. Whatever it was, however, neither Mattie nor Donald seemed to be in any doubt about it. On November 19th, in the sixth of her letters, she was looking forward to his return for a long break over Christmas and Hogmanay:

It seems almost impossible to believe that I will be seeing you again in about three weeks time. It was very good of Mr MacLeod to allow you home for such a long time. It will be nearly a full month. Your mother must be overjoyed to be having you at home over the holiday time.

Perhaps one day soon I'll be able to meet her. When I'm Mrs MacKillion too she'll not be able to object too much. I can understand why she wants to keep you to herself, I don't feel that much different myself. Still I'll be able to get up to Glasgow and if you come down we can meet up in Castle Douglas as usual.

Donald's point of view was not quite the same, but, then, he was looking at it from a different place:

My mother's such a fuss-pot. Yesterday I received a package she'd sent with a month's supply of clean socks and soap. She seems to think that there is neither water nor the inclination to use it on this side of the Channel. Or perhaps it's just me she has no faith in!

Again, writing a few weeks later, on 31st October:

It feels strange not to be home at Hallowe'en this year. My mother has always been a great one for a family party. I suppose she will find it difficult without my father there now and perhaps I ought to be there, but she's got to start somewhere. My sisters will be there with spouses and children, seven children in all now. Eileen has three, Kathleen two and Mary has two also. You remember Mary, we bumped into her that afternoon in Kelvingrove Park. She had the baby in the pram.

There'll be dunking for apples, apple pie with a threepenny piece in it, nuts and ghost stories. It'll be strange alright, but I don't think I'll miss it. Being the only boy and the youngest I always end up feeling like

I'm still in short trousers. Christmas is the same too. It'll make quite a change to walk down to M. Gautier's café this evening, for a glass of wine on Hallowe'en.

There was a lot about his mother in Donald's letters. She wrote to him regularly and sent parcels nearly as often. The picture was of a close relationship, loving and warm, but one which Donald was beginning to feel that he had outgrown. And although his mother was such an enthusiast for family celebrations, he did not talk about her probable reaction to being denied her only son's wedding. Gregory wondered how old he could have been. Twenty? Twenty-one? At least that if he was contemplating marriage. Volunteering to work in Lille might have been his way of breaking away. His father was not long dead – in one of the letters Donald talked about his father having 'passed away' in May – and perhaps there was no other way he could do it.

By comparison, Mattie found very little to say about her mother. Gregory knew that his grandfather, a first mate on the Head Line, had been lost on an Arctic convoy during the war. A framed photograph of him had always been on the dresser in the parlour: a young man, he sat poker straight, cap on his knee, the three brass buttons on his jacket done up. As a child, the most interesting thing about this photograph to Gregory had always been the tiny black and gold label on the back. Sometimes when his mother's back was turned he would sneak a quick look at it: Bingham's Photo Emporium, 86 West Queens Street, Toronto. What horizons those few words opened up, what vistas of the exotic and the marvellous. Charlie probably still had the photo somewhere.

As for his grandmother, Gregory had never known her and he could not remember ever having seen a photograph. She had died when he was a small child, of the same thing that had killed his mother, heart trouble. That much he knew because Charlie had told him. But that was about all. Uncle Charlie was the source of his meagre awareness of family history. His mother had never talked about the family, nor had she encouraged questions.

'What's the use,' she would say, 'of going over the past? You can't change it and it won't help you get on with your own life. It's nothing more than a lot of silly nonsense.'

And that was that, whether it was in reply to a child's question about his grandfather or a comment upon a sixth former's ambition to be an archaeologist.

The one time in the letters when Mattie did talk about her mother at any length was in her last letter, written on 21st January 1947:

It seems a dreadful thing to marry without any family there. I do not know what your mother will say, but I don't think mine will ever forgive me. Once she gets something into her head there's no shifting it. She's very sure of herself and what's right and wrong. She will just have to like it or lump it I'm afraid. I think she's already suspicious. She keeps asking me if I've had any post.

I can be quite stubborn myself sometimes. Do you think you will be able to live with someone who's as pig-headed as I am? (Only joking!) I've had to be stubborn to survive.

In Mattie, Gregory was starting to recognise his mother, although only with the benefit of nearly forty years' hindsight. But in his grandmother he recognised her immediately: always right, giving no ground because she had no ground to give, always quicker to find fault than favour. No shifting her. That was his mother to a tee. Although, in the end, something had stopped her...

It was becoming almost too clear. Too sad, too miserable, too familiar in its waste and its repetition. An unbroken chain of command and refusal stretching back in the female line. And across how many generations? For all Gregory knew, it might go all the way back to Eve herself. Even his mother, the most stubborn character he had ever encountered, had not been able to break free.

At which point the mysteries started to pile up again in front of him. Mattie had nearly flown the coop but not quite. The most obvious and the greatest puzzle was, simply, what had happened? What had happened to frustrate their marriage plans? They were only a few days away from the wedding, after all. Even if they had been discovered, would that have been enough to stop them? This question raised once again the issue of why their mothers would be so certainly opposed to the match. Gregory could think of nothing that would have been insurmountable, even then.

Before that again, in terms of the strict historical order of things, there were a number of other, less momentous, questions to which Gregory would have dearly liked answers. How they had met was one such which persistently presented itself. From what he had read, Glasgow seemed a likely bet for the 'where', but there was no indication of either the 'when' or the 'how'. And what was this about his mother working in a hospital? Throughout his childhood and teens she had been part-time housekeeper for the Reverend Taggart, but he couldn't remember her ever working in a hospital.

Donald's death was an equally obdurate mystery. Nothing in the letters was any help here. Gregory pushed his chair back and stared at the table, with its tidy piles of paper. Thinking about it wasn't getting him anywhere.

But there was another angle of inquiry, something more to be figured out about Donald. His work. It was perplexing, although Gregory wasn't sure why. What was this Scottish Joint Council and what was it doing in Lille? It didn't seem to be the obvious place for that kind of work. It even seemed to perplex young Donald at times: 'more like a policeman than anything else' was how he had described himself in one letter. Gregory smiled to himself – young Donald, indeed – although he couldn't've been very much older than most of his students. Gregory looked over the stuff in front of him and, after a slight indecision, picked up one of the letters:

There was a bit of an incident here yesterday. The French police, or at least I presume that they were the police (they didn't say very much to me), picked up a man in the office. A Czech, or so he said, he had been in to see us a couple of days earlier. The police seemed to know that he was coming back and when.

Thank goodness he wasn't one of my cases. There was such an air of forlorn hopelessness about him as they took him away. Like an old cow that knows what awaits her at the slaughterhouse.

That was written on 1st October 1946. Twelve days later, in his next letter, there was more, this time about Mr MacLeod's 'little foibles', in particular his weakness for young women refugees:

I don't know what we are doing here. We never seem to do anything for anyone. That's not true, of course, we distribute the old clothes and blankets and what have you that the folk back in Scotland collect, but there doesn't seem to be much else. If it's just for Mr Mac to vanish in the afternoon with one of his 'special cases', then, quite frankly, I'd sooner be back at home, swotting.

There was nothing for a while. Gregory quickly read the letters through, then he found something else. On November 26th, at the end of a very long letter which was largely about the eagerly awaited weeks which he was soon going to be spending at home, there was another glimpse of life at the Lille office of the Scottish Joint Council for the Relief of Refugees:

It'll be a marvellous Christmas for us, but for some of the poor creatures we deal with, there might as well be no Christmas. Mr MacLeod is going to be here. He's not married so there is no pressure on him, and he's hoping for some food and toys from back home. There's so much misery still and we can do so little.

Most of my time this week has been spent liaising with the Canadian authorities in Paris about a Lithuanian family who arrived here last week, by way of a Red Cross camp in Switzerland where they'd spent most of the last year. It may take months to arrange a passage for them to Canada, that's if we can trace the relatives which they say they have over there, and in the meantime they have to be found somewhere to live and food. If the French were more helpful life would be much easier for everybody. They regard everyone who isn't French as suspicious by definition. Mr Handler, the man of the Lithuanian family, has been subject to particularly close attention because he's originally of German stock.

Anyway, I'm sure that you're not interested in listening to me rattle on about the ins and outs of our squabbles with the gendarmerie.

There was only one other passage that seemed significant, and that was in Donald's last letter, dated 15th January:

The Handler family continue to provide us with work. The oldest son, Eric, has just been arrested. It's something to do with the black market. If I was Mr Mac I'd just tell them to go to hell and let somebody else worry about them. Since that's where they've probably come from there doesn't seem much point, however.

Gregory was hard pushed, on the evidence of the letters, to appreciate the point of any of it. Perhaps Donald had fulfilled his original purpose in volunteering. At least it had got him away from his mother. Permanently, as it turned out.

Outside the light seemed to be growing and a hint of blue sky was visible in the day's high gloom. On the table, under the cold light of electricity, his mother's unexpected legacy waited to be claimed. In one bundle Mattie, in the other Donald. And now, in between them, Gregory.

One way or the other, in the end it was all permanent.

CHAPTER FIFTEEN

REMEMBRANCE DAY

Thompson Alexander. The name stood on its own, separated by several empty lines of granite from the last line of the 1939-45 list. In brackets after the name was the explanation for this distinction: U.N. Forces, Korea. He was the only Alexander to appear on the memorial. Close inspection revealed the hand of a different mason from the earlier names, a subtly different way of carving letters in stone, but there was nothing else to be discovered from the monument itself.

Gregory stood in the twilight of a wet November afternoon, as lonely as his father's name. A persistent drizzle was turning his heavy grey shorts into a soggy felt that would chap his legs. The blazer which had been bought several sizes too big hung saggy and sodden on his narrow shoulders. He could almost smell the must of it drying in the hallway and hear his mother scolding him for dawdling on the way home from school. And she would, soon enough.

He would let her think that he had been dawdling, it would be the easiest thing. Martha Alexander's refusal to attend the Remembrance Day service was, this year as every other year, an injunction to her son. And her injunctions were not lightly flouted, even if only indirectly, as today.

'We're not going down there to stand with that crew of hypocrites,' she had said over an unusually late Sunday breakfast. 'They wouldn't give him the time of day when he was alive, I'll not give them the satisfaction of fussing over him now he's dead. He's gone. Moping over it'll not bring him back.'

And that was that. Gregory got no more out of her. It was the only service that she ever missed, and she missed it every year. Every Sunday morning he was made to go to Sunday school and church except one, and on that day they were forbidden to him.

And so it was that on this miserable and bone-chilling Monday afternoon, Gregory made his first worm's turn. His fall was neither dramatic nor the simple impulse of a child thwarted. He had made and laid his plan the previous Friday, when the poppies had been sold in school. Lacking the money to buy one himself, he had volunteered to sell them. Being in the top class and always top of the class, that bit had been easy. If he had waited, the Headmaster, Mr Cupar, would probably have asked him anyway, but he wanted to leave nothing to chance. Gregory stole a poppy. He didn't tell himself that it was only fair, since he had, after all, sold them. He didn't blame it on his mother for refusing him the penny he had asked for that morning. He just took one without paying for it, and he knew that was stealing. It had been drummed into him often enough for him to recognise the act.

Now the rain trickled off his nose, his eyebrows, the peak of his school cap, his chin, but he stood, as he imagined it to attention, ignoring these minor distractions in the solemnity of his own ritual. Bending down stiffly, he gently placed the red paper flower next to the wreaths that clustered together at the bottom of the Cenotaph. Taking a step back he stood in silence for what he thought must be two minutes. Then, shouldering the leather strap of his satchel, he walked across the square and up the hill home.

That was all his mother had ever told him about his father, that 'they wouldn't give him the time of day when he was alive.' Beyond that, nothing. She had photographs, hidden away in her wooden chest, which she had once shown Gregory. Once only he had seen the two pictures, when he was eleven. It was the day after his private ceremony of remembrance, the only one time he had ever asked her what his father looked like.

Each photograph was as revealing and as enigmatic as the other. In one his father was evidently young - sixteen or seventeen, perhaps - and he stood bashfully holding a large fish up for inspection in his right hand, while the other held firmly on to a fishing-rod. In the background were the masts and cabins of a busy quay side. When asked, his mother didn't know where it was taken or when. In the second, he was in uniform: battle dress, kilt, Glengarry on his head. He was older now, but the difference did not show in the open boyish face that looked straight into the camera. It had been taken just before he had left for Korea.

His father was not a subject on which it was possible to draw Uncle Charlie, either. 'I didnae know him very well, you have to understand. He wasnae from Glenvie, you ken. But he was a good enough man Gregory. What I knew of him. And I was sorry when he was killed.' That, more or less, was what Charlie had to tell him.

And until this moment it had, more or less, been sufficient. On the one hand there was his mother, on the other the war memorial, each made of stone as stubborn as the other. The one had nothing more it would give, the other nothing more it could. A child who grew up to master the necessary arts of private and infrequent rebellion, recognising the immovable obstacle when it presented itself and keeping a tight check on his debts and commitments, Gregory took enough to be enough and left it there.

But now it was no longer enough. Now the greatest puzzle of all presented itself amid the ruins of Donald and Mattie's romance. His father. And, standing behind his father, his mother.

CHAPTER SIXTEEN

THE DENBIGH

Every year it was the same. The examination season arrived suddenly, catching the lecturing staff as unaware as the students. Hot, dry days and warm, muggy nights arrived with it. The best of the summer squandered itself while examinations were in full swing in gymnasiums and dining halls up and down the country and before the school holidays or the tourist season had started. When the wind dropped, the Bristol Channel looked as much like a mill pond as it ever would, and in Llanorgan's parks prized azaleas and rhododendrons drooped their leaves and looked too soon past their best. There was the usual talk on the television of a water shortage. The young and the not-so-young alike contributed enthusiastically to its prevention by drinking ice-cold imported beers, or alcoholic fruit drinks with ridiculous names, straight from the bottle in pub gardens and courtyards. In between bursts of head-down activity in the library and elsewhere, undergraduates of both sexes loafed around the campus wearing little more than shorts and suntans. A hundred romances which would not survive beyond the last exam paper hatched liked cicadas in the heat.

Gregory was even more oblivious to the ferment around him than usual. Since unearthing his discovery - which is how he saw it in his mind, even though he'd had nothing to do with actually finding the packets - the days had very quickly passed, one hurrying after the other. He had thought of little else. He had marked all of his examination scripts. He had done his stint of invigilation without any mishaps. He had passed the time of day with colleagues and discussed the grading of borderline cases. He had even managed long conversations with both Ellie and Faye, about Mothercare and some new exhibition at the Watershed in Bristol, respectively. But none of this required more than the surface layer of his consciousness. Everything else, to some degree or another or from one angle or another, was focused upon the two linked puzzles: Donald and Mattie, on the one hand, his father and his mother, on the other. They had even managed to exorcise the obsessive - and laughable too, it seemed now - images of Faye and her rugby playing accountant which had been such an uncomfortable part of his daily round just a couple of weeks earlier.

Donald and Mattie. Father and mother. Only when he was sleeping was he free of them. Now Gregory rose early and went to bed late, and it was his waking hours which were filled with dreams.

So it was on a bright Friday in the middle of June. The exams were over and Gregory had only a handful of papers left to mark, Part One scripts which Adrian hadn't yet finished first marking. He sat in his office in the early afternoon, staring emptily at the wall planner tacked to his noticeboard just above eye-level while the pencil in his right hand tapped an irregular staccato on the desk top. Had anyone offered him a penny for his thoughts they would probably have been disappointed with their bargain, but he was beginning to sense a resolution in the offing to a problem which had been proving particularly obstinate: what to do next.

'Gregory.'

The voice repeated itself.

'Gregory.' There was a knock, knuckles on wood. 'Gregory...for goodness sake Gregory, do I have stand here all day?' Faye's head was poking round the door.

'Oh, hello.' He sat up straighter in the chair and swivelled around to face her. 'I was day-dreaming... Miles away.'

'And I suppose you were day-dreaming this morning?... You walked right passed me in the Library. Said hello to you and you just walked right on by. I felt such a fool, stood there looking at your back.' She sat down, rooted around inside her bag, took out a packet of Marlboro Lights and lit one.

'Sorry. I'm a wee bit distracted at the moment.' He looked around. 'And I'm afraid I don't have an ashtray.'

'I'll use the bin, don't worry. Here, pass it over. And I won't spill any ash on your carpet. My God, you're worse than my mother.'

'Faye, I'm sorry...'

'And stop apologising.'

'What d'you expect me to do? Not apologise?' Gregory stood up and closed the office door. 'Anyway, I can't imagine what happened this morning... It's lovely to see you.' He bent down and gave her shoulders a quick squeeze. 'Did you come just to tell me off, or do you actually want something else?'

'Bit of both, I suppose. I wanted to find out what the hell was the matter. I could see you were distracted... That was the easy bit. And anyway, I wanted to see you, we haven't had a chance to talk since you were up at the house last and I've been missing you. Weeks ago. What with exams and everything...Anyway, that was the prepared speech.' She laughed. 'Corny or what?'

'No. Not corny.' He swivelled in his chair and stared out the window.

Faye waited. For a good thirty seconds.

'Well?'

'Well what?'

'What's the matter?'

'How long've you got?'

Faye looked at her watch. 'Twenty minutes? I've got an internals meeting at half past three.'

'It'll need longer than that, I'm afraid.'

'Tell you what then, what're you doing tonight? How about a drink? Let's celebrate the end of marking for another year at the same time.'

''Fraid not. I only wish you'd popped in earlier... I'm having dinner with Ellie and Art, at that woman, Antonia Grimaldi's. She rang me this morning. I can't get out of it now.'

'No reason you should either. She's not the world's worst, you know... Can't you even give me a potted version of whatever's bothering you?'

'Believe me, it doesn't condense.'

Faye stubbed out the cigarette on the rim of the bin and dropped the butt inside. 'I hope that doesn't make your office smell too much. Well, why not meet for a drink, before you go? What time d'you have to be there?'

'About eight. The usual.'

'Okay, that's fine then. How about the Denbigh... I know, I know, it's not the most salubrious place in town, but at least it's still got some character... Come on. How about it? Six o'clock?'

'I don't know...'

'If you don't want to walk in on your own, I'll call for you. Alright?' She stood up. 'I'll collect you about six then. It's only five minutes from your place.' Faye walked over to Gregory and kissed him gently on the top of his head. 'There. Cheer up now. See you later.'

Gregory did not say anything to her back as she opened the door and left. He had already returned to his own preoccupations.

Faye didn't exactly have to drag him, kicking and squealing, to the pub, but it was a close-run thing. All the way there Gregory protested in silence. Every step, every angle and line in the set of his body, every pause in the desultory conversation was an exclamation mark of discontent. He was the only black cloud the streets had seen in weeks.

The Denbigh itself, or, to give the pub its full name, The Marquis of Denbigh, did nothing to improve him. On the main road between Llanorgan West and the town centre, it shared a substantial double-fronted Edwardian building with the Conservative Club. On one side of the party wall they read The Telegraph and The Express. On the other, it was The Guardian and Socialist Worker. Everyone read The Sun and The Western Gazette. G and Ts and bridge gave way to draught cider and pool. Visible tattoos were probably against the Club's rules, the pub's clientele probably smoked more dope.

The Denbigh was one of the few remaining oases in Llanorgan to have escaped the attentions of a brewery bent on improvement. Strictly speaking that wasn't true, it had been renovated, but the job had been only half-heartedly done. The auction room assortment of second-hand settees and easy chairs which had been one of the place's great delights had been thrown out some time in the late 'eighties, replaced by equally ill-matched bar-room tables and chairs, the survivors of other pubs which had long-since been themed, modernised, or otherwise made to look older than they were and more authentic. It had also been redecorated. The nicotine and grime had been covered over with magnolia and grainy toffee-coloured varnish. It looked cleaner but not too different.

The people who drank there had not changed much either. Most of them lived in the Victorian terraces which climbed up the knees of the steep hill behind the main road. The area was close enough to the centre to be cheapish, but on the western side of town, so only cheapish. Various housing associations had invested heavily in the area, as had private landlords. The Denbigh drew its regulars from the neighbourhood's distinctive mixture of social workers, academics and the like, old people still hanging on in the streets where they had lived long lives, unemployed young women and men subsisting in bedsits, students in shared houses, and a miscellany of flotsam left over from the 'sixties.

It was still early and the long, gloomy public bar was nearly empty. A couple of youngsters, one with dirty mock-dreadlocks, the other with a shaved head, both wearing tattered brown fatigue trousers and ripped tie-dyed singlets, stood at the counter. Some older men, who looked as if they might work on the buildings and sounded as if they had been in the pub since opening time, were busy with a noisy game of pool in the darkness at the back. One of this group who was at the bar buying a round of pints passed the time of day with Faye and Gregory in a soft Irish accent.

When Faye had bought their drinks they moved over to the front bay window and sat looking out over the pavement and the street. She raised her glass, a half of bitter.

'Cheers... You know this place's not the same without old Jimmy.'

'Cheers.' The usual scotch and ginger. 'Who's old Jimmy?'

'Jimmy the boxer? You must remember him. I sometimes used to think he lived here... He was always here. An old fellow, over seventy maybe, used to shadow-box up and down the room. He'd stop and dance in a circle round you. Harmless enough, just seemed to be a part of the place. Funny old bugger, his clothes were always a bit down at heel, but his shoes... Used to wear immaculate shoes. Italian loafers, they looked hand-made. You must remember him.'

'No...'

'You've never been in here before?'

'I didn't say I had.'

'Fair comment... Now you're here, what d'you think? They've tidied it up a bit.'

'I shudder to think.'

'Get away with you, it's great.'

'It's different.'

'It's not the only thing that's different, either... What the hell's up with you anyway?'

'Nothing's the matter. It's nothing like that... I really don't know where to begin.' His glass was empty. 'Another?'

'You could try the beginning, I suppose... Not for me, I've still got most of this and I've got to drive home...Has something happened?'

'Wait a minute 'til I get another one.'

'You're knocking them back.'

'It's been a hot day.'

Gradually, Gregory told Faye about the letters. The progress of the story was uneven; there was a certain amount of moving backwards and forwards in the tale as he remembered things which he should have mentioned earlier or responded to one of Faye's infrequent questions and there were several interruptions for further trips to the bar. By seven o'clock he had more or less finished his story, he was on his fifth scotch and Faye was less than half-way down her second half. He looked down at his glass.

'That's the trouble with these, they go down a wee bit too quickly.'

'You want to be careful. We can't have you turning up at Antonia's pissed.'

'I'll blame it all on you.'

'And I'm sure they'll have no trouble believing it. Did you say that Ellie and Art were going as well?' Gregory nodded. 'I saw her the other day. I don't think motherhood can ever have been the same for anybody before... Honestly, some women. To listen to her, you'd think nobody else had ever had a bloody baby.'

'It's a big thing...'

'I know that. I just don't see why such a big thing has got to be made of it... Anyway, enough of bloody Ellie. What are you going to do? About the letters, I mean.'

'Well that's the problem isn't it? I don't know...I don't know what I want to do, and I surely don't know what I ought to do. For the best, I mean.'

'Are you sure you want to do anything?'

'I don't think I have a choice... It's driving me up the walls. I can't think of anything else.'

'Why? Why is it so important? That might be a good place to start thinking about what to do.'

'Why d'you think? It's the first time I've ever felt any sort of, I don't know, empathy I suppose, with my mother. All my life, literally as long as I can remember...' Gregory was raising his voice. The bar was starting to fill up and he noticed the couple at the next table looking in his direction. He continued, speaking more quietly. 'As long as I can remember, she was always this aloof, distant creature. Stern and remote. I was always afraid of her, for God's sake. Look at the dreams I've been having... They seem to have stopped, by the way... Well now, for the first time, it's like there was this chink in her armour. Maybe I can find out why... Something that'll explain the way she was, why she never...' He finished his drink.

'I'll get this one.' Faye stood up. 'I need a pee anyway.'

When she returned with another scotch, Faye lit a cigarette for herself and joined him staring out of the window. A girl with short black hair, flat white face make-up, dull red lips and startlingly heavy eyes, dressed all in black except for black-and-white striped leggings, was arguing on the pavement with the dreadlocked young man who had been at the bar earlier. A silver piercing twinkled in her exposed navel. The altercation appeared to reach its climax when she spat at him, full in the face, and stormed off down the road. Abandoned, he stood there for an instant, spittle dripping from the end of his nose, before noticing the audience in the window. He seemed to be about to say something but, instead, raised his right hand with a solitary middle finger extended straight in the air. Honour satisfied, he too moved off in the same direction as the girl. Faye laughed quietly.

'Wouldn't be Friday night without a bit of drama, I suppose.'

'Aye. 'Twas ever thus...' They turned back, away from the window. 'But it's not just my mother, you know.' Faye looked at him but did not comment. 'I never knew my father, I told you that didn't I? Never knew either of them really, and...well, it's the first time I ever felt like doing anything about it. It's that as much as anything else, the fact that I want to find out...' His voice was quiet and steady but his eyes were drifting somewhere in the middle distance.

'What're your options then? If you want to get to the bottom of all of this.'

'I'm not trying to get to the bottom of anything. Nothing so ambitious. But I should be able to find out... I mean, Charlie's the obvious place to start.'

'So...what's stopping you?'

'I don't know. It's just, I always said, you know, that I'd never go back. To Glenvie.' She began to say something but he stopped her with an upheld hand. 'No, it's not what you think. It's not pride, nothing daft like that. I'm in dread of the place, I suppose. It has hardly anything good attached to it in my mind...Just unpleasant memories.'

'Maybe it's time that changed too. You can't spend the rest of your life running away... Sorry, that's not for me to say. Mind my own business...but it's worth thinking how many birds this particular stone might dispatch.'

'There's nothing else for it anyway. It's either that or forget it...and I don't think I want to.'

'And I don't think you should.'

'Thank you Marje Proops.' Faye made a face and stuck out her tongue. 'That really isn't a very attractive habit, young lady... And I bet it puts the men off.'

'Them! I'm off men, so who gives a shit.'

'Since we're on that subject, how're things on the Ioan front?'

'You know me, I'll get over it. Live to fight another day.'

'Not what I asked.'

'No, it wasn't. But it's the best answer... Fuck it, Greg, there's nothing I can do about it so there's no point moping over it. Think I'll embrace celibacy. At least it might embrace me back...sorry, that was a pathetic joke.'

'Well I didn't come here for the cabaret.'

'Just as well.'

'I'll believe it when I see it.'

'You might just be surprised.' She drained her glass. 'What time is it? Christ, it's nearly half past seven. We'd better be getting a move on. Don't want you being late. Do you want me to drop you at Antonia's?'

'Where does she live?' The whiskies were starting to make their presence felt in Gregory's bloodstream.

'Down by the marina. One of the new flats. It's either me or a taxi. You're not fit...'

'Can we stop at an off-licence?'

'Isn't there one on the way back to your place? We left the car there.'

He belched quietly as he stood up. 'Lead on Macduff.'

Leaving the pub, Gregory and Faye bumped into a man hurrying in through the doorway. He was passed them and halfway to the bar before he turned round.

'Greg?...Greg how are you?' Hand held out and smiling, it was Trevor Thomas. In floral Bermuda shorts, Hawaiian shirt and nut roast tan, he was the brightest thing in the room. 'Good to see you. It's been ages.'

'Yes, yes. Trevor...'

'How are you then boy? Good? Fabulous.' He turned to Faye and shook her hand. 'I'm Trevor, friend of Greg's.'

'Me too. Faye.'

'Delighted...got to be honest, can't stop. Only popped in for some fags...if you'll forgive the expression.' He laughed at his own joke.

'We're on our way out anyway...Faye's giving me a lift.'

'Great. Lovely to see you. I'll give you a bell...' And he was off, disappearing into the back of the room towards the cigarette machine while Gregory and Faye continued out into the warm evening.

CHAPTER SEVENTEEN

HICCUPS

The evening seemed to become warmer as night gathered in the sky. Although it was getting on for ten o'clock, the small living room was hot and airless, even with the French doors open onto the balcony. Three candles burning in the middle of the small table were the last straw. Gregory was sure that they were the reason he was sweating. He sat opposite Antonia while Ellie and Art faced each other. It was simply much too warm.

'More wine Greg?

'Thanks.' He offered his glass to Art, who filled it with red. Gregory recognised one of the bottles which he had brought. The off-licence didn't carry a huge stock at the best of times. now, in the middle of what passed for a heat wave in south Wales, its shelves were half empty apart from the very expensive or the very cheap. The Valpolicella was on offer: a pound off if you bought two.

Still, Antonia had seemed more than happy to receive them as she welcomed him in the hallway of her flat on the second floor of one of the ersatz warehouse blocks overlooking the marina. An enormous, flowing, ethnic-print smock in green and yellow, which she appeared to inhabit rather than wear, filled out like a racing spinnaker as she moved. 'Valpolicella. You must be psychic,' she said. ' We're eating Italian. Mama Grimaldi's home-cooking. Come into the kitchen and we'll get you a drink. There's not much space but you can entertain me while I finish the pasta.' Gregory had been worried that she might offer her cheek in greeting, but there was none of that. By the time the others arrived, the half-empty bottle of Tesco's Chianti – some of it had gone in the sauce – was empty and they were busy discussing the uses of nutmeg in Italian cooking.

The Valpolicella was okay. Robust would have been the kindest description. The food, though, was much better than Gregory had expected. Antonia could cook. The wind which had been bothering him all evening gently expelled a small and swallowable burp of garlic, basil, peppers, nutmeg and wine up into the back of his throat. Careful... It was perilously close to something more solid and a good deal less manageable. Perhaps he should ease off on the wine. He could taste acid in the back of his throat as well. Fizzy water might be the thing, although there was always the danger of hiccups with that. And after the hiccups...better not to think about it.

'Have you all had enough?' Antonia's enquiry seemed to be genuine enough. There were meatballs left in the cast-iron pot in front of her and a tiny amount of tagliatelle in pesto sauce could still have been scraped cold off the bottom of its glass serving dish. But everybody had, certainly for the moment, eaten enough.

'Gee, not right now, thanks, I'm hanging fire here for dessert...'

Art was interrupted by Ellie. 'And even though I'm eating for two I don't think I could manage another meatball.'

Gregory was beginning to sympathise with Faye's earlier complaint about Ellie. Her smock was bigger than Antonia's – although more subtle in its delicate blue floral print – and she probably wasn't even four months gone yet. It didn't seem to be possible to talk about anything without coming round to babies or pregnancy within three sentences. And Art was nearly as bad. He'd already been out pricing a car seat for the 'little guy'. There was even talk of buying a new car. Gregory knew it would have to have a 'Drive Carefully – Child On Board' sticker in the back window. And, at least once, he thought he detected impatience on Antonia's part, although the others seemed to miss it.

'What's this little guy business?' she had asked Art, smiling over a spoonful of potato soup heavy with cream and garlic. 'Have you had it sexed then?'

'Not yet, Ellie was going to...'

'Anyway Antonia, in the States guys can be either. Boys or girls. But the consultant says that I can...'

And so it went on. Gregory was almost beginning to feel sorry for Art. At the same time, however, watching him fight to get a word in was at least distracting.

Antonia cleared away the dishes and the remains of the main course. She returned from the kitchen carrying an ashtray.

'And now I'm going to indulge one of my small luxuries.' In her other hand was a packet of San Toy cheroots. 'Anybody mind?' If Antonia noticed the mute protest and distaste on the faces of two of her guests she did not acknowledge it. She was looking at Gregory as she asked the question. He shook his head cheerfully. 'Good. Time for a smoke break before pudding.'

In fairness to Art and Ellie it did smell foul. Gregory was hard put not to wrinkle his nose in solidarity with their's. Antonia, in a small gesture of deference towards her obligations as host, moved back a couple of feet towards the open doors, allowing the smoke a chance to drift out over the marina on whatever whisper of a breeze it could find. Art poured more wine for himself, Gregory and Antonia. In his hand, the bottle wavered uncertainly over the glasses on its way round the table. Ellie was drinking still mineral water.

'What about this protest at the graduation ceremonies then?' Antonia blew a passable smoke ring as she spoke. 'Not bad, eh? My ex taught me to do that...at least he was useful for something.' She laughed. 'What are you going to do, Gregory?'

'I don't know anything about it. What protest?' He appreciated the way that Antonia didn't presume the familiarity which calling him Greg might suggest.

'Didn't you get the circular? About that man, what's his name? Standup. Tory councillor.'

'No, what's...'

'It's Philip, Greg.' Ellie answered the question. 'It's about Philip not getting his grant.'

'I think there's a little bit more than that going on Ellie,' Antonia said. She was smiling gently but the correction was emphatic. 'Councillor Standup is going to be a guest on the platform at one of the graduation ceremonies. Management and Social Science, I think.' That was her faculty, and Philip's.

'But what good's a boycott gonna do? Or a demo?' Ellie's voice had risen in pitch. Anxious self-justification elongated every syllable into something that fell just short of a whine. 'He's gonna enjoy a protest. Just what he wants, all that publicity. It won't stop him turning up. Quite the opposite.'

Art nodded vigorously. "Sright.'

'Okay Ellie, you've got a point.' Antonia moved back closer to the table. 'If it was just graduation. But it's not. And even if it was, you're still talking about having to do something. You can't just let someone like him...I mean...' She turned back to Gregory. 'Think about it. He's bad-mouthed the College, what he said about Philip's probably libellous...'

Art started to mumble something about, 'Why didn't he see a lawyer then?', but shut up abruptly. Gregory thought he had felt a kick from Ellie under the table.

'...The arsehole's managed to get a large and important grant withdrawn – and let's not forget that this was a piece of research which might, at the end of the day, have helped to do something about the HIV problem, and that there were people employed on that contract, people who're on the dole now...'

Art mumbled something again. Gregory couldn't be sure, he was trying to listen to Antonia, but it was something about a bunch of fucking something-or-others. God only knows...he was pissed. So was Art. Antonia, whether she was drunk or sober, continued as if she hadn't heard Art at all.

'...So what are we supposed to do, sit back and pretend that it's fine? And what do we do the next time? When it's overseas students, or whatever his next target is? Ellie, I'm afraid you're being a teensy bit naive.'

'Naive? I'm being naive? I'm the only one...'

'And as I said, it's not just graduation anyway. Word is that he's going to be invited to sit on Council. Apparently the V-C thinks that it's important to open a dialogue with him...

Something about improving communications between town and gown. A heap of shit is what it is, more like.'

'But what good is it going to do, washing all this dirty linen in public? Is it going to help Philip?'

'Ellie, this is not about helping Philip. It's about...it's about academic freedom.'

'Jesus H. Christ.' Art wasn't mumbling now, he was laughing. Out loud. 'Academic freedom, for Chrissake. And you're calling her,' he pointed at Ellie, 'naive? Lady, you could give her lessons. Not to mention the art of being patronising. Teensy bit naive...'

'Art...'

'No Ellie, someone's gotta say it. I'll tell ya what's a heap a shit... Academic freedom. It ain't gonna pay the fuckin' bills. Look at her.' Once again he jerked his thumb in his wife's direction. 'Why should she give a rat's ass about academic freedom? She works hard and what does she get for it? I'll tell ya. All the backstabbing she can handle from her so-called colleagues and...'

'Art, that's not fair. They're not all... I mean, there's Greg.' She shot her erstwhile colleague a look that said, 'He's drunk, it's nothing to do with me.' Gregory just sat in his chair, rolling his glass between his palms. He needed another drink. Or maybe he didn't.

'...He's as far in the hole as you are. You're neither of you exactly top of the popularity stakes in that fucking place. For different reasons, granted, but, er, result's the same. At least the College...it may have been too fucking long coming, but now you've got your Senior Lectureship...'

The kick under the table was definite this time. It was almost audible and it stopped Art dead in his tracks.

'Shit Ellie.' He pushed his chair back, its legs scraping on the floor, and wrenched his knee up to eye level to inspect the damage to his shin. 'Wha's'at for?'

'You know very well what that's for... Gregory, I'm sorry. I was going to tell you myself, but it's not official yet and I told Adrian I wouldn't broadcast it, you know, until the letter came through. I'm sorry you had to find out like this. Drunken ape...'

Gregory smiled and shrugged his shoulders. He was feeling hotter and stickier by the minute. 'No, no...'salright. Calls for a toast.' He raised his nearly empty glass. 'Congratulations. Well done. Richly deserved.' He suppressed a hiccup.

Art would not be suppressed, however. Playing second fiddle did not come naturally to him. 'But it just proves my point. Why, why should you,' he was stabbing his finger at Gregory now, 'why should you stick up for those guys? What the fuck've they done for you? And Philip of all people...buncha lousy faggots...'

The silence that followed this remark was so brief that nobody at the table noticed it. Ellie and Antonia spoke at once.

'Art! How could you!'

'That is quite enough.' Antonia stood up and leaned over Art, slumped in his chair and the knowledge that he'd gone too far. 'You, mister, have pissed on your chips. You don't call me lady, and you don't call my friends faggots. Not in my house.' She stood up straight. 'I'd like you to leave please. Now.'

'Antonia, I'm sorry, he's drunk...'

'I don't give a toss what he is. You're welcome to stay, but he goes. Now. Art, out.' This time Antonia jerked her thumb as well.

Five minutes later they were gone. Ellie had not stayed. Antonia hadn't really thought she would. She came back in from the front door and sat down opposite Gregory again. The light from the two candles which remained alight reflected on the French doors. She relit her cheroot.

'I don't know what to say...'

It took a minute for Gregory to answer, and when he did he sat up straight in the chair at the same time. 'You did a minute ago...hic. What was that about pissing on chips? Where d'you learn that?'

'This's all I bloody need. You're drunk too.'

'You're not so sober yourself. And I'm not...not very.'

'You're a bit ahead of me. And I told you, I'm a Cwmbran girl originally. Anyway, I am... Shit, I'm just sorry. I probably shouldn't have brought it up.'

'What? Brought what up?'

'God alive!' She threw her hands up. 'Graduation, and that man...Standup.'

'I don't know...art did nothing more than come out with it. It's what he's always thought.'

'Doesn't mean the bastard has to say it. And not at my table. Anyway, what're you gonna do? About graduation, I mean.'

'What am I supposed to do? I don't know.' Another silent hiccup went down the hatch.

'Well we want...

'Who's we?'

'It's not the bloody union, that's for sure. They don't want anything to do with it...they called a special meeting. Wasn't even quorate...There was this creep turned up, from Physics somebody said he was, bloody God squad, said perverts should be sacked...what can you say to someone like that? It's just a staff-student committee, I suppose...not even that. We sent everybody a circular. You must have got it.'

'Sorry...I tend to throw things in the bin without looking at them.'

'Hopeless.' She shook her head.

'Didn't Philip tell you? I used to get told off,' he giggled, 'for being a-po-lit-i-cal. Any more plonk?'

'I haven't discussed you with Philip.' The tone of her voice was just dry enough to be unmistakeable, even to Gregory. 'Sure you're up to it?'

'Prob'ly not... Any fizzy water?'

'In the fridge...Hold on, sit there, I'll get it.' She brought in a big green plastic bottle and passed it across the table to him. 'We're asking staff to boycott the platform for that particular ceremony and for everybody else, that's you – you're Humanities, aren't you? – to join a protest outside.'

'What kind of protest?'

'I don't know. Placards. Leaflets. That sort of thing.'

'Has anybody senior said what they're going to do?' Gregory could hear his own voice from a sufficiently drunken distance to notice the broadening of his native accent. Distance didn't seem to have much effect on the hiccups, however.

'Chance'd be a fine thing. Only Geoff' – Professor of Social Work – 'and we made him an offer he couldn't refuse. Although, to be fair, he's supported Phil all the way along. Not that Phil sees it that way, of course.'

'He wouldn't.'

'No...not the world's easiest person. Doesn't make all of this easier. He makes enemies the way some people make their beds.'

Gregory looked at her, puzzled.

'Every day...never mind, it was something I just thought up. You know, to say... Anyway, I'm afraid sometimes I'm tempted to think that he, shall we say, thrives on adversity? Still, that's not the issue.'

'I'm still not sure exactly what the issue is.'

'Come on...for you? You don't know what the issue is? Bullshit. I'm sorry, but that's complete crap.'

'Well there we are then.' Gregory's elbow slipped on the chair arm. 'That's alright. I bow to your authority,' he was laughing again, 'or at least I will when I gather myself together again.' He straightened himself up. 'Is that the time?' It was ten past eleven. 'I'd better get a taxi. Home to bed.'

'You'll be lucky this time of night. Closing time. You'll have to wait hours.'

'Doesn't matter. Prepared to wait hours.'

'Right. I'll ring. While you're waiting I'll make some coffee. There's pudding as well, you know. Home-made Italian ice cream. We never got round to it. Could you handle it?'

Gregory could feel the surge rising in his throat before Antonia had finished her sentence. This time it wasn't a hiccup.

CHAPTER EIGHTEEN

ACADEMIC FREEDOM

On Tuesday morning a re-usable - and much re-used - orange internal envelope appeared in Gregory's pigeon hole. He had no other mail. Inside were two pieces of paper. The larger, a sheet of standard lined A4, was attached to the front of the smaller by a bright red paper-clip. Written in a large, round and roly-poly hand, a green-inked script of rumbustious calligraphy and irresistible punctuation, it read as follows:

Monday 22.6.92

Dear Gregory,

Here's another copy of the circular about the protest. Just in case you're still interested... More important, I hope the other evening wasn't too awful for you. I know a host isn't responsible for the behaviour of her guests, but I can't help thinking that perhaps I shouldn't have brought the subject up. Not the right time or place. Anyway, my apologies once again.

Excuse the formality of this note, but your department office said you weren't coming in today and I don't have your home phone number. I didn't want to ask Ellie for it. I do hope you won't be put off accepting another invitation in the future! Cheers,

Antonia

Gregory felt little enough like smiling, but he couldn't really help himself. Among her personal qualities Antonia Grimaldi clearly numbered tact. Not a mention of the evening's grand finale. Fortunately Antonia's living room had a polished wooden floor and there were no rugs down near the table. More by force of gravity than judgement he'd managed to miss the table cloth as his dinner made its explosive exit. Afterwards he just sat there, useless, his head hanging in drunken confusion as she wiped up the mess. She had only said one thing, after checking that he was alright: 'Never mind, when you've worked in a chippie on a

Saturday night this is just a drop in life's great ocean.' Well, she had said something like that. And it had seemed funny at the time. At the time, he'd even been too drunk for the embarrassment which had depressed him for most of the rest of the weekend.

He put the circular down on his desk after looking at its headline: STAND UP FOR ACADEMIC FREEDOM – BOYCOTT STANDUP. A bit obvious, but perhaps subtlety wasn't called for. He couldn't recall receiving it before. If he had he certainly hadn't looked at it before throwing it away. He would have remembered. Sod it, he wasn't going to look at it now. It was nearly ten o'clock and there was a meeting to go to. Gregory gathered the thick bundle of files which rested precariously across the top tray of the stack – the one marked 'Done' (the others were 'To do' and 'Essays') – and made his way to the Archaeology Examinations Board meeting.

Adrian waited until the meeting had effectively ended. The usual congratulatory and self-congratulatory noises had been made, the pass lists were circulating for signatures and people were starting to talk among themselves. The external examiner, that silly old fart Mackintosh from Leeds, displayed avuncular feelings towards Hugh Brimsley, one of his old pupils. Mackintosh had only a year or two to fill in before retirement, but age had clearly not diminished his interest in women. Every few seconds his eyes would dart over Brimsley's shoulder to where Ellie sat.

Today she was wearing a smart and flattering sun dress in a pastel batik design, rather than a smock. Every now and again she would meet Mackintosh's eye with a shy half smile, while Adrian expounded the difference between a real First and a bureaucratic First. Martin Griffiths, this year's success story was, apparently, the latter. She and Gregory had greeted each other cordially enough, but she did not meet his eye and he did not give her much opportunity to. Although Ellie's promotion was clearly not a secret to everyone – congratulations were muttered here and there – it was carefully not being mentioned. She excused herself finally and went over to talk to Pauline, who was busy gathering all the documents into some kind of order.

'There is one thing more.' Adrian had trouble making himself heard, so he banged on the table with his diary. 'Excuse me, just one more thing.' He lifted a letter from an open manila folder and looked at it over the top of his spectacles. 'Erm...I have a letter here from the Vice-Chancellor. Concerning the, erm, threatened protest during the graduation ceremonies. In my capacity as Departmental Head I am required by the Vice-Chancellor to let him have the names of any members of, erm, staff who indicate that they are intending to join any such protest.' He continued to look down at the piece of paper in his hands. It betrayed a slight shake. 'I would, therefore, be, erm, grateful if those of you who do so intend would let me know. That's all.' He replaced the letter in its folder. 'Now, if someone will lead the way, the examiners' lunch calls, I believe.'

Gregory made his excuses and left the lunch as soon as he decently could. The private dining room in Tŷ Ogwr – known to the students as the Ogre's Castle – felt more like a dentist's waiting rooms than a venue for sociability, and the food, as ever on these occasions, was imaginatively awful. Today's special was locally caught sewin, that managed to be simultaneously dried out and greasy. The broccoli looked like a washed-out bottle brush and tasted like school cabbage, while the duchess potatoes... Well, as Mackintosh dryly remarked, it was the Duchess of York who came immediately to mind. Sherry trifle for afters. Adrian's idea of a good wine was Liebfraumilch, so that's what they had. Bloody Blue Nun. And all together it was costing the Department something like ten pounds a head.

Nor did the company improve from one year to the next. It didn't change at all, in fact. For Gregory, it had been worse than usual without his usual companion at his elbow. Ellie had spent the meal entertaining Mackintosh, laughing loudly at his jokes while ostentatiously refusing alcohol. She seemed perfectly happy when he lit his pipe with the coffee and After Eights.

It had been impossible to make even the smallest of talk with any of his colleagues. Every time Gregory tried to think of something to say – about the weather, perhaps, or the chances of young Griffiths getting a British Academy scholarship – his mind dragged itself round to Adrian's announcement. Nobody mentioned them, of course, but for Gregory those few stammered words flickered over the table like a failing fluorescent light tube. The man rather than the message was the affront. Now that he was Head of Department, Adrian would be unbearable. Even more unbearable, if that was conceivable. Gregory's own future prospects receded ever further, back into a familiar, even if anxious and uncomfortable, distance.

Having escaped, Gregory did not know, however, what to do next. The afternoon was hot and there were sticky patches under his arms. He took off his tie and put it in his jacket pocket. Then he took off his jacket. The sky, although cloudless, was overcast with haze and dust and its own glittering grey reflection off the sea. In the car park behind the Humanities building, Gregory put his jacket safely in the car, pocketed his wallet and keys and began to walk.

'Gregory.' A female voice hailed him before he had gone fifty yards. Turning round he saw Antonia coming towards him. 'Gregory...I thought it was you.' She gestured to the bundle of bright yellow papers under her left arm. 'Just doing my bit...sticking notices about the protest under windscreen wipers. Here, here's one for you.'

Gregory was reluctant but he accepted it nonetheless. His life was becoming circumscribed by pieces of paper. Letters, notices, circulars, literate lockstitches hemming him in. He did not try to read it.

'It's nothing you won't have seen before.' She waited for a response but none came. 'You okay? Still under the weather?'

'No, sorry. I'm fine, thanks. We've just had our examiners' meeting...I was a million miles away. And I should have called you to apologise...'

'Not at all. Forget it. Did you get my note?'

'Yes. Thanks. And I am sorry about the other night. It was an awful mess.'

'Wasn't your fault...that shit, Art, honest to God, I didn't think anybody could be so bloody crass, not these days.' She leaned with heavy emphasis on the end of the sentence. 'Speaking of crass, have you seen Ellie?'

'Yeah, she's probably still fluttering her eyelashes at the External Examiner... She's in her element.'

'She say anything?'

'No. Not much chance...'

'Probably just as well.' Gregory stayed silent again. Antonia went on. 'Have you thought any more about the boycott, I mean the protest, you know?'

'I don't know. There's that message from the V-C...' Antonia looked at him with obvious puzzlement. 'Haven't you heard?' She shook her head. 'All Department Heads have been instructed to report staff members who participate in any protest.'

'First we've heard of it...the bastard! Are you going to...'

'I really don't know.' The sharpness of his reply cut across Antonia's building head of agitation and enthusiasm. His voice softened. 'Sorry, I didn't mean to be rude. Sorry...I'm feeling a wee bit under pressure over this. Like the bloody meat in a sandwich...'

'And I'm sure I'm not helping... Judge not and all that. I'd better get on anyway, there's a meeting at three. Just before I go though, you know this has got nothing to do with Philip any more. Speaking for myself, it's on my own behalf I'm angry. That's why... And that's why you should be...Gregory, I'm not asking you to do anything for Philip. It's for yourself. Nobody else...there. Sermon over.' Antonia was flushed, whether with heat and exertion or screwed-up gumption was impossible to tell. 'You do what you must.' She smiled and squeezed his arm. 'I must go. Give me a bell.' She returned her attention to the line of parked cars. Gregory turned back towards the building.

Fifteen minutes later, Gregory carefully licked the gum and sealed the envelope that he held in both hands. With equal care he placed it in Adrian's pigeon hole. Pauline's office was still, quiet and tidy. Everybody was still over at the lunch. The phone started to ring. Gregory ignored it. He locked the door behind him as he went out to the lift.

CHAPTER NINETEEN

SILVER FRUIT

It was late afternoon before Gregory turned the key in his front door. For a couple of hours he had wandered in the heat. Down by the front, around the Marina, along the Esplanade, back through the High Street to the multi-storey where the car was parked. The day had turned into a half-smoked butt, stubbed out and abandoned in the gutter, nothing left in it but temptation for a down and out's shamelessness.

Gregory's fingers were slow on the latch, his feet dragged, his head hung. There was no post, not for him anyway. A couple of envelopes which looked like bills awaited Jacqui Evans upstairs. He hadn't seen her for weeks. Was she still seeing that pretty fellow with the curly hair? Years younger than her. Not that Gregory cared.

But what did he care about? God knows. Not much.

And what did God know anyway?

He used to believe that his mother thought that she knew the answer to that. Now he was beginning to think that perhaps he'd been wrong. And always had been. Gregory went into his flat and closed the door quietly behind him.

In the dark, the view from the parapet was straight down into the black chasm of Devil's Leap. Gusts of wind sighed and shivered in the trees on up the glen. A howl rose up to Gregory's ears and was followed by another, and another. The Devil was down below, standing guard over a heavy wooden box held fast by a brass padlock.

Still in the dark, Gregory woke to see the corners of his bedroom, right and left, back and front, shadowed by the delicate light of the bright round moon in the sky beyond his window. There was no noise apart from his heart pulsing in his ears. Then there were words to accompany it: 'Slowly, silently, now the moon...' What was the rest of it? He could recall learning it by heart in school. Something about 'This way and that...' If he only could remember it, perhaps he could sleep again.

The digital clock by the bed said 4:37 and the moon was long since lost in the thin light of earliest day. Outside, the gardens were full of bird song. Gregory lay flat on his back. The bed was clammy with sweat and his mouth was sticky and dry. Blood pulsed in his temples and thundered in his ears.

He had been dreaming, he was sure he'd been dreaming...something about a garden in the moonlight. And a bridge. He shivered, his shoulders suddenly cold above the bedclothes. Pulling the duvet around him more tightly, Gregory turned onto his side and tried to sleep.

At six o'clock he was up, making coffee in the kitchen. The birds were quiet now and the light of day was already full. Gregory sat down. Mattie and Donald's letters were still on the table, beside the tablemats and coasters, where they had been since he had first opened the parcel. Absent-mindedly he shuffled the pile into tidiness, levelling its long edge on the table top between his hands. One persisted in sticking out at a slight angle, snagged on another envelope. It was one of his mother's, he could tell that from its cheapness. Worse than Jacqui Evans' bills. It wouldn't push back into the rest, so Gregory cut the pile in two. He could not resist a look, just as he had not been able to resist every other time he had moved them in the last weeks.

It was dated October 6th, 1946. Like all of the others, he had read it so many times that he could almost have recited it by memory. The thought pushed aside something in the back of his mind. He had a glimpse of a garden in strong, bright moonlight. It looked like a cartoon. A well-drawn, old-fashioned cartoon. Very clearly he could see a dovecot, he could hear the quiet bubble of its inhabitants. And fruit trees. The words of a poem followed this brief vision...

'Slowly, silently, now the moon
Walks the night in its silver shoon.
This way and that, it peeks and sees,
Silver fruit upon silver trees.'

He'd probably got it wrong anyway. Never could remember poetry. He always used to be the one standing up in class, stuck on a word. If it wasn't the last verse, he could feel the impatience of the rest of the class gathering around him. One more reason for their resentment... 'Eh, clever clogs. If ye're sae rotten smart, why can ye no remember yere verses?' If it was the last verse, the tittering would soon start and his face blushed redder and redder. He was no better with scripture, either. Well, a bit better, perhaps, the costs of ignorance in Sunday School were that wee bit higher.

There was something else...that he couldn't quite remember either. His head was thick and muzzy. He looked around for the paracetamol. He took a deep drink of coffee instead and stared down at the letter for several minutes, looking but not seeing. Nothing there. He stuffed it back in its envelope, crumpling the coarse paper as he did so. Remorse coloured his cheeks immediately and he carefully took it out again, smoothed the creases and replaced it. Tidying the pile of letters, he put them back in their place. No, there was nothing there to jog his memory.

At about nine o'clock Gregory, shaved and showered but not much else, left the flat. The same post was waiting on the hall table. On the mat just inside the door was today's. One small, colourful packet addressed to Miss J. Evans. Photographs back from the processor's. Wonder what they were of? He remembered again that there was something at the back of his mind, something which he was trying to remember... He took another look at the packet, shook his head and placed it beside the rest.

As he closed the outside door the sun twinkled in his eyes, reflecting off the fittings of the lock.

A brass lock. Photographs. A wooden box.

He remembered. Faye did not get back to him until nearly lunchtime. Her department secretary hadn't been sure whether or not Dr Watson was going to be in today, but yes, if she did she would be sure to give her the message. Yes, said Gregory, I have tried her at home. No, I don't think she could have been in. Bloody stupid woman. Sat in her office all day flirting with American exchange students and polishing her nails...well so Faye said, anyway.

In the meantime he had been holed up in his office like a badger with a sore paw, safe with the door locked. There wasn't one of them that he felt like facing. Not one. Adrian would have read the letter by now. Ellie would've had nothing to say to him anyway. She was probably more embarrassed then he was. Or perhaps not. And the rest? To hell with them...the door had been knocked once, probably a student looking for a late essay, but whoever it was hadn't even tried the handle.

No-one rang him. By eleven o'clock he was almost starting to wish somebody would. Anybody. He had tried to put the time to good use by reading a review article on computer modelling in the latest number of Current Archaeology, but gave up when he found himself nodding off in the heat. It was too late in the morning to go for a trawl around the Internet: America was waking up and trying to download anything would just take ages. He looked around the office. Titles of books bought years ago and never read stared down from the shelves, a sheaf of conference papers in a blue folder that he had never even skimmed. Second-year essays, still waiting to be marked. The light in the room was heavy and indistinct with the blinds fully drawn. A south-facing window was ideal for the spring and autumn, but much too warm today. Opening the window did nothing to relieve the pressure. Time took its time, and the soft shadows did not move. Why didn't somebody ring? He was marooned in this bloody College, Ben Gunn without the goats, nobody worth knowing and nobody who wanted to know him. Not a sail on the horizon. The phone rang.

'Hello petal.'

'Faye?'

'Who else, you daft bugger?'

'I don't know...'

'So...I got your message. What're you up to?'

'Sitting here feeling sorry for myself, and getting better at it by the minute.'

'That's not like you.'

'Listen you...one of the things Oscar Wilde was right about was sarcasm.'

'Pardon me dear...'

'It's your birthday next week isn't it?'

'Uh huh, on Sunday.'

'Christ...that close. I thought it was Monday or Tuesday.'

'Why? What difference does it make?'

'I don't usually miss it, do I? And I didn't want to miss it this year.'

'Where you off to then?'

'Thought I'd go home for a wee while.'

'Home? You mean...'

'Aye. Glenvie. Just for a couple of days.'

'After all you've said about...'

'I know, I know. Shake the dust of that place off my feet, and all that. It's just...Well there's a few wee things I need to sort out. And besides, weren't you the one telling me the other night that I ought to?'

'That's true... What's the time? Half past eleven. What're you doing now? For lunch I mean?'

Lying on her back on Gregory's sofa, an unchilled can of Miller Lite in her hand, Faye was finding it difficult to drink. Every time she tried, beer and foam dribbled out of the corners of her mouth, while the little bit that she did manage to swallow threatened to choke her.

'For God's sake, would you not make such a bloody mess. Why don't you just sit up?'

Gregory was in the chair by the glass table, one leg draped over its arm, a cold-misted glass of white wine in the hand that was resting on his bent knee.

'Shut up... Oops! Sorry...it's my shirt. Look, you're just making me worse. What're you so worried about anyway?'

'If it was going on your shirt I wouldn't worry about it. I don't know if those covers are washable... Boy oh boy, am I tired.' He yawned and took another sip of wine. The bottle, Penfold's Chardonnay, was on the floor by the chair. The remains of lunch – cheese, bread, a wooden bowl of fruit, a couple of plates and a scattering of crumbs – littered the table.

'So anyway, you were going to tell me about the meal, at Antonia's. How'd it go?"

'Absolute bloody disaster. Ended up throwing up all over the place. Sitting at the table. Ugh...' He shuddered.

'Didn't even make it to the loo? Umm... Yup, that's pretty bad. What'd she say?'

'Who?'

'Antonia. Who did you think?'

'Nothing. She was marvellous. Just went and got a cloth and wiped up the mess. I think she was more worried about me than she was about the floor.'

'You could try taking a leaf out of her book.' This was immediately followed by a coughing fit as Faye attempted another mouthful. She raised up on one elbow, trying to find her breath again.

'And you could try a straw.'

'Bog off.'

'I hate to say I told you so, love, but she's always been an ambitious, conniving bitch. Nothing's changed.'

'You're one to talk. It never stopped you going to her parties.'

'Once a year. Once a bloody year. And they're good parties. No point cutting off your nose to spite your face.'

'Bloody hypocrite.'

'Bollocks. Anyway, if I remember correctly you asked me to the first one. What was it? "Come on, for my sake, otherwise I'll have no-one to talk to." Something like that. Couldn't leave you to play wallflower...senior lectureship my eye. Bloody cow.'

'It's not that. That's fair enough. She deserves it more than most.'

'That's not the point. That bastard Art could've kept his mouth shut. Faggots indeed!' She laughed. 'Mind you it would've been worth it to see Antonia in action... I told you that she wasn't the world's worst. Shouldn't go on first impressions.'

'I'll remind you of that. The next time you take one of your famous dislikes on sight to someone...or the other way round... Anyway, did you get that proclamation from Rees?'

'About the graduation protest? A load of crap. Fucking fascist. I'm not going to pay any attention.'

There was a long silence. Gregory looked at her over the top of his glass.

'Ah, but that's not really the point is it? Not pay it any attention. What're you actually going to do on Graduation Day?'

'I'm not even sure I'm going to be here. I might just go down and see my mother for a couple of days. She's due a visit.'

'You are a hypocrite. A whited bloody sepulchre.'

'Not me. I haven't been making a huge great fuss about this. I haven't been handing out leaflets. Going to meetings.'

'Why not?'

'Why haven't you?'

Faye looked at her watch. 'Christ. Gone three.' She was sitting up now with her legs tucked up underneath her. Her shoes were crossed over each other on the floor, beside two empty beer cans, one upright, one on its side. She had just opened a third. The half-empty glass of wine on the table was the last of the bottle. 'I'll go when I've finished this.'

'You be alright to drive?'

'Probably not.'

'Stay for a cup of coffee then.'

'I'll see. Are you going to do it then?'

'I don't know...there doesn't seem to be much point, having told Adrian I'm going to if I don't.' Gregory's head was thick with the peculiar weight which only descends during afternoon drinking. 'I'm going to make some coffee in a minute anyway. It was just when Antonia said about doing it for myself, it made sense, kind of...I don't know.'

'And what about Scotland?'

'I thought I might head off in the morning.'

'Are you sure it's wise?'

'No. But if I don't go I'm never going to get this thing sorted out. And it's got to be sorted. D'you know I never used to have dreams? Well, not often anyway. It's crazy...maybe it's me that's crazy.'

'Don't be silly. It's just the old subconscious at work. Back of your mind talking to the front. That's the trouble with you archaeologists, you've never read Freud.'

'Well apart from apologising for the gaps in my education, there's not a lot I can do about that. And subconscious or no subconscious, when you start dreaming about the Devil, it's probably time to do something about it.'

'I'm just not convinced that going looking for him is it.'

'Now you're being silly. It's the box... I still don't really know why I did it. It seemed like a grand, great gesture at the time. Making a clean break and all that. Suppose I should've known better.'

'But it won't still be there. It'll be gone.'

'But that's not the point...and maybe Charlie can tell me something.'

Faye swigged some beer. 'How do you fancy celebrating my birthday in Scotland then?'

'What d'you mean...you? Come as well?'

'Only if you want. I don't want to impose...but there's nothing to do here now. Not until graduation anyway. And a few days away'd do me the world of good. I always wanted to see that place anyway.'

'Glenvie? Don't be expecting too much.'

'Does that mean I can come?'

CHAPTER TWENTY

SILVER TREES

Gregory finally capitulated just south of Kendal. Faye had asked several times to do her share of the driving – and that she should do her share of the driving had been part of the agreement – but he kept putting her off... She wasn't to worry, he'd let her know when he'd had enough. And anyway, he enjoyed driving, didn't find it a bit tiring... Not until they swerved abruptly in and out of the outside lane of the motorway, in front of a large BMW which just managed to squeeze by next to the crash barrier, headlights flashing, horn screaming and fist shaking, did he admit defeat.

'If I'd wanted to be in a fucking road movie starring little Noddy I'd've made bloody sure he didn't get anywhere near the M6.' Faye was white with fear and anger, fists balled tight in between her knees, eyes fixed straight ahead. 'Typical bloody man... You nearly killed us! And that other guy.'

'Sorry...I just got very tired all of a sudden. I was fine until a minute ago. Sorry.' He shook his head and ran the fingers of one hand backwards through his hair. 'And he shouldn't have been going so fast.'

'Crap. You've been nodding off for the last half hour. I don't know what the bloody hell you think you're trying to prove. I know you don't think much of my driving, but...'

'It's not that...'

'Then what? Men! Not fit to be behind a wheel.'

They switched over at Killington services, overlooking the reservoir. Gregory said he needed to stretch his legs anyway. Faye needed a cigarette. That had been another part of the agreement: no smoking in the car. Neither was hungry so they settled for coffee and a soggy Danish pastry each. Gregory didn't finish his. Faye had an extra cup of coffee.

They filled the car and set off again. Within ten minutes Gregory was dozing. By the time they passed Carlisle he was fast asleep.

His neck was stiff, his head angled awkwardly against the cold glass of the window. The seatbelt was tight under his armpit. A trail of spit had dribbled down onto his chin. The first thing that he saw was stone and grass. A bank with a hawthorn hedge along its crown. The shadows were long in the thin yellow sunlight of a late summer evening. Sitting up, he realised that he was alone. It took a minute to shake himself properly awake. Undoing the seatbelt, he found a handkerchief in his pocket and wiped his face.

The car was parked tight in to the side of a minor road. To the front, on the other side of the valley which the road bisected, rose a steep hillside, boxed with dry-stone walling and dotted with heavy green patches of whin bushes and the occasional stand of trees. It was a minute before Gregory saw Faye, a hundred yards or so down the road, and another before he recognised the place. She stood on the bridge at the Devil's Leap, leaning forward over the dark grey stone of the parapet, smoking.

The sound of the car door slamming turned her head. She watched Gregory walk towards her.

'Back in the land of the living?'

'Aye...God, I must've been tireder than I thought.' He stretched and leaned on the bridge beside her.

'You were completely bloody bushed.' Faye took one last lungful of smoke and threw the end of the cigarette into the air in front of her. 'Feel better now? What were you trying to do anyway? It wasn't the Indianapolis 500 you know.'

'How did we end up here?'

'I stopped the other side of Dumfries and had a look at the map. You were out cold. This was the shortest road. And when I saw the name, it's marked Devil's Leap on the map, that made my mind up.'

'So...what d'you think?'

It's smaller than I imagined. You know, not as high. Down there.' She gestured towards the tumble of rocks and water rushing and crashing a hundred or so feet below them. 'I don't know what I was expecting...Niagara or something.'

'Aye, well, when your only tall enough to rest your chin on the edge, let me tell you it's enormous. And when it booms – it does it when the river's full – let me tell you, it's the Devil himself.'

'But it is lovely. Look at it. Beautiful. And it's so quiet... Even with the waterfall.' She turned round and the view changed abruptly. From a patchwork history of walls, ditches and the occasional farmhouse, to a straight-lined and sharp-cornered plantation of Trafalgar Square-sized conifers, which muffled the contours of the top of the valley. The forest's peaked canopy shone an iridescent silver green, but, even though the sun was still an hour or so above the horizon, beneath its bald bottom branches night lurked, waiting its moment to creep down into the lowlands. Faye turned round again. 'So, where does the name come from? Devil's Leap.'

'There're different stories. St Patrick, although why it should be him I've no idea, he was supposed to be fighting the Devil and the old fella got away by jumping across. There...d'you see that sort of V-shaped cleft? No...over there.' He pointed to the top of the ravine, on the right beyond the edge of the falls below them. 'See where the wee tree is? Just beyond it. That's where he's supposed to have caught one of his hooves as he was jumping. Another story has it that it was where the witches used to meet. They used to jump backwards and forwards across the gap. God knows why.' He chuckled. 'My favourite, though, is the one about the hare. Apparently some old farmer came out one morning and found a hare up on the roof of his cowshed. He chased it as far as here and when it got to the edge it turned into the Devil, jumped across and got away. The bit about the hoof getting stuck's in that story too.'

'So how d'you know all this?'

'From Uncle Charlie. Sometimes he'd babysit if my mother was working up at the Manse, I must have been five or six, no more, and he used to scare the pants off me with his tales...And when I got older he told me about Rabbie Burns. All kinds of exploits. To hear Charlie talk you'd think half the countryside around here had Burns for a great-grandfather. He's full of stories.'

'I can't wait to meet him.'

'Aye...' Gregory looked sceptical. 'We'll see.'

'Getting nervous?'

'What d'you mean?'

'About going home. And with me.'

'No, it's not that. I always get a bit, I don't know, anxious I suppose. Coming back home.'

'We moved around so much when I was young. I'm not sure where I'd call home. Funny old business...home. Anyway, where did you throw the box?'

Gregory leaned out over the edge. Below him a wreck of boulders and white water crowded the river for twenty or thirty feet, as far as the precipice over which it vanished down through the Leap. 'Straight down there. It must have gone in among the rocks.'

'Is there any way down?'

'Don't know. I've never tried.'

'Well, tonight's not the time.' Faye shivered. 'It's getting cold.'

'Aye, and we'd better get on. Uncle Charlie'll be expecting us.' They started back to the car.

'He sounds an interesting old cove. Imagine, having an answering machine on his phone. Not quite the country bumpkin you paint him. What does he do? His job, I mean.'

'The County Council. Supervises road gangs and that sort of thing. Started out as a labourer. He's done well for himself.'

'Not your run of the mill by the sound of things. Was he ever married?'

'No, not him. He's a confirmed bachelor.'

'Just like his nephew.'

'Not quite. Got the car keys?'

CHAPTER TWENTY-ONE

PHOTOGRAPHIC MEMORY

Uncle Charlie had already gone to work by the time Faye came downstairs in the morning. Gregory was in the kitchen.

'Morning. Coffee? It's only Maxwell House, I'm afraid. And its powder, not granules.'

'That's fine... You know, you sound just like one of those bloody silly adverts. Next thing you'll be popping out to the neighbours to borrow some because you've run out and falling in love with the handsome young man who answers the door.' Faye lit a cigarette. 'And don't make faces. I'm going to give up.'

'You haven't seen the neighbours. Anyway, I think that's your department...falling in love with handsome young men, I mean.' He brought her the coffee. 'How did you sleep?'

'I was so tired I could have slept standing up.' Faye, after Uncle Charlie's initial misunderstanding that she and Gregory would be sleeping together, had been given sole occupancy of Gregory's mother's room and her bed. 'What was the settee like?'

'Alright. Better than where you were anyway.'

They moved through into the lounge.

'Poor old Uncle Charlie. I think he was quite disappointed.' Faye sat down in a low modern armchair by the empty fireplace, Gregory on the matching settee, next to the neatly-folded sleeping bag and blanket which had been his bedding.

'About the food? No, that'll not have bothered him.' They had arrived to find a hot meal in the oven which neither of them could manage.

'No, not that, silly...about you and me, not sleeping together. I think he quite fancied the idea, bless him.'

'Well, never mind. But it took me a wee bit by surprise, that did. Didn't think he was so...so modern. Anyway...And the dinner'll keep, so it's lamb casserole tonight.'

'Great. It smelled wonderful. You never told me there were two men in the family who can cook.'

'Nobody told me either.' Gregory looked around. 'I'm beginning to think old Charlie's a wee bit of a dark horse. This is all new, you know. He's only been in the house a few months and already... There used to be a wall there,' he waved in the general direction of the open-plan kitchen and dining room which was separated from the rest of the long living room by an archway, 'and there. There were three rooms. And all the walls, that brickwork, for example, it's new too.' The brickwork of the chimney breasts had been exposed and cleaned, in sharp contrast to the white plaster and dark wood panelling of the rest of the downstairs. 'He says it was only finished the week before last.'

'It's certainly not what I was expecting, after all you'd told me. That, for example.' Over the fireplace hung a framed print of a grainy black-and-white photograph of a beach scene which looked as though it might be somewhere in France, a Doisneau or something like that. A little boy with wide, dark eyes looked on in silent wonder at a man with a curly moustache entering the water in a striped one-piece bathing suit. 'It's, well, it's just not what I was expecting.'

'The kitchen's all new too.'

'I noticed that. He must have spent a fortune...although that bedroom, it's something else. I don't think he's done anything to that. Gives me the creeps.' It was a dark and cluttered grotto, entombed by heavy curtains, dark over-sized furniture and threadbare carpet. 'It's sort of crowded and empty all at the same time. As if no-one had ever slept there, but full of this... I don't know what you'd call it. I was almost embarrassed to undress.'

'There's some things you can't rush... But he's made an amazing start on the place. It feels a wee bit strange, for me, seeing all the changes, but it was about time...'

'Where did he used to live?'

'Down in the village. In lodgings with Mrs MacClintoch. He'd been there for years... He was telling me about the answering machine, by the way. He has to be on call sometimes for work, something to do with that. The Council put it in for him.'

'Did he never marry or anything?'

'You asked me that yesterday... I never even heard of a girlfriend. But sure you wouldn't know. He's always played his cards very close to his chest. They were two of a kind in that respect, him and my mother.'

'Look who's talking.'

Gregory looked at his watch. 'I'm sure you're right. Anyway, isn't it about time you had some breakfast?' He got up and walked back into the kitchen. Faye shook her head, stood up and followed him.

Before Faye had finished her breakfast, she had also fallen out with Gregory about what they were going to do for the rest of the day. He wanted to go for a drive, to show her 'some of the countryside'. She accused him of 'bloody well bottling out', 'running away'... They hadn't, after all, 'come all this way just for a sodding holiday'. Gregory was prepared to concede this, but could see no reason why they shouldn't 'make the most of it while we're up here...and anyway, we can't do anything until Charlie gets back.' Leaving Faye to stub her annoyance out along with her last Marlboro Light, in the end Gregory had gone for a walk down to the village. There might still be a newspaper left and he fancied some fresh air. He hadn't even attempted to conceal his disapproval when he agreed to get her some more cigarettes.

Charlie let himself in the front door at about midday, not more than ten minutes after his nephew's departure. Faye was in the kitchen making another cup of coffee.

'Anybody home? Oh, there you are. Making yourself at home I see lassie. Good, good. Aye, I'll have one too. Two sugars.' He sat down at the kitchen table. 'Thanks. Where's his nibs then?'

'Gone to get a paper.'

'Has he now? That's funny, I came up that way and didnae see him. Still, if he fancied a wee walk he's maybe gone on doon the other way, by the burn. If he's gone that way he'll be a while yet.'

'He wasn't expecting you back 'til teatime.'

'That'd be right. I took the afternoon off. Sure it's not every day that he's home, is it? If they want me, they can always ring. There's nae reason they should, though. We'll see if he fancies doing anything when he gets back.'

Today the kirk's small graveyard was a different place. Sunshine reflected on polished granite here, a chrome-plated flower basket there. The hillside beyond was far away now, a distant backdrop of dull grey rock, yellow whins and purple heather. Even the kirk itself seemed to Gregory newly-scrubbed and wholesome. He closed the gate and walked slowly towards the rectangle of earth, as yet still unmarked by a stone, which covered his mother.

Faye's comment had been innocent enough: 'Being here, you know, in this house. It makes me wonder what he was like. When he was younger, you know? He's always seemed so, I don't know, middle-aged...not that there's anything wrong with middle-age...'

'I know what you mean.' Uncle Charlie patted her hand. He stood up. 'You're awfu' fond of him, aren't ye? Aye, well, I'm fond of him myself. Wait there 'til I fetch something. It'll likely interest you.'

He returned with a black photograph album, worn at the corners and faded, bulging under his arm.

'I bet you'll no ha' seen any of these.' He sat down opposite Faye. 'He must hae his mother's photos, not that she was a great one for that sort of thing, but if I know the same boy he'll no show anyone them.' Faye was about to tell him what had happened to his sister's stuff but thought better of it. Charlie continued. 'I was mad keen on photography when I was younger... I was thinking mind you, now I have this place, I'd maybe take it up again. I could make the roof space up there intae a fine wee dark room, and they've got night classes you can sign up for, in Castle Douglas. That wouldnae be tae far tae go...here, would you listen to me, blethering on. Anyway, I was saying, I had this old Brownie, an old bellows camera, and I would always be called upon if there was ever a snap to be taken. There's a few of Gregory.' He opened the album in the middle and turned a few pages, backwards and forwards, before he found what he was looking for. 'Here's one.'

He turned the album around and shunted it across the table towards Faye.

The few flowers and wreaths had been cleared away long since. Now there was just the earth, dry and dusty on top of the plot in which she lay. As burial mounds went, there wasn't much to it. Hardly enough to show that it was anything special at all. Gregory lifted a handful. It crumbled between his fingers. There was hardly a breath of movement in the air to scatter the soil as it sieved slowly away. He'd have to talk to Charlie about a stone. The words were the problem...name and date. Maybe they could find something from the Bible that would please her. But what about anything else? His father was buried in Korea, so...

He got no further. Why did he think it was Korea? He didn't actually know where his father was buried. He had never once even given the matter any thought. Nobody had ever told him. Nobody had ever really told him anything. Not that he had ever asked. Not since he was very small. He had never once asked. And he had no idea how he was going to ask now.

It was unmistakeably Gregory, yet at the same time Faye wouldn't have recognised him if she hadn't been told. He must have been eighteen months old, maybe two. Dressed in a crocheted woollen jacket and some kind of trews or leggings. No shoes, just his feet and toes.

But it wasn't Gregory she was interested in, it was the woman who was holding him. A strict, formal face, and a strict formal pose. It was in the open air, there were trees in the background. She was dressed in dark clothes, they could have been black, it was hard to tell. Hair either very short or tied back. No smile. An awkwardness and distance in the eyes and arms. She held her son at arm's length, although she held him close.

'That's his mother. It wasn't very long after his father died.'

'I thought it must be.'

'There's some more.' Upside down as they were to him, Uncle Charlie flipped over the pages. There was the same serious boy's face - wide eyed, no smile in any of them - as Gregory grew up before Faye's eyes. In one he was standing by a river, holding a fish up by its tale, gingerly, with thumb and forefinger, as though he was not yet convinced that it was dead and harmless. Charlie smiled.

'I was trying tae teach him tae fish. But he wasnae really interested'.

In another he was standing to attention in what looked like a sailor's suit. Charlie explained again.

'That was when he was in the Life Boys.' Seeing Faye's puzzled look, he continued. 'I suppose it would be something like the Boy Scouts. It was run by the kirk. When you were eleven or twelve you went on tae the BB...that's the Boy's Brigade. His mother thought it'd make a man oot o' him, but he never liked that either.'

'What did he like?'

'Reading, he'd read anything. You could hardly get him oot the door tae play. There was an old set of encyclopaedias, I dinna ken where they came from, but he must ha' read every page. And he loved listening tae stories when he was wee.'

'He told me that. Said you used to frighten the life out of him.'

'It never stopped him asking for more.' Charlie laughed. The laughter stopped abruptly and he closed the album. 'You know. since his mother passed on, I've been thinking a lot aboot... It must be being back here...when he was a wee boy, he was so, he never had anyone tae...it was his mother, you see, she seemed tae close up, he never had... I dinna really, what I'm trying to say is that I suppose it was a father he never had. I used to try and take him fishing and that, but she was never happy, always worrying. Took him to Dumfries once and, d'you know, she was there in the Square, waiting for the bus when we got back? And yet she never, it wasnae that she ever did much with him herself.' He was silent for a moment and Faye let the silence be. 'Anyway, you must hae better things tae do than listen tae me rattling on.'

'No. There's nothing I've got that's better to do.' This time it was Faye who put her hand on his. The decision had been made in an instant. 'In fact, Charlie, there's something I need to talk to you about.'

Gregory returned shortly after three o'clock, apologising that he had gone for a walk and lost track of the time. Since he had not brought back either newspaper or cigarettes, Faye went down to the Square herself. The village store didn't stock Marlboro Light, so she settled for forty Silk Cut instead. By this time it was nearly four, and the idea of going out had faded from view completely.

The lamb casserole had survived its postponement without taking any discernible harm. While waiting for his nephew to return, Uncle Charlie had busied himself in the kitchen assembling a fruit salad from a mixture of tinned and fresh fruit. He served it with the top of the milk.

Gregory washed the dinner dishes and came back in to the living room. Faye was curled up in a chair watching the end of the Channel Four News and Uncle Charlie was reading. The photograph album was under the lit lamp on the low table by the settee. Gregory noticed it as he sat down.

'What's this?' He lifted the heavy volume and looked over at Uncle Charlie.

'Uh? Och, that.' Charlie marked his place with a brown envelope which had been tucked into the back of the book, and closed it. 'It's just my old photo album. I was showing it tae Faye this afternoon. I was saying, maybe I'll take it up again...You know, photography.'

'Can I have a wee look?' Gregory held up the album as part of the question.

'Help yourself. They're only a load of old snaps. I didn't take all of them...and they're not in any order. But there's a couple of you when you were a wee fella.' Charlie opened the book again and resumed his reading.

Gregory turned the heavy black front cover. Inside there was no name, no identifying address. The first pictures were of places: the Square, a large, detached house that he didn't recognise, then, with a start of recognition, he found a photograph of Castle Haven dun, its dry-stone walls and walkways crisp and clear in the contrast and grain of old-fashioned black-and-white film. He didn't know Charlie had any interest in that kind of thing. It was a good photograph. He looked at it for a moment, thinking about the fort's restoration before the Great War – he was never sure about these things, whether it wouldn't have been better just to leave it alone, there were always two sides to that argument – and moved on.

Eventually he raised his head.

'Who's this?' He turned the album round and showed the picture in question across the room. Faye turned her head to look as well. Uncle Charlie took off his reading glasses as Gregory passed the album over to him.

'Let's have a look. My goodness, Gregory, that's your father. That'd be not long after he met your mother.'

And so it started. With the aid of a photograph here and there, Uncle Charlie began, for the first time in thirty years or so, to tell his nephew a story. Faye listened, to a history which had too long been hidden beneath layers of private pain and public renunciation. Every now and then she nodded or shook her head. Every now and then she asked a question. She lit a cigarette. Every now and then she found herself watching Gregory, as the little boy and the man gradually began to find each other.

CHAPTER TWENTY-TWO

FATHERS

'I couldnae hae been very old myself when you look back on it. No more than twelve or thirteen when you were born. And tae me, well it was all... There was Martha, that was Gregory's mother, and his grandmother. My mother. And I was just a wee lad, it wasnae any o' my business. There was little or no talk aboot it. Not in our hoose anyway. So I only found out what I picked up here and there, and I was more interested in fishing up the burn or getting off school.

'Of course there was the war. You know, in Korea. Every day on the wireless you'd hear how this was going or that was going. And there was talk in the schoolyard. You'd be playing Yanks and Commies. We'd play at being aeroplanes... What was it now? I remember, Sabres and Migs. Running roond the yard with your arms bent back, screaming and banging away...and I can always remember the name of General Douglas MacArthur, I thought that must be an awfu' big man... There'd always been something, ever since I could remember, and if it wasnae that it'd be British and Gerries.

'I can still mind V-E Day, it was all flags and cheering. I was, let me see, six. Aye, six I would've been. Stood in the Square, waving a wee Union Jack along wi' the rest of them. Then there was Berlin, the Berlin Airlift. It seemed like there was always something, that was just how you grew up then.

'And before that...I was just a wee baby when my father got killed. He was a sailor, Merchant Navy. Charles Hume, First Mate on the Bengore Head. A Head Line boat, out of Belfast. She was torpedoed in the Denmark Strait. May 9th, 1941. This is him.' It was a large wedding photograph. The groom straight and proud, smiling in best dress uniform, cap under right arm, the bride, firm-faced and serious in white, holding a small black book but no bouquet.

Charlie was quiet for a moment. 'It must hae been terrible cold in that water... D'you ken where the Denmark Strait is? It's up between Iceland and Greenland. Freezing. You couldn't've survived once she went doon.' He shivered, as though a breath of the tempests which stir the waters of that remote green waste had somehow found their way in through the window of Finlay's Terrace. He shook his head. 'Anyway, he wasnae a Glenvie man. He was from near Belfast originally. A wee place called Castlemillan. What he was doing over here I've no notion. I know nothing aboot it really.

'It's funny when you think on it. There's so much missing when you look back. Nobody ever told you anything. In the end you just stop bothering your head over it. I heard tell my mother and him met in Stranraer, but whether there's any truth in that I couldn't say. He used tae come and go tae join his ship through Stranraer, right enough, but that was after they were married... I can remember one day, I canna mind exactly when, I'd've been eight or so, it was just after the war anyway, and there was a dreadful disaster came over on the radio. The boat from Stranraer to Larne went down in a big storm. There was a terrible lot of people drowned. That was when she said something about him catching the boat there.

'It couldn't hae been very convenient for him, all the same, but they lived here because o' the hoose. It was my mother's and she'd not part with it. She liked her own way, did my mother. She inherited the hoose from her mother...and her stubbornness.' Charlie laughed and shook his head, for his own benefit rather than his audience's. 'From what I know, it was bought when it was first built, with money from my grandfather, he was a Graham. Money he made in South Africa. Something tae do with gold or diamonds... Anyway, little good it did him, he died not long after they moved in. They were only just married. I dinna ken the exact date. He had TB or something. To do with the mines. His lungs gave out.

'My mother was the only child and my granny never married again. In those days, if you were a widow...anyway, there was relatives of my grandfather living in the village until not too long ago. Remember the Strachans? Lived the other side of the old mill? Well, auld missus Strachan was my mother's aunt. It was from her that I got a lot of this. She must've been over ninety when she died.'

'Are there any other relatives?' Faye spoke through a cloud of smoke from a newly lit cigarette.

'Not that I know. Not in Glenvie anyway. No, not that I'm aware. People moved away, died... The Strachans now, there's a couple over in Castle Douglas, I think. And I once came across a fella in Dumfries, he was a Graham...but it wasnae that kind of family. They always kept themselves tae themselves. So, even if there was, it'd likely be no different.'

Faye spoke again, delicately ticking off the ash from the end of her cigarette into an ashtray at the same time. 'What about your grandmother's family?'

'Well now, she was a McGregor. Edith McGregor. There's lots of them aboot, but I'm not sure which of them belonged tae her. Or if any of them did. Suppose some of them must... There's McGregors in Glenvie now, down on Flack Street, Walter McGregor, and there's Billy too, but I dinna ken if they're connected. My mother never took anything tae do wi' them.'

'What did my mother do, before she got married?'

'Like I said, I was only a wee boy at the time Gregory... But I remember her going tae Glasgow, tae be a nurse. She was in her uniform on V-E night...and bonny she looked in it too. Glasgow Royal Infirmary, she showed me her wee badge, sort of enamel. It was her took me doon tae the celebrations, my mother would take nothing tae do with it. I stood there holding her hand in among all those people.' Charlie shook his head and smiled. 'You know, tae a wee boy it seemed like the whole world was there. Your granny wasnae that keen on the idea, the nursing, not keen at all, but Martha went anyway. There was a few cross words spoken.'

'Why not?' This time it was Faye who interrupted.

'Why not what?'

'Why did your mother not want her to do nursing?'

'Och, it was something tae do with going and leaving her on her own, after my daddy died, you know. But I think she didnae like the idea of the big city. She was very good living. Glasgow was Sodom and Gomorrah itself... And maybe she wasnae far wrong.' Uncle Charlie laughed again.

'Anyway, Martha went. It'd no be easy for you tae imagine, but she was very different then tae what...well, tae what she was like when you... Later, like. To me, when I was wee, I thought she was great...she was always a good laugh.' Charlie sat for a moment silent, he did not laugh, then he stood up to switch on the standard light in the corner of the room. 'Anyone fancy a wee drink?'

He returned with a small trolley. 'There's beer, and whisky. There's nothing tae mix it with but ginger ale. Sorry aboot that...but there's ice.' The ice bucket bore a large Canada Dry logo. Gregory couldn't resist a smile, remembering the last time he had a drink with Charlie. After he had poured them all drinks, Uncle Charlie continued.

'Where was I then?'

'You were talking about Gregory's mother.'

'Aye, so I was.' He fell quiet again, looking into his drink.

'You were saying that Gregory's mother used to be...I think you were saying that she changed in some way.' Faye was trying to choose her words carefully, but she had no idea what could and what couldn't be said.

'Aye well, right enough, she did change... I was never really sure what happened... She came back from Glasgow and got a job in the Cottage Hospital...' He turned to Faye. 'It's gone now. They closed it doon aboot ten years ago. If ye take sick now you hae tae go all the way tae Castle Douglas, and I hear tell that they'll be closing doon the maternity there next year, so ye'll hae tae go all the way tae Dumfries. I dinna see the point...it's daft.

'Anyway, whatever it was, there was a big row with my mother. I mind being up in my bed, I could hear the pair of them, going at it hammer and tongs they were. And it wasnae very often it came tae that. It was something tae do with going away again. My mother wasnae well, it was her heart. Not that she was that old, but she was always up at the doctor... Angina I think it was, something like that. Whatever it was, that time she got her own way... Aye, go on, help yourself. Are y'alright Faye?'

Gregory stood up to refill his glass. 'Do you remember a friend of my mother called Maggie?'

'Aye.' Charlie looked surprised. 'I do indeed...where d'you hear of Maggie? That's a funny question tae be asking, after all these years.'

'Not really. It just came into my head.'

'Well, it's a wee bit odd that's all, that you should mention her now. Because she was something tae do with all the bother. I dinna ken what, mind, no-one ever told me anything. Anyway, my mother wouldn't let her in the house after that. Maybe her and your mother were planning on going off together... You see, she was a nurse too. They trained together, up in Glasgow... She was a wee bit older than Martha.'

'Is she still alive?'

Charlie looked at his nephew for a moment before he answered. At last he put his glass down and leaned forward.

'Aye, she's very much alive...and kicking too, I shouldn't wonder. Gregory, what's all this aboot? Why're ye so curious all of a sudden? ...Don't be getting me wrong now, I dinna mind. It's no skin of my nose, and maybe you should've been asking these questions years ago. You've a right to know whatever there is to know after all. But it's no like you.' He kept Gregory firmly under his gaze, eyes steady, no blink.

Of course, Uncle Charlie had a very good idea what it was about. Faye had told him some of it, enough for him to steer his nephew through the shallows and banks of the strange waters in which they both found themselves. Gregory knew none of this, of course, and his explanations did not at first come easily. Ten minutes later, however, he appeared to have satisfied Charlie's curiosity.

'Well, that's a tale and a half and no mistake. Donald you say this fella's name was? I can't say I ever heard any talk aboot him...but anyway...'

'So, what about Maggie?' Gregory had stopped worrying about interrupting.

'Och aye. Maggie Burns.' Now he looked at Gregory with a twinkle of mischief in his eyes. 'Maggie Knox, once she was married. Married Willie Knox, a few years after your father and mother married...Willie was the doctor hereabouts for a long time. He was a good wee bit older than she was. They met when she was working at the Hospital.' This aside was addressed to Faye.

'Mrs Knox?'

'Aye Gregory. That's your Maggie. A strong big woman, you might say.' This too was directed at Faye. 'If she hadnae wed Dr Knox, she'd've finished up matron, sure as anything.'

'And where would I find her now?'

'She's no moved. They'll carry her oot a' that big hoose feet first, and she's no showing signs o' that yet.'

'So what's the problem with this...this Mrs Knox?' Faye had visions of a cross between Bette Davis and Margaret Rutherford, living in a gingerbread cottage with the oven turned up full.

'Nothing really.' It was Charlie who answered. 'She's just, well, for a long time she's been used tae getting her own way. Doctor's wife, ye ken.'

'She scares the pants off me.' Gregory stood up and poured himself another drink, lighter on the ginger ale this time.

'Here, you can get me one while you're at it.' Faye passed him her glass. 'I can't wait to meet her...but Charlie, what about Gregory's father. What about him?'

'Well...it's the same auld problem. I tell you, it was like living wi' the three monkeys, living in this hoose. Hear no evil, see no evil and speak no evil...well, the first and the third monkeys anyway.' Gregory nodded as his uncle spoke. He knew well enough what Charlie meant.

'They were that bit older than me, so all I ever heard was what I could pick up here and there. I dinna ken how they actually met, but she brought him home one day. Just turned up wi' him. I know he came from Ardrossan, but he never talked much aboot his family. I mind the wedding, at the wee kirk it was, there were a couple of folk from his side there, but I canna think who they were.

'But what I do mind is how bonny she was. For a wee while she was just like her old self...like she, I dinna ken, like she'd got her second wind or something. He was on leave when they met. First time I saw him he was in uniform. They needed special permission tae marry. My mother kicked up a terrible stink...she stood in the kitchen out there' – he nodded in the general direction of the back of the house – 'shouting at Martha that she'd only known him for three weeks and now she was marrying him... Marry in haste and repent at leisure. That's what she said.'

'When was this?' Faye asked the question.

'Well, it's funny, you dinna often know exactly, dates I mean. But it was a week after my birthday. I mind it well because I was so cross. Not aboot the wedding itself, no, it was the suit. The suit I had for the wedding. Nothing fancy, plain brown tweed and too long in the arms and legs, but it was my birthday present. I had my heart set on a wee telescope and I got that bloody suit instead.' Charlie chuckled. 'My mother stood there and told me I'd tae consider myself lucky tae hae anything at all, what wi' all the expense of the wedding and him a soldier without two baubies tae rub together.'

'So?'

'Aye?'

'When was it?'

'March. End of March 1951. The regiment had tae leave a couple of weeks later, that was why there was the hurry. Off tae Korea.'

'Which regiment was it?'

'King's Own Scottish Borderers.' This time Gregory answered her.

'So you have been paying attention.' Charlie looked at his nephew with new interest. 'Aye the Botherers, as they're known up here. Or the Kosbies. They're sort of a local tradition. If you joined up, that was the regiment tae go for. There's families that go back generations...that's why there's so much aggravation aboot this proposal tae merge them wi' the Royal Scots. Royal Scots my arse... Pardon the language Faye, but that's another bloody daft idea if you ask me.'

'Don't worry, I've heard worse.'

Gregory laughed. 'She comes off with worse, all the time.'

Faye made a face and rummaged in her bag for her cigarettes. Charlie continued.

'And then the next thing I can remember was a soldier at the door. An officer. In the pictures it's always a telegram from the War Office, but it wasnae like that.' Charlie leaned back in his chair and avoided Gregory's gaze. 'Your daddy was killed at a place called Kowang-San...Hill 355. There was the Kosbies and the Royal Leicesters. Not many, just a few companies, a few hundred men. Thousands of Chinks there were, they kept it up all night. Our lads were outnumbered ten tae one.

'I mind talking tae one of the men that was actually there. Big Archie Crossan, he used tae work for the Council over in Dalbeattie. He's the one you should be talking tae...but he's dead this last three years. Said he'd never been more afraid in his life. Real bad scared.

'It was the cold he said he remembered most, the cold in the wind. That and the noise. When the Chinese attacked they'd blow trumpets and bugles and all sorts of things. There was an artillery barrage, hours it went on, with everybody dug in and keeping their heads doon. Then, then there was a wee moment's silence before the other noise. The horns and stuff. And then they came on, line upon line upon bloody line. Like insects.

'There's one famous story aboot that night, I dinna ken whether it's true or not, but I've heard it a few times. They had mortars, our lot that is, and they were firing off so many shells they turned red hot. They had tae cool the barrels doon by pouring beer intae them... And it wasnae as if they had enough beer tae waste it. Apparently there were a few grumbles.' Charlie smiled and emptied his glass.

'What happened?' Faye came over and took his glass. 'Another one?'

'Aye, sure, why not. What happened? Well, after being driven off the hill, they took it again. If you say it like that, it doesnae sound like much, but tae hear Archie, and he wasnae the sort tae boast you understand, you'd have tae ask him aboot it, he wasnae forever telling stories aboot it, it must have been something terrible. There was a VC won that night, so that maybe gives you some idea. A big fella called Speakman. He wasnae from roond here, he wasnae even a Scot. I think he was from somewhere near Manchester, I'm no sure. What he was doing in the Kosbies I never did discover. Anyway, he took the Chinks on all on his own, and then a few more followed him. And eventually they took it back... All that for a bit of a hill. Sounds daft...unless you were there. Thanks.' He took the fresh drink from Faye.

It was quiet for a moment.

'And my father? What happened to my father?'

Charlie looked at Gregory.

'Your daddy?'

'Yes...what happened to my...to my daddy? What happened to him?'

'Killed by a shell before they took the hill. During the barrage.'

It was quiet again. It was a silence in which the echo could be heard of bugles and mortar fire, the squelch of boots stuck in freezing mud, the screams of wounded men and worse.

'Where's he buried?'

Charlie looked surprised. Perhaps he had been expecting something else.

'That I couldn't say. Somewhere in Korea, a war grave I suppose. Martha got a letter telling her, but she said nothing aboot it. It's probably in that box, with the rest of her stuff.'

They told Charlie nothing about the box. Nor about their plans for the next day.

CHAPTER TWENTY-THREE

MAGGIE

The name plate mounted on the wall to the right of the door had been worn smooth by years of dutifully applied polish. Still bright, obviously a duty not yet shirked despite death, it read: W. A. Knox, B.Ch., M.R.C.G.P. Gregory paused, his hand stretched out to the round bell-push, framed in similarly aged and glistening brass, and looked up at the house.

Built of irregular blocks of granite that betrayed the hand of quarryman and mason in their shaping and trimming, 'Hilltop' was every inch and corner a country doctor's house. On the outskirts of the town, it had been built by a local mill-owner for his son, just before the turn of the century, and stood on a rise with a clear view across the valley to the kirk and the moorland beyond. Double-fronted, one bay looked down a long gravel drive towards heavy gateposts boasting another brass plate, the other across a neat lawn, bordered by shrubs and flower beds full of roses, sloping down to a wall made of the same stone as the house and topped with ornate wrought ironwork.

The surgery entrance had been round the side of the house, in a low extension at the head of the drive, but Gregory had never been there as a patient. His mother's doctor had always been Dr Snoddy, Glenvie's other GP, who lived down in the town itself in a more modest house and whose surgery had been entered through a plain glass door straight off the street. He remembered his mother once saying something to the effect that 'Willie Knox was all very well for those who could afford him', but, having heard Charlie's story last night, he wondered now whether there wasn't also something else behind her choice of Dr Snoddy.

'Yes? Can I help you?'

Gregory's thoughts were interrupted by a question from the doorway of the house and a simultaneous gentle dig in the small of his back from Faye. He recognised the woman who stood in front of him immediately. He had known Mrs Knox as a distant figure of local eminence ever since their first encounter, when she was giving out the prizes at a Life Boys' annual Display. He must have been only nine or ten. What the prize was for he couldn't remember, but he remembered her saying, ‘Very well done, young man’, and her firm handshake. This afternoon Mrs Knox did not offer her hand. She just stood, staring him quietly in the face, as tall as he was, erect and straight despite her years, waiting for an answer. When it did not immediately come, she spoke again.

‘Young man, I am not going to stand here all day waiting until you can be bothered to address me properly. I would have expected Martha Alexander to teach you better manners than that.’

‘It’s...Mrs Knox...I was wondering if...’ He stopped. He was flushed with embarrassment. ‘So you know who I am then?’

Mrs Knox nodded, once.

‘You knew my mother?’

She nodded again.

‘I was...I was wondering if we could take a few minutes, if we could... I’d like to talk to you, about my mother...if it’s not too much trouble.’

She continued to look at him. He managed to look back.

‘I don’t suppose it can do any harm.’ Mrs Knox looked over Gregory’s shoulder, one eyebrow raised almost imperceptibly.

‘Oh, yes, sorry. This is, this is my friend, Faye Watson. Dr Faye Watson. Faye, Mrs Knox.’

Faye stepped around him and extended a hand. ‘Call me Faye. Please.’

The other woman took it. Her grip was as firm and cold as the set of the small smile which she offered Faye in return. She moved to one side and gestured them inside.

‘I’ve wondered many times whether all of this might not come up again some day.’

Mrs Knox smoothed her skirt over her knees as she spoke, sitting in a high-backed chair in the bay of the formal and evidently little-used sitting room. All trace of what must once have been her original accent had been lost in a smooth middle-class diction and delivery that would have been as at home in St Andrews as in the doctor’s circle locally. Faye was reminded strikingly of Gregory’s own accent. She sat awkwardly beside Gregory on a well-upholstered Chesterfield sofa, not knowing how best to create a proper impression, not sure why she wanted so badly to do so. Their host, with the light behind her, appeared to be staring out of the window into the garden. She had taken that chair, she explained, because it gave her back support.

‘Your mother was one of the most stubborn women I ever met.’ She paused, ‘At least I see you’re not given to contradiction,’ and turned back round to face them. ‘And I’m afraid there’s very little I can tell you. I didn’t even know that Donald was dead until you told me. I haven’t spoken to anyone about it. Not since...she, your mother that is, Martha, was told to have nothing more to do with me. By your grandmother... Actually, she might have been the most stubborn, your grandmother, now that I come to think about it. When she discovered that Martha had been getting letters sent to my...’

'Excuse me, I'm sorry to interrupt.' Mrs Knox nodded to Gregory, permitting him to continue. 'But how did she find out? About the letters?'

'In a wee place like this? The postman, of course. What was his name now? Gordon, Hamish Gordon. It was the postcard that did it, I think, from Paris. Not very discreet...but who knows, love's a funny thing. And it was love. Oh yes.' She stopped and looked down at her hands. 'Where was I? Oh yes, Hamish. I'm sure it was him. He told somebody, somebody told somebody else. It was only ever a matter of time. Anyway, after that she was forbidden to have anything more to do with me, and I was told not to come back. Stood on the doorstep, your grandmother that is, all the neighbours watching, told me I was a slut and a liar.' Mrs Knox was quiet for a moment, the lines around her mouth deepening and creasing.

'But why did you get the blame?' Faye rustled inside her bag. 'Do you mind if I smoke by the way?' She looked around in hope of an ashtray.

'I'd rather you didn't. Why? Mrs Hume was not what you would call a charitable woman. And she never did approve of me. Never really approved of anyone. Calvert Row, that was where we lived, wasn't good enough, not for her dear Martha. She owned that wee house and she never let anybody forget it.' She sat up straight, her face set, every inch the doctor's wife now, the mistress of a substantial stone house, set in its own grounds, looking down from its own hill on to Finlay's Terrace. 'I'd hardly ever even spoken to Martha until I came across her in Glasgow. We were at school together but she was a class ahead of me. And she was hardly allowed out of the house. We were both training at the Royal, at the Infirmary, and I think she'd had to fight her mother every inch of the way to get there. If it hadn't been for the war I don't think she'd ever have made it.'

'Martha.' Gregory, nervous, cleared his throat. 'Did she never get called anything else?'

'Not that I ever knew. She was always Martha to me, and in the Infirmary. Why do you ask?'

'Oh, it's nothing, just an idea I had. And the Infirmary, that was where she met Donald?'

'That's right. He was a medical student. She met him the year after I finished and came back to the Cottage Hospital here. I never met him myself. I saw a couple of photographs. And I heard a bit about him.'

'But...' Gregory leaned forward, the leather of the sofa creaking as he moved. 'Why was my grandmother so set against it? I would've thought that...'

'Aye, so would I. A nice middle-class boy, going on to be a doctor. He'd only taken that year off to go and work in France... You see, he had a conscience, or so it seemed. I remember Martha telling me once – she didn't have much to say about him, but you could see that she was so proud of him, completely head over heels – that he wanted to help to make the world a better place.' She laughed, a dry, empty chuckle that sounded as if it had nothing left in the world to laugh at. 'Not that it did him much good...' She paused and looked out of the window again, before looking at them. 'And you really don't know? Why Martha's mother, your grandmother, took against him?'

Gregory shook his head.

'He was a Catholic. What my late husband would've called a left-footer. My goodness,' It was her turn to shake her head, 'I would have thought that even someone...someone as naive as yourself might have guessed. From the name. Still, perhaps not...times change.'

'And that was all there was...'

'What do you mean, all? Young man, that was quite enough, certainly in those days. And anyway, no, that wasn't all. Not really. I don't think it would have mattered who she brought home. Your grandmother just didn't want to let go of her. Or poor old Charlie, for that matter, and I sometimes think she still hasn't let go of him. It was always a wonder to me that Martha ever got married at all.'

'And she never spoke to you again?' Faye was itching for a cigarette. Asking a question was a poor substitute.

'Not once. I used to think that in her own way she might have blamed me for what had happened. I don't know. In the end I gave up trying to catch her eye in the street. And besides,' Mrs Knox turned away once more, 'I wasn't having anybody thinking I was scraping for their approval. Martha may have had her pride...fair enough. Well, I had mine too.' She faced them again. 'Who did she think she was? Accusing me? It was her daughter...'

The room was silent. Finally Faye spoke again.

'Mrs Knox, I'm really sorry that we've dug all of this up again. But once Gregory had found the letters, there was nothing else for it.'

'If there had been any other way...' Gregory tried to catch the older woman's eye. 'But the letters are all there is. There's nothing else. We asked my Uncle Charlie...and all he could come up with was you.'

And the letters were, indeed, all that there was. The Devil's Leap had turned out to be no more of a disappointment than Faye had said – and Gregory, in his heart, had known – it would be, but there was still nothing there. And it was still a disappointment. Nothing but an undignified clamber down from the bridge over barbed wire and through thorns. A dizzy and slippery scramble, hand in hand, hand over hand, along the edge of the narrow gorge. A trembling attempt to peer down into the rush and riot of the torrent, which was still, in the driest months of the year, full enough to wet all but the very largest of the boulders which were piled up at the bottom of the falls. A futile exertion. A breathless and miserably silent return.

And now, sitting here with a stranger, in a cold and strange room, there was nothing more. The silence was as intimidating as the thunder and crash of the waterfall. For what seemed like many more minutes than it was, they remained still, each looking for something – a thin ridge of dust on the skirting board, the pattern on a set of ornamental plates in a glass-fronted cabinet, a thrush on the lawn, anything – with which to divert the unwelcome persistence of their thoughts. An enormous grandfather clock in the hall, its tick-tock unnoticed until then, eventually broke the spell by chiming the half-hour.

'But you're wrong, you know.' Mrs Knox looked at Gregory again. The smile was only a hint this time, unsure, diffident. 'It's not all there is...thank goodness. What did Charlie tell you?'

Quickly, Gregory gave her the gist of the conversation of the evening before.

'Good.' Mrs Knox shook her head, almost imperceptibly, as if in reflection upon some internal dialogue. 'Good...but here, would you look at me. I've been rattling around this old place so long on my own, I'm starting to forget my manners.' She looked at her watch. 'Will you take some tea?'

Mrs Knox replaced her cup in its saucer, and cup and saucer on the trolley. Plain but delicate, white bone china with a thin gold rim, there was a full set to match. 'Another scone? No? Well, help yourself if you change your mind. I'll make a fresh pot in a minute.' She seemed to have come to a decision. Sitting suddenly upright, her posture bore within it a powerful formality and seriousness of purpose. 'I must apologise. There's no excuse for bad manners. After all, it's not you I was angry with all these years. And not even your mother either, not really...poor Martha, she was probably more sinned against than sinning...' An apology was one thing. Waiting for it to be accepted was, however, another. Mrs Knox hurried on without a pause. 'Now, you were saying Gregory...I may call you Gregory? Good. You were saying that the letters are all there is.

'Well there is more to it than the letters. Not that I have any idea what was in them, you understand... We were friends, your mother and me, but we weren't that close. She didn't tell me very much, always kept a lot to herself, and I never liked to ask. I knew that she was planning to run off to France and marry him. She told me that. I suppose she had to tell someone. Oh, my goodness, but it seemed so romantic at the time. An adventure.

'Charlie was right you know. Your mother used to be a very different person...I can remember, the first time I bumped into her in the Infirmary. It was in the canteen. She was with a whole gang of other new girls, she'd only just started and, you know, I nearly didn't speak, I'd always thought she was very stuck up. But she said hello to me. Once she was away from Glenvie, from her mother, she wasn't the same girl. Not quite the life and soul of the party, you understand, but a good laugh. We used to go the dances. There were Americans, Canadians, all sorts. And our boys, of course. Glasgow was full of life in those days. She had another boyfriend too, before Donald, he was an American, in the Navy, a lieutenant – sorry, a lieutenant.' She laughed. 'What was his name now? I forget. It was never that serious. He was a big chap, well over six foot. Chuck? Something like that.

'Anyway, I finished my training and not long after that I came back here. I'm still not sure why. I suppose really I'd gone with the intention of coming back, and then when the moment came there was nothing to keep me there anyway. It was the end of the war.'

Faye was about to say something, but thought better of it. Mrs Knox didn't miss it.

'To save you asking, no. There was nobody. Martha was...Gregory, you'll find this hard to believe, but it was always her the boys were interested in. It wasn't that she was very pretty, I mean she was attractive enough, but it was a way she had with her. She was...bonny.'

Gregory remembered his Uncle Charlie the night before. The same word: bonny.

Memory often plays tricks. The act of remembering feeds upon itself, and behind every door as it opens is the possibility of another. So it was, a fresh pot of tea later, that in the middle of a story about Martha Hume as a student nurse finding herself locked out of the Nurses Home after midnight in the pouring rain and trying the risky ascent across the bicycle shed roof and up the back fire escape with her coat over her head in an attempt to keep dry and her shoes clenched between her teeth in an attempt to keep quiet, Mrs Knox suddenly stopped.

'Goodness me. Here I am, carrying on like a silly old windbag, and I've forgotten...' She paused. 'Sorry, you must think I'm doting. I'm just trying to remember where I put something. Will you excuse me for a moment?'

After ten minutes upstairs she returned. In the meantime Faye had lit a cigarette. Mrs Knox had brought an ashtray in with the tea trolley and, without a word, placed it beside her plate and cup and saucer. The taste was vile and Faye stubbed it out less than half-smoked.

'I hope you didn't put that out just because I'm back. You'll be making me think I'm even ruder than I am.'

'No, it's not that.' Faye's smile was as broad as it was wide. 'Honestly. I'm smoking too much, it tasted terrible. I'll have to give up one of these days.'

'Aye.' Mrs Knox looked down at the biscuit box she held before her, and then at the ashtray with its crumpled butt. 'Aye. Well, make it sooner rather than later. You wouldn't credit it, would you? He was a chain smoker. Willie, my husband that is. And him a doctor. God knows he might still be here today... Anyway,' she wiped her eyes with the back of her hand, 'that wasn't what I wanted to say to you.'

The box on her knee, Mrs Knox sat down in her chair again. From the angle of where he sat, Gregory could make out a picture of a large, old-fashioned looking factory and the name, Huntley and Palmer's, on the box. It looked as old as the knee it balanced on: colours faded, paint scratched here and there, metal dented, the lid warped at one corner so that it no longer fitted properly. Mrs Knox could have been reading his mind.

'It's a bit like me, this old box. Battered and bashed, maybe even a wee bit twisted.' She smiled, looking at Faye as if to say, don't worry, I don't really mean it. 'We've certainly both got a few of our own wee secrets to keep.' She patted the lid gently with the flat of her hand.

'There's something in here for you.' She opened the box and, after a moment's searching inside, produced a manila envelope. 'It arrived after the dust-up with Martha and her mother. I never really knew what to do with it... I suppose I should've passed it on, I could have done something. It was wrong, I know, but I never really was able to...' She looked at the envelope, weighing it in her hand. 'Anyway, here it is.'

Gregory took it. He turned it over, looking for the flap.

'No. No, please don't open it.' Mrs Knox's plea was surprisingly urgent in the still room. 'Not now. It wouldn't seem right, not after all these years. Whatever's in it, I don't want to know.'

Within ten minutes Gregory and Faye were on Mrs Knox's doorstep again. Gregory turned round and offered her his hand. He had to transfer the letter, still unopened, to his left hand in order to do so.

'Mrs Knox, I hope we haven't been too much bother. You've been very helpful. I can't thank you...'

'Not at all.' Her grip was still firm. She put her other hand over Gregory's, resting on the bond between them. 'No, you've helped an old lady lay one or two things to rest. You know – well, of course you do – but I couldn't even bring myself to go to the funeral...Whoever it was said that age brings wisdom must have been a stupid old fool himself.' She let go, bending down to absent-mindedly pull out a broken leaf from the lilies growing by the door. 'They're in need of some water.' She stood up again. 'Can you remember the first time we met? I do. I was Mrs High-and-Mighty herself, handing out the prizes to the Life Boys. It must be nearly thirty years ago.'

Gregory nodded. How in the name of God did she remember that?

'Do you know how I remember that? It was the last time your mother and I ever spoke. It was afterwards, we sort of bumped into each other, although, truth to tell, I think maybe I was hoping we would. Anyway, she was waiting for you to come out with the rest of the boys. She looked at me, it seemed as if she stood there for a lifetime, just looking at me. Not a hint of embarrassment. And eventually all she said was, "Good evening, Mrs Knox", and then she turned and went on her way. Nothing else. And I just stood there, looking at her back.

'But I remembered you, young man. Can you remember what your prize was for?' She turned to Faye before Gregory had a chance to reply. 'Och, but you should have seen him, all polished and shining. He was a picture. It was for recitation, the prize. Do you remember what it was you recited?'

'No, no...I'd forgotten even what it was for.'

'Well I'll have to remind you, then won't I? It was one of my favourite poems, that's how I remember it. I learned it at school when I was wee. Once learned, never forgotten.'

Mrs Knox drew herself up into a formal pose for public speaking. Her voice dropped its tenor, her diction became even more precise than usual. Faye had a sudden vision of elocution lessons, and the transformation that they must have achieved. The sheer determination, the pride.

'Slowly, silently, now the moon
Walks the night in her silver shoon;
This way, and that, she peers and sees
Silver fruit upon silver trees;
One by one the casements catch
Her beams beneath the silvery thatch;
Couched in his kennel, like a log,
With paws of silver sleeps the dog;
From their shadowy cote the white breasts peep
Of doves in a silver-feathered sleep;
A harvest mouse goes scampering by,
With silver claws, and silver eye;
And moveless fish in the water gleam,
By silver reeds in a silver stream.'

Gregory's lips began to move in hesitant synchronisation as line followed line. His face was flushed and his eyes were edged with tears by the time Mrs Knox, letting out a deep breath, returned to conversational mode.

'Walter de la Mare...what's the matter? Come on now man, it's only a silly old poem. Not even a very good one... "Couched in his kennel like a log" indeed!' Mrs Knox turned to Faye, who had been watching Gregory closely out of the corner of her eye. 'You'd think he could've done better than that now, wouldn't you? And that daft wee mouse. If it was real life there'd've been a big silver owl as well.'

'I always thought that was what happened next.' Gregory's voice was frail and distant. 'You know, I can remember thinking that when I was learning it. That there was another bit to the poem that nobody ever got to see. With an owl, or a fox in among the doves.'

'And they say children don't understand the world.' Mrs Knox put a hand on Gregory's arm. 'I sometimes think it's when we're wee that we understand it best.'

Faye looked from Gregory to Mrs Knox, then back from Mrs Knox to Gregory. She looked away. There was nowhere else to look.

CHAPTER TWENTY-FOUR

WORDS ON PAPER

'I was never any good at memorising poetry. That was the point, you see. I used to come home in tears from school, they would make fun of me, the others, in class, because I couldn't ever finish the poem or whatever it was. I was always top of the class, or near top, but standing up there and doing a recitation, I never could do it. And the others, the rest, they'd jump on this like a ton of bricks.

'It's funny, you think you've forgotten about all this stuff...and it doesn't mean anything, it didn't mean very much even then, but it all comes back anyway. Just like that. I can remember standing there in the classroom, I can see the dust floating in a beam of sunlight, and everybody waiting and that last bloody line, or whatever it was, it just wouldn't come. It would be alright the night before, at home, but the next day...gone.

'And it was no better at sunday school. I had a slap from Reverend Taggart more often than not because I couldn't get my verses right. Every week you had something to learn, Matthew 9, verses 1 to 10 or whatever, and there was the Catechism, and the Creed. But I always got it wrong. In the end he talked to my mother about it. She was the housekeeper up at the manse, part time; he wasn't married. Anyway, they put their heads together and decided that nothing would do it but putting me in for the Life Boys recitation prize. My mother must have spent weeks drumming those lines into my head, hours and hours a night. That's what it seems like, anyway.

'And the thing is, of course, that it only made the whole thing worse. Anyway, I won the prize, like Mrs Knox said. Can't even remember what I got now. But it wasn't really the memorising, it was the standing up in public, the exposure of it, having everybody watching you, just waiting for you to make a mistake, that's what the problem was. Not the memorising, not really.

'I think I only managed it because, between my mother and Reverend Taggart, I was more afraid of them than I was of anyone else. I can remember my mother telling me that I needn't think I was going to let her down in front of everyone. God, I was terrified. I can remember, there were four of us in for the prize, and you had to stand up in front of everyone at the Display and speak your piece. And there she was, sitting in the front row of the parents, and he was sat up on the table – come to think of it, he was probably one of the judges – it was terrible. She just sat there and stared at me. I can remember I was busting to go the toilet. Nearly wet myself.' Gregory shook his head. 'Funny how you forget about these things, isn't it?'

Faye lit a Silk Cut and wound down the car window. It wasn't funny at all.

She finished the cigarette and closed the window. 'What about the envelope, then? Aren't you going to open it?' It lay on top of the dashboard.

'Aye, in a minute. We'll stop somewhere. I don't want to be opening it in the house, not with Charlie there.'

The Square was lit by the soft sun of a late afternoon in June. From where Gregory had stopped, the sun twinkled on the polished stone of the Cenotaph. Apart from the odd person on their way somewhere else, the Square was empty. There were no seats, and no other encouragements to dawdle. The motor car had long since demolished the horse trough that had once squatted in front of the hotel and mains water had similarly dispatched the pump that had stood beside it.

Now, there were just a few restricted parking bays – 'Mon to Sat, 8.00 am to 6.00 pm, Waiting Limited to 45 min, Return Prohibited Within 1 hr' – amid an otherwise comprehensive circumference of double-yellow lines. Since they were all full, Gregory risked putting two wheels on a broad stretch of pavement and left the engine running. He looked over his shoulder, then around the Square and finally at his watch.

'We should be alright for a minute here.'

'For God's sake Gregory, it's Saturday afternoon. There won't even be any traffic wardens working now.'

'It's not a matter of traffic wardens... Never mind. Pass that over here, would you. Thanks.'

Faye passed him the envelope. It bore a faded mauve 3d stamp with the head of George VI on it. Or at least it looked like mauve to Gregory, it was the sort of colour about which you could never be absolutely certain. The postmark was too smudged to make out either the date or place of posting. He opened it. Inside, there was a sheet of paper, folded, and another envelope, simply addressed, in a handwriting that Gregory recognised immediately by now, to Miss Martha Hume, with 'Please Forward' written in the top left-hand corner. He unfolded the sheet of paper. It was written in a different hand, neat and bureaucratic, devoid of excess or flourish, straight up and down, black ink on white paper:

Forres
4th March 1947

Dear Miss Hume,

I do hope that you will excuse my writing to you like this, but I had hoped to see you personally, in Aught last week. I can, however, understand your reasons for not attending the funeral. I can only hope that your grief will heal and mend and offer you my deepest condolences. Donald will be sorely missed by everyone.

If it is any help to you in your time of trouble, the police in Lille are of the view that he was probably unconscious before he hit the water. Apparently he seems to have knocked his head on some masonry after he missed his footing. That section of the bridge has been dangerous and in need of repair for some time. He could have felt no pain; nor, in the dark, could anything have been done to save him that was not done. It was a tragic accident. I hope you will excuse my talking in this manner, but sometimes it can be a comfort to know these things.

I also enclose a letter which I found in Donald's desk. I hope, once again, that you get over this sad business soon. Life must go on, although it may not seem like it at the moment. If I can be of any further assistance, please do not hesitate to contact me. I must return to Lille tomorrow and you can reach me there. I think that you know the address. In the meantime I trust that you are well and that this letter has not been an intrusion.

Once again, my condolences,
Yours sincerely,
Andrew MacLeod

'Who's it from?'

Gregory looked up at Faye and passed it across to her.

'There's a man who knew how to write a smooth letter.' He remembered Donald's remark about 'Mr Mac's special cases', and something about 'little foibles'. A lady's man. 'Further assistance', indeed.

'Who was Andrew MacLeod?'

'Donald MacKillion's boss. In Lille.'

'Where's this place Forres?

'I think it's up near Inverness somewhere. I'm not completely sure. He probably took some leave when he came home for the funeral.'

'And...how do you pronounce it? Aught?'

'No idea. Probably Aught.' Gregory pronounced the 'g' and the 'h', rolling them into one guttural consonant. 'I've never heard of it. Could be anywhere.'

'And the other one?' Faye nodded towards the smaller, white envelope which Gregory was turning over in his hands, slowly and absent-mindedly, his forearms resting on the steering wheel.

'Uh? Oh yes. Better have a look, I suppose.' But he did not have a look.

'Go on then.'

'Yes, I suppose I'd...you know, it doesn't really seem right. It's not the same as the others. I mean, she'd read those, she'd left them, tied up in a wee bundle, under the floorboards... This, this is...'

'Shall I open it?'

'No. I suppose I'd better do it.' And he did, slowly, with a tender and delicate precision, gently finding the spot where more than forty years of gum and spittle were vulnerable to an insistent fingernail and easing up the flap. It was short and the handwriting desperately familiar:

Dearest Mattie,

By the time you read this, it will be too late. You have not written and I do not know what to think. I waited for you in Paris, in the vain hope that you had perhaps missed the train or something. Now I have accepted that you are not coming, I can no longer go on without you. Do not think too badly of me.

Your ever loving Donald xxx

Gregory read it again. And again. He passed it over to Faye and she did the same. She returned it to him and he replaced in its envelope without reading again.

'What a fuck-up.' Faye lit another cigarette and inhaled the smoke deeply as she threw the dead match out of the window.

'Do you think MacLeod knew?'

'Who's to say? Why would he send her the letter if he did? He probably wouldn't want it coming out.'

'No, I suppose not...I wonder will Maggie Knox ever know how much good she probably did, sitting on this all these years?'

'Only if you tell her.'

'Aye.' Gregory stared down at the white envelope. 'What a fuck-up indeed. What a fuck-up.'

CHAPTER TWENTY-FIVE

WORDS ON STONE

'A problem your mother had wi' the rest o' Glenvie?' Uncle Charlie seemed genuinely puzzled by Gregory's question. 'What d'you mean?'

'Something to do with my father, something to do with when he died. I don't know, she never really told me very much about it. I can remember her forbidding me to go down to the Cenotaph on Remembrance Sunday, when I was just a wee lad. Saying something about them all being hypocrites. Does that make sense?' Gregory was having to work hard himself to make sense.

Charlie paused to reach down and pull a can from the plastic collar of an unopened four-pack of Draught Guinness that was on the floor at his feet. It was ten to one in the morning. Faye had gone to bed a quarter of an hour earlier, bouncing gently off the walls as she went.

'Och aye, that makes sense. I'm afraid it does that.' Charlie concentrated upon the delicate art of opening the can and successfully getting it to the rim of his glass before the gas pellet in the bottom sent the froth squirting everywhere. He poured the beer to his satisfaction then looked back at Gregory. 'But like everything else in this bloody family, it goes way back.' He took a drink. 'Remember I told you about my father? His ship was sunk during the war?'

Gregory nodded.

'Well, at the end of the war, the British Legion here in Glenvie was in charge of seeing tae the names on the Cenotaph. You know, one side's the Great War, the other one's the Second? Anyway, my mother got tae hear of it, I dinna ken how, but sure in this place isn't there always someone ready tae make sure bad news travels as fast as possible?

'Anyway, whatever happened, it turned out that they didnae put my father's name on the War Memorial. They said it was because he was a merchant sailor, not in the services, you know. But my mother never believed them. She was very bitter. Said it was because he wasnae from Glenvie, because he was from Ulster. She thought they were just being spiteful. Never forgave them.

'So whenever your daddy got killed, your mother was already waiting for it, tae see what was going tae happen. And she waited, this was after Korea finished, and nothing happened. So eventually she wrote tae the Legion, asked them what they were going tae do. And they hummed and they ha'd, but eventually she got her way. I can remember somebody saying that it wasnae fair, he'd have his name up in two places, here and in Ardrossan.' Charlie shook his head. 'In the end, she embarrassed them in tae it. She wrote tae The Sunday Post, aye, all the way tae Glasgow, she wrote tae your daddy's old commanding officer. Wrote tae all kinds of folk.

'I think in the end, mind you, it was the Reverend Taggart that did the trick. He went down tae a Legion meeting and gave them a sermon. On the Good Samaritan, asked them who did they think was their neighbour. I'm not sure they understood the finer points of it, but he got his way.'

'He always did.'

'Aye. He did indeed. Even so, it must hae been a good two years late.'

'So that was what it was all about?'

'Aye, your mother never forgave them either. I think she felt that she'd had tae beg for something that was hers by right. And maybe she had a point. There should never hae been any question aboot it.'

'And how did the Reverend Taggart come into it?'

'Och, sure you know what he was like. Had tae have his finger intae everything. I think it was just about the time when your mother started working at the Manse. And you know what him and your mother were like, thick as thieves.'

Gregory was still for a moment. He thought better of what he was about to say and stayed quiet. As deep as that he did not want to dig.

CHAPTER TWENTY-SIX

A BRILLIANT DAY

Faye wrinkled her nose and pushed the cup away from her across the wood-effect table top. Gregory was sipping a mug of hot chocolate with only moderately greater enthusiasm.

'Coffee's dreadful.' She tapped her finger nails on the formica. 'God, but I could kill a fag.' It was late on Monday afternoon, and they were in the motorway services at Killington again, looking down over the reservoir and across to the bulking shoulders of Calf Top, filling the sky to the east.

'Homophobia isn't going to make you feel any better.'

'Aren't we the funny one then?. Mister bloody PC...alright, dear, I could kill a cigarette, then. Okay?'

'That's better.'

'I think I preferred you before you decided to experiment with a sense of humour.'

'And I think I preferred you before you decided to give up smoking.'

'Fuck's sake, who is it's been...'

'Sorry, sorry. I shouldn't tease you.' Faye's temper was as genuine as it was immediate. Gregory put his hand out and rubbed the top of hers. 'Anyway, who am I to talk? If you've never smoked it's impossible to imagine what it must be like.'

She pulled her hand away. 'Oh, well that's very understanding of you! Very! Thank you ever so much for...' She stopped, then she shook her head and laughed. 'Listen to me would you? Look, don't pay any attention, that's all. Just don't try and be bloody understanding... Be patient, be quiet and let me be a pain in the ass for a while. And before you say it, I know you've had lots of practice, okay? I'll get over it. Giving up's easy. I've done it hundreds of times.' She laughed quietly again and took a mouthful of coffee. 'Well, at least it's hot and wet.'

Ten minutes later they were back on the M6, heading south. Faye was taking her turn to drive. It was easier not to fret over cigarettes when she was at the wheel.

'You know, I think yesterday was the best birthday I ever had.'

'Then you must have had some very dull birthdays, that's all I can say.'

'No... You and Charlie were wonderful. D'you know that was the first time I've ever had a champagne breakfast?'

'And judging by the effect it had on you, it'd better be the last... Anyway, that was Charlie's idea, not mine. He said he'd read about them and always wondered what a champagne breakfast would be like. And it wasn't champagne either.'

'Don't be such a bloody killjoy. Who gives a fuck what it was? I had a brilliant day.' Faye looked at the wing mirror and put her foot down hard on the accelerator, swinging out smoothly past the coach that had been in front of them since leaving the services and into the now-empty outside lane. The needle of the speedometer settled down at eighty-five and she kept it there.

And, indeed, it had been a brilliant day. The sky was high and blue with occasional rafts of soft white cloud drifting across the sun, the breeze light and salty from the west. After a late breakfast in bed - fresh carnations in a vase, orange juice, a bottle of Veuve du Vernay which had been in the fridge overnight, percolated coffee, smoked salmon, toasted white bread from the bakery down by the Square, and Keiller's marmalade, brought up on a tray by Uncle Charlie with The Sunday Times - Faye rang her mother. Gregory gave her the birthday present which he'd bought for her weeks earlier, a hardback copy of Greil Marcus's *Lipstick Traces*, and Charlie kissed her on the cheek.

With Charlie's help she had the wine finished by half past eleven. Gregory excused himself on the grounds that he had to drive later. Half an hour later, after several false starts while Faye got herself ready and, just at the last minute, decided that she needed to pee now, he finally got them into the car and they set off for what Faye - who had by this time had 'one for the road' with Charlie, a large scotch - kept calling 'the magical mystery tour'. Indirectly, the drive had been her idea. The night before she had half-heartedly complained that she'd come all this way and, so far, hadn't even seen the inside of a pub. Gregory told her to be patient and she'd end up seeing more than that.

He took them on a sweep through the landscape of his teenage years, a mental map originally traced during geography field trips and solitary bus-rides on Saturday afternoons. At Stanshiel Rig he tried to get Faye to take an interest in the inconspicuous humps and hollows of an Iron Age field system, although even he had to admit that there wasn't actually a lot to see. At New Abbey, in the shadow of Criffel mountain, he had another disappointment as they stood outside the gate of the Cistercian Abbey which wasn't due to open until two. In the car, driving away, Charlie, who'd been there the year before on a local Historical Society outing, told the story which gave the ruins their name, Sweetheart Abbey.

Devorgilla, who founded the abbey in the thirteenth century, was married to John Balliol, and he, in his turn, was famous for founding Balliol College. Balliol College, Oxford. After he died, she kept his heart in a casket and, when she died, it was buried with her. Gregory remembered the weight of a casket of wood and brass.

At the Mote of Mark, on the road to Dalbeattie, he had one listener who appeared to be interested in what a timber-laced wall was and how it vitrified when it was fired by attackers. Faye, on the other hand, was having trouble staying awake. In Kircudbright town itself, they stopped in The Selkirk Arms for a late lunch. Faye and Charlie perked up sufficiently after a couple of whiskies and some sandwiches to suggest a walk round the town. They looked at the Tollbooth without going in, and at the Stewartry Museum which, they discovered, didn't open on Sundays at all. On the bridge over the Dee they looked out across the sands of the Solway Firth towards the distant shadow of England. They listened to the high and lonesome song of the gulls.

Gregory had more success as they drove on to Borgue, conjuring up for Charlie and Faye the romance of the Master of Ballantrae. Past and through the long main street of Gatehouse of Fleet, he parked the car and a short climb took them up to Trusty's Hill. This time he didn't bother with the subtleties of timber-laced construction as they stood in front of the small fort, nor did he point out to them the outer defences, which still showed their ups and downs on the surrounding land. He had brought them to see something really special: the carvings - circles and discs and jagged, angular strokes - which were antiquity's claim upon a low outcrop of stone near the fort's entrance.

Faye seemed disappointed when Gregory explained that they were not that old: they were Pictish, not Stone Age, probably not much more than a thousand or twelve hundred years old. She cheered up again when he told her that nobody had any idea what they stood for.

'Well, at least that's something.'

'What is?'

'You archaeologists, with all of your science. I don't know...all this dating and laboratories and stuff. Give me a bit of romance and Indiana Jones anytime... There's no romance in a bloody laboratory. How are we supposed to use our imagination if you guys are busy pinning everything down and digging everything up? It spoils it. This...' She knelt down and traced her finger in an interlinked circle design on the rock. 'I'd rather just imagine this was Stone Age. Much more exciting than the bloody Picts.'

'But it's not. Stone Age, I mean. And it's exciting enough. Look.' His hand described a sweeping proprietorial circle in the air around where they stood. Charlie had disappeared inside the fort. 'Here you've got the remains of a set of earth defence works. Bank and ditch. Now I've got a good idea how those were made. And I've an even better idea about this wee fort, how it was built. I was explaining to you at the other one we stopped at, but I don't think you were very interested.'

She stuck out her tongue. Gregory stuck his out back, and continued.

'Anyway, the point is that knowing things like that doesn't spoil the romance. Not at all... It just gives you more to work with. More for the imagination, not less. And, well...think about it, when you hold something in your hand, a polished stone axehead maybe, and you know that somebody, maybe five thousand years or so ago, whatever, that somebody sat and made that thing. And they took time and trouble over it, and had a pattern for it in mind – you know that because similar ones have been found in different places, here and there – they knew exactly what they were doing. And not just that, but you know where they got the stone from, and maybe that's a couple of hundred miles away from where the thing itself was found. And you know, or at least you've a good idea, how it was made, because they've been found at all different stages in their manufacture, and people have tried to make them today in the same way. And you're holding this thing in your hand. A direct, tangible link to all of that...and to that real person somewhere. Now that's romantic!'

Faye looked up at Gregory as he stopped talking. He looked down at his feet. Standing up, she rubbed her palms on the seat of her jeans, lifted his chin with one hand, tweaked his nose with the other, then, starting to laugh, gave him a big hug.

A moment later Uncle Charlie reappeared, doing up the top button of his fly. Releasing Gregory from the hug but keeping half a hold on one hand, Faye guided him gently over to where Charlie stood. She linked arms with uncle and nephew.

'Right then, you two wonderful romantic men. Where next?'

On the way to where next, Gregory shifted literary tack from Stevenson to Scott. Guy Mannering offered them Dirk Hatteraick's Cave near Ravenshall Point – 'There's five or six bloody Dirk Hatteraick's Caves,' Charlie muttered – and Barholm Tower, the novel's 'Ellangowan', among the trees behind the road. 'That's not Ellangowan,' Charlie added, 'Ellangowan was Caerlaverock. Everybody knows that.' Gregory gave up on literature.

Ten minutes later, they stood in the early evening sun by Carsluith Castle, a steady stream of cars and container lorries from one of the Irish ferries winding impatiently along the A75 behind them.

'Even with all this traffic, this is one of those places that just takes you back. You know, romance and all that.' Gregory was talking to Faye. 'I can remember coming here with the school once. They were doing some work, I don't know, it must've been some kind of conservation work or something. Anyway that had a big trench dug and you could see bits of masonry and stuff. And I can remember thinking that I wanted to do that. Not the digging so much, but the business of finding out.'

'They'll put a big blue plaque up on the wall one day. Just wait and see... This is where Gregory Alexander first got his inspiration. I can see it now.' Faye took her cigarettes out. 'One, two, let's see, six left. I'll make these last me tonight. Tomorrow morning I'm going to stop.' She replaced the packet in her bag.

'What's brought this on?'

'Been meaning to do it for weeks. Don't know, I just made up my mind, that's all. See how it goes'

'Good luck... And, by the way,' Gregory spoke to his uncle now, 'I'll tell you something that you don't know, clever clogs.'

'And what might that be?' Charlie asked, walking ahead towards the gate.

'Did you know that the last Abbot of Sweetheart was born here. Gilbert Brown.'

'Is that right?' Charlie turned round, shaking his head in exaggerated surprise. His eyes twinkled with mischief. 'And tell me, did you ever read Scott's *The Abbott*?'

Gregory threw up his hands in disbelief. 'I should have known...bloody smart alec.'

'Not me. One smart alec's enough in any family.' Charlie smiled. 'Come on, let's have a look at this place before they close it up for the night.'

CHAPTER TWENTY-SEVEN

KNOWING WHO YOU ARE

'Alright, alright, I see you.' The red Sierra that had been flashing its lights behind them swept past, horn blaring as Faye let the car drift back into the middle lane. 'I haven't had a chance to say thank you...you know, for letting me come home with you... Just what the doctor ordered.'

'Glad you enjoyed it. I was a wee bit worried you were getting fed up, traipsing around... Anyway, it should be me thanking you.'

'Don't be daft. Honest to goodness, the way some people drive. He must be doing well over the ton. I had a brilliant time. I told you, it was the best birthday I ever had.'

'I think Charlie enjoyed it too.'

'Meaning that you didn't?'

'Not at all. I was quite happy running the pair of you around. No...it was good to see you both having fun. At one stage I was beginning to wonder whether I was playing gooseberry.'

'Don't be so disgusting. Anyway, I don't think that was what Charlie had in mind.'

'And you did?'

'That doesn't even deserve a silly answer.' She looked over her shoulder, indicated and pulled out again. 'Joking aside though, all the time we've been away, you know, I haven't thought about Ioan and that silly business once. I think some time out was what I needed, and we've been so busy playing detective that I haven't had... Sorry, that sounded a bit sarcastic.'

'It's alright. Quite appropriate really... Who did you have in mind? Poirot and Miss Marples? Or...' He smiled broadly. 'How about Holmes and Dr Watson?'

'Very funny...and pretty bloody elementary too. Anyway, I was thinking about it a bit today. You know this morning, when you and Charlie went up to the grave? Oh, and I meant to ask you...did you decide about the stone?'

'Aye, sort of. Something as plain as possible. We're still not definite but we thought probably just "Martha Alexander". With the dates. There's no call for anything else.'

'She probably wouldn't want it anyway.'

'No. Probably not. Anyway, you were saying, before...'

'Oh yes. About Ioan. Well actually it's not about him as such. Sort of brought on by him, if you know what I mean.'

'Not really...'

'I didn't mean it literally, stupid. Anyway, if you'd let me finish? I was about to say that it made me think, about myself more than anything else.' She braked. The Sierra was in front of them, held up at the tail end of a fast-lane wagon train of six or seven cars. 'See? Flash bastard. Didn't do you much bloody good, did it mate?'

'Easy now, easy. I'd hate to have your blood pressure at the end of this.'

'Sit there and enjoy the ride and let me worry about that. So...I was thinking. Maybe he had a sort of a point. Ioan, I mean. Maybe it's time to change my life-style a bit.'

Gregory wasn't sure whether Faye intended to say more or not. Eventually it became clear that she didn't.

'What d'you mean...life-style?'

'Don't be so bloody obtuse. Sex, what d'you think? What else could I be talking about?'

'I don't know, do I? It's not like you to beat about the bush, that's all...so, how change?'

'Well, I don't know, be more careful I suppose. No, that's not it. It's not as if I'm not careful. I'm always bloody careful. No, I suppose it was when he called me promiscuous. PRO-MISS-Q-US. That's what really pissed me off.'

'So what're you going to do? Get thee to a nunnery?'

'Oh yeah, sure. Listen you, I'm trying to talk seriously here.'

'I know you are, I know. It's just that... Well, what are you going to do? I mean, you are who you are, after all. How are you going to change that?'

'What d'you mean? You are who you are? What's that supposed to mean?'

'It doesn't mean anything. Calm down. Christ, I think I preferred you when you were smoking... Sorry, sorry. That's twice now. No more. Promise. All I meant was that, well...I don't know how to put it.'

'Try.' Faye's eyes stayed fixed on the cars in front.

'Well, perhaps you...we've all got different...needs, right? It's a case of being true to yourself, I suppose. Not trying to be something that you're not. So, all I meant was that, well, I would think twice. Before trying anything drastic.'

'Needs? What are these fucking needs? Do you mean maybe my biological programming tells me to go and screw as many men as I can find? Is that what you mean? That I can't fucking help it?'

Gregory took a deep breath. His ears were burning and he could feel a flush rising into his cheeks.

'No that is not what I mean. What I mean is...I mean that you've got to know who you are. That's all.'

'That's all? Sounds like a hell of a lot to me.'

'I didn't mean it was...'

'How're you supposed to know who you are anyway? It's a bit of a tall order.'

'I don't know...I didn't say that I was sure of what that is, in my case for example. But we were talking about you.'

'And you were suggesting that I wouldn't be able to stop being...'

'No I did not. Look, if you're going to go on like this, let's talk about something else.' She said nothing, so he continued. 'Right. Right then, all I was meaning to say is that it's not that simple. Knowing who you are. And you can't just change, become somebody else, just like that...apart from anything else, other people won't let you. It's just not that easy. My God Faye, do you think I haven't tried?'

Faye took her eyes off the road for a moment and caught a quick glimpse of him, staring out of the window in the opposite direction. Out of the other corner of her eye she saw the brake lights of the lorry in front. She turned her attention back to matters of life and death.

CHAPTER TWENTY-EIGHT

THE MOST IMPORTANT THINGS

The digital clock on Gregory's bedside table said just before ten. He felt terrible, his head thick and dull, aching and naked before the light of the day. Tight pain knotted in the small of his back and along one stiff side testified to a restless night. The bedclothes smelled and felt as though they needed changing and the air in the room sat smug and heavy on his face.

It had been long past midnight when Gregory finally arrived home the night before. Dog-tired from the journey, he went straight to bed. Since there was nothing scheduled for the next day, he left the alarm switched off. But although he had been struggling against exhaustion for the last hundred miles of the drive, once he turned out the light sleep was beyond him. So was rest. Uncertain in the end whether he was dreaming or hallucinating, Gregory eventually dropped off into a choppy, fragmented storm of half-glimpsed faces and unidentifiable bodies: his mother, Donald, Charlie, Mrs Knox, Faye, a ten-year-old boy in a sailor's hat, Philip, an old sea captain, a soldier in a kilt whose back was always turned, Adrian. Jumbled up and sometimes impossible to tell one from another. At one stage, they were standing on a bridge peering over the edge. 'Where is it? What have you done with it?', some of them demanded, while the others peered in vain for somebody down below: 'There he is. No. Over there. Where is he now?' His mother held out to him a red flower on a single green stem. He tried to tell her that she was offering it to the wrong person, that it was the soldier's poppy, but this was a world in which he could not speak.

A shower, orange juice and several mugs of coffee made the business of beginning the day seem more plausible. More manageable anyway. The mail which he had brought in with him from the hall the night before was on the kitchen table, but there wasn't much and none of it looked interesting. Nothing in the flat needed to be done urgently. It was Tuesday; the binmen came on Wednesday morning, but the rubbish would have to wait until the evening. Nor did it take him more than five minutes to put the dirty clothes he'd brought back into the washing machine. He attempted a bit of half-hearted dusting and looked in the freezer to see what he might be able to defrost for dinner. There wasn't much. That meant shopping at some stage in the day.

Gregory knew what came next, he just didn't want to think about it, let alone do it. But he would have to go in to College, and he would have to see Adrian, and he would have to discover what was happening on graduation day, the protest. The ceremony was on Friday, only three days away. At least there was one small mercy, some of that he could find out from Antonia. He wouldn't actually have to capitulate to Philip, face to face. Not yet.

Why had he written that bloody letter? Stupid. What did he think he was doing? He knew why, he knew that Antonia had been right, that it was nothing to do with Philip and everything to do with himself. But where was it going to get him except into trouble? 'Into trouble', that was a phrase straight off his mother's tongue. Well, he was going to be in trouble this time, and no mistake.

Looking for something to do as much as anything else, he picked up the mail. The white envelope on top was his phone bill, a final demand, then there were some which looked like circulars of one kind or another and underneath that again something from the bank. It couldn't be his statement, he'd only had one a couple of weeks ago, so they were probably trying to sell him something. Putting the bill to one side, he moved over to the sink, opened the cupboard door and was just about to throw the junk away when he realised that there was a piece of paper, folded, below everything else.

It was notepaper. On the outside in large round letters – he wasn't sure where he recognised them from – was one word: 'Gregory'. Opening it out, the message inside was simple: 'Please ring me, it's urgent. Antonia.' Below this was printed a phone number.

He tried the number, but there was no reply. He had moved no more than three short steps beyond replacing the phone gently in its cradle when it rang.

'Gregory Alexander. Oh, Antonia, hello, gosh that's a coincidence, I've just been trying to ring you.'

'Telepathy, eh? So you got my note. Sorry I had to put it through your letter-box like that, but I wasn't sure when you were due back. I just bumped into Faye, Faye Watson, she told me.'

'Faye's in work at this hour? Wonder what's got into her?'

'Said she'd had a wonderful time, felt like a new woman. But anyway. It's about the protest...'

'That was what I wanted to talk to you about...'

'It's off.'

'Off?'

'That's right. Cancelled.'

'What's happened? I mean, Philip...'

'Philip has called it off. And Standup refused the invitation to attend the ceremony anyway.'

'Why?'

'Why what? Which now?'

'Both. Both of them.'

'Well Philip's done some deal with the Welsh Office. Says it's a great victory. And Standup couldn't resist the opportunity to kick them in the nuts, I suppose. He got to hear of Philip's promotion, I don't know how, and well, you can imagine it in the paper, last night. What was it now, "Promotion for gay propaganda lecturer", something like that. Kicked up a right stink.'

'Promotion?'

'Oh shit. I'm sorry, Gregory, I don't know why, I'm not thinking very clearly, I just sort of took for granted you'd heard. Senior Lectureship. They told him last Friday.'

'I was away then... Still...it's not as if he doesn't deserve it, I suppose.'

'Well, whatever, that's what's happened. It must have been in the pipeline for a while, before all of this blew up... I'm not sure who comes out of it smelling worse.'

'But what about the people who told their Heads of Department that...'

'I don't think many have. I think most of them were waiting 'til the day before.'

'I didn't.'

'You mean...bloody hell, that's why I was ringing, to tell you not to. If you were going to, that is.'

'Too late, I'm afraid.'

'Jesus. What...at least we can rely on Geoff, I don't think he's said anything yet. Hasn't reported us to teacher yet, I mean. Which is probably a bit of a cop-out too. And not much comfort to you.'

'Not really. But, well, it's done now. No point crying over spilt milk.'

'No but...what's your Head of Department...what's his name, Wallbutton or something daft like that is it? What d'you think he'll do?'

'What he's already done more like...'

'You think so?'

'I'd put good money on it. It can't be helped.'

'That's very understanding of you.'

'Not really...it's not the most important thing in the world, is it?'

A minute later, as Gregory put the phone down again, he realised that it really wasn't.

On first glance, there appeared to be lots of mail waiting for him in the office. On closer investigation, however, most of it was a bundle of Senate minutes with a departmental circulation list attached. He was the last person to whom they had to come. Without even pretending to look at them he ticked off his name and shoved the lot into Adrian's pigeon-hole. That left a couple of book catalogues, a rolled-up piece of paper held together by a computer-addressed internal sticker, a white envelope bearing the University of Southampton dolphin logo, and a medium-size manila envelope without a stamp and nothing more than Gregory's name typed on the outside. Half-suspecting what Southampton had to say, it was this last one that he opened first.

It contained another envelope, addressed in Gregory's own handwriting to 'Mr Adrian Wallbutton, Head of Department, Department of Archaeology.' Turning it round, the self-adhesive flap was torn at one side. It had been opened and re-sealed. It tore again as Gregory looked inside. The letter was there. Gregory heard a noise and turned around to find Pauline standing in the doorway watching him.

'Hi. Good time?'

'Aye, aye, fine.' He looked down at the open envelope, then back at her. 'Fine. Is, um... is Adrian in?' He looked again at Pauline. 'Are you alright? You look like death.'

'I'm tired. That's all.' There was a sharp edge there, just within the human range, but audible nonetheless. 'Come into the office.'

Gregory followed and she closed the door before taking her place, facing him. She waited for him to speak.

'What's the matter Pauline? Something's up isn't it?'

'You missed all the excitement while you were away. It's Adrian. He's in hospital. You may as well know, I'm sure everybody else does by now.' She ran a hand through her hair and then passed it slowly across her face. 'He took an overdose. Saturday night.'

'Shit.' Gregory sat down and looked at her across the desk. 'Adrian? An overdose? He's not..?'

'No. No, thank goodness. It could've been worse. He managed to phone 999 before he passed out.'

'And Meg?' There was no answer. 'Meg. Is she...?'

'I expect she's fine. I don't even know if she knows yet. That's why he...she told him on Saturday morning, from what I can gather. Packed her bags and left. Gone off with some fellow from Cardiff.'

'You mean, Meg's been...'

'I don't know. I think it's been going on for a while. God knows.'

'Sorry, I didn't mean to...'

'Oh, it's alright. It's not you. I'm just fed up talking about it.'

'Has anyone been to see him?'

'Do you know?' Her eyes were filling up, not for the first time that morning by the look of things. 'You're the first person that's actually bothered to ask that? I don't know, I really don't.' She shook her head. 'No, no-one's been to see him. His sister's come down. They discharged him yesterday, and she's going to stick around for a while, keep an eye on him.

The doctor's got him doped up to the eyeballs. I spoke to her yesterday. He doesn't want to see anyone, and I can't say as I blame him.'

'No.' He sat for a moment, looking at his shoes. 'What about graduation? The ceremony.'

'What about it?'

'Who's going to be on the platform? Someone's going to have to present Martin Griffiths. For his First, I mean.'

'Yes, yes, of course. Thank God you mentioned it, because I hadn't even thought about it. I'd better talk to Ellie. She's the next senior...well, she will be anyway.'

The quiet between them in the small office grew quieter and even quieter. Finally Gregory stood up.

'I suppose I'd best be off then. You going to be alright?'

Pauline nodded. She poked around in a desk drawer, found a tissue and silently dabbed at her running mascara.

'Look, I don't know if...give me a ring, if there's anything, we can go up together and see him if he changes his mind.'

'We'll see Greg, we'll see. I'll let you know.'

'There is one other thing.' He showed her the envelope. 'Know anything about this?'

'About what?'

'A letter, from me to Adrian. I found it in my pigeon-hole.'

'I don't know anything about it.'

'It's about...'

'If I were you, I would just treat that as returned to sender and forget all about it.' She looked him straight in the face, one eyebrow slightly arched. 'And, when you do see Adrian, I wouldn't bother him with it either. He's got quite enough on his plate as it is.'

'But...'

'No buts. Now, if you don't mind, I've got work to do, and I'm sure you have too.

In his office Gregory opened the window and sat down. The letter from Southampton dared him to open it, too. It turned out to be what he'd expected, they didn't want his paper for the conference volume. At least it had the virtue of obviously being a standard letter which had presumably gone out to a few people. Sod it: in the bin with it. The roll of paper, however, was a circular of a different sort...

CHAPTER TWENTY-NINE

DEFEAT FOR STANDUP!

Following the announcement last week of the promotion to a Senior Lectureship of Dr Philip Braithwaite, Bill Standup, Tory Councillor for the University Ward has refused to accept the College's invitation to attend the graduation ceremony and sit on College Council. Despite the refusal of the Vice-Chancellor to issue a statement in support of academic freedom, this, combined with the settlement which has been reached with the Welsh Office about the funding of the HIV research, means that we have decided to call off the planned protest at the ceremony. Nothing further would be served by spoiling a day which is primarily a celebration for students and parents. We would like to thank those of you who have supported this campaign, despite the opposition and indifference of the union, the College authorities and many colleagues.

Defence of Academic Freedom Committee

Gregory screwed up his face. He screwed up the paper and dropped it on the desk. He had had enough of letters. Whether they were addressed to him or not. He had enough of all kinds of things.

'Did you know?' It had taken Gregory less than five minutes to get to Philip's office. It was the first time he had made the journey in nearly a year.

'Did I know what?' Although he leaned back casually in his chair, Philip's voice was tight and high. His hair was growing out into tidy anonymity and he wore a light brown linen suit over a white T-shirt with the right amount of creased carelessness. A small silver stud shone on his ear lobe.

'Did you know? About your promotion. When all this fuss started.'

Philip picked up a copy of the circular. 'Haven't you had one of these?'

'Yes I've seen that. But it doesn't answer the question. Did you know?'

'It says it here, look. It was announced last week...Last Friday, in fact.'

'So?'

'So what?'

'I don't believe this... Did you know about your Senior Lectureship when you started this protest?'

'It was announced last week.' Philip sounded tired, as if he was rehearsing a routine. 'I told you.'

'And that's all? That's all you've got to say? What about the...the Sunday-go-to-meeting bloody Welsh Office? That was the expression used if memory serves.'

'That was last week too. The first phase of the contract was always only a feasibility study. And they're not actually withdrawing the funding. Well, only in the first instance. They're going to fund a Welsh part of a national study next year, but they'll do it through the Department of Health. They reckon it's better value for money that way. And we'll get that.'

'Just like that?'

'Well, there'll have to be tenders, of course. But, we'll have a head start over anybody else...'

'So what about these redundant researchers? And the people who supported you? And what about academic bloody freedom?'

Philip was red in the face now and didn't answer.

'I tell you what, Philip, my dear. I took you to be many things, but never a liar and a hypocrite.' Gregory was close to Philip now, a slight stoop and he would be bending over him. 'Not until now. Are you listening to me?'

'I hear what you're saying.'

'My God, spare me the social-work talk.'

Philip stood up suddenly, forcing Gregory to take a step back. 'Don't you dare lecture me. Don't you dare! And why this sudden concern anyway? Getting worried are we, now that sugar daddy's not well?'

'What?' Gregory started to laugh. 'Sugar daddy?' He frowned, shook his head and laughed again. 'Adrian? Sugar daddy? If that's a joke, it's in not in very good... What are you talking about?'

'Certainly not poor Adrian Wallbutton, that would be nearly as ridiculous as you. That neanderthal, from the club. What's his name, Trevor?'

'Trevor Thomas? What's the matter with him?'

'Don't tell me you haven't heard? That's just too funny. He says it's cancer.'

'What do you mean says?'

'What do you think I mean? It's pathetic...I don't see why he can't just admit it. Trying to get back in the closet at his time of life. Pathetic.'

For the first time in his life that he could remember, Gregory wanted to hit somebody.

Later, he was glad that he hadn't, but at the time it took every year, every day, and every long moment of his mother's upbringing to turn him around, without another word, and walk him out of Philip's office.

CHAPTER THIRTY

GRADUATION DAY

Llanorgan was hot, even for July. A deep and cloudless sky framed the hats and dresses, the suits and gowns, and the rented mortar boards perched delicately upon heads of every irregularity and size. The graduates no longer knew what do with themselves in a place where they had belonged for three years. Parents bickered. Estranged parents did their best not to. Girlfriends and boyfriends from home drifted around the edges of family groups and were introduced awkwardly to college friends. Very awkwardly to some college friends, for whom, it seemed, the awkwardness was mutual. Some tears were shed. Not a breath of air moved to disturb or cool any of them. Meanwhile, sunshine sparkled in the wine which washed down strawberries and cream and overflowed during a thousand toasts, the lenses of a thousand cameras and camcorders sparkled back, and the stars of the show, upstaged in every direction, looked at the world with eyes confused by their own emotions. Hope, fear and indifference bloomed and withered in the same pot.

Gregory saw none of this. As he hurried out of Ede and Ravenscroft's impromptu robing rooms at the back of the Guildhall he bumped into Ellie. The ceremony had gone well enough and she had practised hard, at very short notice, to deliver her formal lines in something approximating to acceptable Welsh pronunciation. But she looked as if it had been an effort. Her face was pale and pinched. The gown could not hide the slight beginnings of pregnancy and she looked tired. Gregory nodded and was about to walk on when she took his arm.

'Greg. Greg, can we talk?'

He eased out of her grasp. 'Well, actually I'm in a bit of a rush... I've got to visit somebody in hospital, and I said I'd be there by five.' He looked up to where a large brass-bound municipal wall clock said ten past four.

'Only a minute? C'mon Greg, a minute?'

He looked at the clock again. 'Alright. I'll wait for you outside.'

Ellie looked more like her usual self again when she appeared at the side door of the Guildhall. Quickly re-applied make-up had restored her colour and some of her ceremonial awkwardness had been handed back with the costume. On the step above where Gregory waited, she stopped.

'So. Here we are. I'm glad we bumped into each other.'

'What did you want to talk to me about?'

'Don't be like that Greg. You know very well what it is.'

'No I do not. And I'm not being like anything. But I have got things to do.'

'Who're you visiting? In hospital, I mean.'

'Just a friend. Nobody you know.'

'Oh. Right. Have you heard anything about Adrian?'

'No, I've not been in work for a couple of days.'

'Apparently Meg's back. Not for good, I don't think, but who knows what'll happen.' She looked at him when he didn't answer. He looked away. 'But that's not what I wanted to talk about Greg. Greg, I'm sorry. I know it's not much to offer you, but it's true, I am. I truly am sorry.'

'I didn't realise you'd done anything to be sorry for.' He still couldn't look at her directly.

'You're not exactly making this any easier are you?. Still, no reason you should, I guess. Look, I know Art was shit-faced, but that's not much of an excuse. Christ, Greg, wha'd'ya want me to say to you?'

'I don't want you to say anything.' Now he knew that he had said the wrong thing. 'I'm sorry. Look, just forget it. It's not...he only said what he's always been thinking anyway, so nothing's really changed that much. And you're not responsible for...'

'No, but...shit, I don't know. Life has just gotten so goddamn complex. And I was gonna tell you about the promotion, I was, really, but Adrian told me not to, had to wait until the unsuccessful candidates had been informed. And I suppose I was a bit embarrassed, you know. I mean you're due...'

'Ellie, please...do me a favour. Forget it. It's well deserved, more than deserved if the truth be told, and I'm pleased for you. Genuinely...pleased. There's nobody deserves it more. And as for Art, well, life's getting just a wee bit too short for...'

'Then what are you being so antsy about?'

'I'm not. Well...I wouldn't be if I knew what it meant.'

She tried half a smile. 'That's more like it.' A barely visible blur of sweat was forming above her upper lip and on her forehead. She rubbed her back. 'It's not much fun, this pregnancy bit. Art thinks it's so wonderful, but he doesn't have to walk round like this. And months and months still to go. God knows what the mummies and daddies made of me up there. Tottering around liked a Goodyear blimp. Not that I'm complaining, Hell no...'

'It doesn't show that much. You did a really good job, the Welsh in particular was very impressive.'

'Well all I can say is thank God we didn't have to go through with that damn protest after all. I doubt I could've lasted out the day. Not in this heat.'

'But I thought you were opposed to it?'

'Yeah, well I was wrong. Worse... Dumb and selfish. I suppose that's really what I wanted to say to you. After that...When we got home from Antonia's that night, me and Art, well, we had what I believe you Brits call "words". First time in years. A real humdinger. I called him a homophobic... Called him all kinds of things, now I come to think of it. Most of them true too. Everything's okay again now, no problem, he was a very sorry boy the next day, still is, but I got to thinking. Asked myself what I would have done fifteen or twenty years ago – before I met Art, when I was at college – and I knew what the answer was.'

'Well, all's well...'

'I suppose. Although I'd be happier if I knew what the V-C's going to do with all those letters... And God knows what Art'll say when he finds out about that. Still, I suppose they can't de-promote me... What's the matter?'

The look on Gregory's face had already been and gone but it could not be undone.

'Oh. Um...the letter. You wrote that letter they asked for? To Adrian?'

'Yep. Handed it to him myself. Real George Washington. Shoulda seen his face. A right picture. Didn't know what to say.'

'Is it official yet? Your promotion, I mean.'

'Why?'

'Nothing, nothing.'

'Like hell it's nothing. C'mon...'

'It's nothing. It'll be alright. It's true. They can't de-promote you. Look, I've got to go. I'm going to be late. Really. Need a lift? It's on my way.'

'No thanks. The car's round the block. What is it with you?'

'Nothing, I told you. I've got to get to the hospital. I don't want to be late.'

And he had to ring Pauline before she left for the day.

CHAPTER THIRTY-ONE

SCRABBLE

Trevor was in a large glass cubicle at the far end of a male medical ward in Llanorgan General Hospital. A nurse in a tiny office just outside the ward, too busy with paperwork to raise her head properly, told Gregory to go straight down, Mr Thomas should be awake. It was a minute or so after five o'clock. Although there were no fixed visiting hours, when they had spoken on the phone earlier in the day that was the time which Trevor suggested. Gregory felt that it was important to be punctual.

At first he had not been able to discover where Trevor was. Ringing round people who he thought might know turned out to be a more protracted business than he had anticipated. Some people who he was sure would know didn't. Others didn't even know Trevor. In the end he rang the Gaiety and one of the barmen, Gwyn, knew.

Now he was here, Gregory was uncertain what to do. Trevor looked as if he was asleep. His eyes were certainly closed. He didn't appear to be particularly ill, but his breathing was harsh and heavy. When he eventually opened his eyes and focused upon his visitor, a dull edge of pain and exhaustion was obvious. Slowly he pushed himself up onto his elbows and rearranged the pillows to sit up. Gregory moved to help.

'No, no, let me do it. I'm alright. There's life in the old dog yet.'

Gregory stopped, helpless in the face of the other man's incapacity.

'Don't just stand there. Take a pew.' Trevor's voice was soft and quiet, there was less wind in his sails than usual. He gestured to the chair beside the bed. In a jug on top of the bedside table there was an assortment of flowers which had Interflora written all over it. Next to the flowers there was an unopened bottle of Barley Water and next to that an unopened packet of cigarettes. 'Nice to see you, Greg...to see you, nice.' He laughed at the bad impression. 'How's tricks my boy?'

'Not bad, you know. But more to the point, how are you? I'm sorry I didn't come sooner. I said on the phone, I didn't know where you were until yesterday.' Gregory wasn't sure what to say next. 'Do you need anything?'

'No, no. Every need catered for. The diet in here's wonderful. Better cocktails than the Ritz... Just wish I knew what the fuck was in them...the chemicals, you know? Never mind.'

Gregory hadn't been there more than two or three minutes but he was already out of his depth. The silence lasted for longer than it would normally have done in Trevor's company. Finally, he forced himself to fill it. After all, that was what he had come for. One of the reasons, anyway. 'What do the doctors say?'

Trevor smiled. 'Well, fair dos, you don't beat about the bush, I'll say that for you.' It was not a very attractive smile. 'If what you want to know is have I got it, the answer is no. Christ knows I probably ought to have, but this time Miss Otis regrets that she's got to disappoint you.'

Gregory's cheeks were burning. For a moment he imagined himself taking offence and walking out. Then he imagined sitting down again and adopting a reasonable tone of voice. So he did. 'No Trevor, I'm sorry to disappoint you. I knew what you've got...I heard that it's cancer. That's all...so, what do the doctors say?'

More silence.

'Look, do you want me to go?' Gregory shifted in the chair. 'I can always come back another time if you're not up to it.'

'No, no. For Christ's sake Greg, don't go. Please don't go. Stay.' Trevor placed one hand on Gregory's arm. 'Sorry boy, sorry. Like a bear with a sore head I am. Literally. Got a headache would kill a horse. My eyes keep going in and out...of focus, like. They think it's the drugs, but they don't know, they're just guessing. I only started on them yesterday, see.'

'What have they told you?'

'I'd love to be able to say that I've got the doctors baffled, got to be honest, that might be a bit more interesting. The consultant's very good. Comes round to see me once a day, whether I need it or not.' Another laugh. 'Leukaemia it is. I've memorised it, acute granulocytic leukaemia. There's a bloody mouthful. They tell me I should consider myself lucky. Mr Desai, that's the consultant, it's one of his specialities. Sort of like his little hobby, I suppose. Like some people grow leeks.'

'Is it..? How...'

'Serious is it? Ask the man in the white coat... He's not making any bloody promises, that's for sure. No, keeps it very close to his chest, he does. Let's put it like this, lovely boy, I don't think I'll bother writing to Santa this year.'

'But I thought...I thought leukaemia could be ...'

'Some kinds of it... It's not all the same, see. And people do, they survive quite a long time with this one. Years, some of them. Well I asked him, straight up, I said, how long do you give me? I'd rather know, I said. Well, he couldn't give me an answer, like. Wouldn't expect him to, really, but the look on his face... He didn't have to say anything. His face said it all for him.'

'What's the treatment? Surely they can do something?'

'There's the chemotherapy.' Trevor's voice was quieter, his breathing ever more laboured. The colour rising in his cheeks was lurid and unhealthy. 'They give you these concentrated doses, over five days I think he said.' A rack of coughing shook the bed. He waited until enough of his breath returned to go on. 'They only started the first yesterday and I feel like shit already. Mind, I wasn't exactly feeling like a spring chicken in the first place. Anyway, so they do that a few times. Three, I think he said. And then they have to see how it's gone.' He shifted under the blanket, fidgeting and twisting in search of comfort. Finally finding some kind of rest again, he looked away, out of the window.

Gregory was struck by how small Trevor looked lying there. What kind of thing is it, that can make a big man like that shrink? His hand still lay on Gregory's arm, and the room was quiet, rather than silent. Before long, Trevor was asleep again.

The next day, Gregory arrived early in the afternoon. Trevor was looking better. He was out of bed and sitting in an armchair by the window which had not been there the previous evening. When Gregory appeared at the door he smiled broadly.

'Greg. Hello. Excuse me if I don't get up...'

'No, that's alright, stay where you are.' Gregory took the plastic stacking chair next to the wall and sat down. 'You're looking a bit more like yourself today.'

'Well, to tell you the truth, I was lying here this morning, feeling right sorry for myself I was. Streak of bloody misery, actually. So I thought to myself, Trev, I said, Trev, you can either lie here like a big girl's blouse or you can get up off your arse and make the best of it. So I asked them if I could get up and they went and found me this comfy chair. A bit of positive thinking, that's what's called for.'

'There's nothing you need, before I get settled in? I can run down to the shops downstairs. It'll only take a minute.'

'It's like a bloody old mother hen you are man. Sit down for God's sake. You've brought yourself, that's more than enough. Tell you what, fancy a game of Scrabble?'

At about half past four Trevor, well ahead on games and points, closed the dictionary which lay beside the Scrabble board on the low table which was sandwiched between the bed and the window. 'Do you mind if we call it a day, Greg? I think I've had enough positive thinking for one day.' He stood up slowly and sat on the bed.

'Suits me, I'm no good at it anyway. Where did you learn to play Scrabble like that?'

'I thought that might surprise you. You being an educated man and all. It just takes a bit of practice and a good memory.' Trevor began to struggle out of his dressing gown, awkward and stiff, still sitting down. He shrugged away the offered hand. 'I can manage. I'm not bloody dead yet you know...sorry, I know you just want to help. But I have to manage on my own.' He dumped the dressing gown in a pile on the end of the bed and rolled in under the covers and lay back on the pillow, sweat shining on his face. 'Fuck me, I'm knackered. You'd never imagine Scrabble could be such hard work. We used to play it on ship. Deep sea. There were some mean Scrabble players. We had tournaments, used to run a book on it. I was never any good by their standards, mind, you'd swear some of them'd swallowed the dictionary.'

'Well, you put me to shame. I haven't played in years, I never really realised how much fun it is.'

'Great game, great game.' He looked up at Gregory. 'I tell you what though, Greg, thanks for coming. I wasn't sure you would, to tell the truth.' Trevor's voice was fading again, the sickness could no longer be pretended away.

'Of course I came. I said I would, didn't I?'

'Yeah, I know, but people don't always mean what they say, do they? And I gave you a bit of a hard time yesterday. Not very grateful really.'

'Don't be daft.'

'Well, you didn't deserve it.'

'And I don't deserve gratitude either. But I'd better be off now. You get some rest. Any visitors this evening?'

'Dunno. There hasn't exactly been a queue forming at the door. There's my sister, Mo, she's over in Neath. She comes across when she can. But she's got her own troubles. Husband, it is... Drinks. And Gwyn, he was here last night, he said you'd been on the phone. He's gonna try and pop in again for a while tonight. A good boy, Gwyn is.' He suppressed a cough. 'Busting for a fag, I am too. Dull bastard, eh?' The cigarettes still lay unopened beside the bed. 'You know, I can't make up my mind. Whether it's just that everybody thinks I'm such a twat they don't want to visit me, or whether it's because...well, you know. They probably just think I'm a twat.'

Gregory shrugged. 'No. I'm sure it's not...'

'But it is funny, all the same. It used to be cancer was the word you couldn't say, a no-no, like. You'd read in the paper that so-and-so had died after a short illness. Something like that. And you'd know. Not any more. Now it's...now it's HIV, it's AIDS. That's the one you can't say. For God's sake, I can hardly get it out of my mouth, and I know...well, I know that I haven't got it. And not likely to now either, I don't suppose. Chance'd be a fine thing, eh?

'It was, that was how they found out about the leukaemia, you know. Round about Easter-time. No, later, May. I was starting to feel tired all the time, felt dreadful, no energy at all. And I had this sore throat that just wouldn't go away. Had it for months. The old mind was working overtime, you can imagine. Lying awake at nights, I was sure I had it. Jesus, it was terrible. And d'you know all I could think? It was how I would tell people was worrying me most of all. And maybe I was right, I don't know.

'Anyway, to cut a long story short, in the end I went for the test. Had to pluck up all my nerve, just for that. Crazy. It was negative, but that was when they noticed that there was something wrong, with the blood, like. When they told me what it was, I didn't know whether to laugh or cry.' He closed his eyes for a moment. 'Still bloody don't, mind. Funny old life, eh?'

'Yes...funny old life.'

'Anyway, off you go. Time for some shut-eye.'

'Okay, see you tomorrow. Sure you don't want anything?'

'Some peace and quiet might be nice.' Trevor yawned. 'Go on now, there's a good boy, bugger off.'

CHAPTER THIRTY-TWO

HEADSTONES

It was another splendid day. A day for the beach or a barbecue. For white wine cold enough to remind you of the fillings in your teeth. A day for shorts and a t-shirt. Outside Gregory's door, the sunshine through the fanlight above the front door fell on the hall table with startling brightness.

Post. He recognised Charlie's handwriting on the envelope immediately. Inside there was a letter and a yellow Kodak envelope. The letter just filled one side of one large sheet of lined paper:

24 Finlay's Terrace
Glenvie

17th July 1992

Dear Gregory,

How are you? I hope you are well. Everything is fine here. How is Faye? Tell her not to forget what I said, she's always welcome. She seems like a grand lassie, full of life. It was good to see you when you were up here. Hopefully you'll come up again before too long.

What I'm writing for is to send you some photographs of what's available for your Mother's headstone. These are the basic types that they have in stock in Cameron's over in Castle Douglas. You remember that was where we said I would inquire. I picked out the ones that didn't seem too fancy. The basic prices are written on the back of each print. Carving costs extra, depending on what you want on it. As you can see I have taken up photography again. That was after talking to you about it when you were home. I took the photos so that you could see the stones for yourself. Basically, unless you want something special, they can do any of them in black or grey or white. I don't much like the white myself. It's marble and I think the others are granite. I'm not sure about that, but I can always ask. Let me know what you think.

Anyway, I must go now. It's my lunch break and I want to get this into the post. Write soon,

Yours sincerely,

Uncle Charlie.

P.S. Have you any ideas about what should be written on the stone? I think it has to be up to you.

P.P.S. I bumped into Maggie Knox the other day. She said to tell you she was asking after you. And Faye too.

The photographs inside the processing envelope were not artistic, but Charlie did not mean them to be. They were clear and sharp, functional and to the point. Six different patterns of headstone. Only one of them was in white in the photos and Charlie was right about that. Not the white. Gregory looked at the first photograph again, then he thumbed quickly through the others again. He nodded to himself. Charlie had done a good job. But he wasn't going to pick now. He'd look at them again and give Charlie a ring to talk about it. He scratched his chest. Time for breakfast.

The Scrabble board had been set aside again. Trevor was so tired that he could barely put a word together. Now he was back in bed, lying looking up at the ceiling. His wrists were thin and bony, too fragile for the hands and sinews which they supported.

'What time is it?'

Gregory looked at his watch, then, remembering where he was, through the glass at the clock at the other end of the ward. 'Ten past four.'

'Doesn't time fly when you're having fun? Sorry, that wasn't getting at you. It's very good of you to bother.'

'Away on, man. Enough of this very good nonsense. I wouldn't come if I didn't want to.'

Trevor was very still. The effort of talking required him to wait for his breath to deepen and his concentration to return from wherever it wandered.

'Why do you? Want to, I mean. Not long ago you wouldn't be seen dead with me...'

'First of all I'm not with you.'

'Alright...you know very well what I mean.'

'As long as you know what I mean.' Trevor said nothing. Gregory continued anyway. 'A lot has happened since then. Nothing to do with you, to do with my mother I suppose. I don't know. I'm sure a shrink could make all kinds of things out of it, but well...let's just say that I've realised that you don't get a second crack at things. Life's very short.'

Trevor looked up at Gregory and slowly shook his head. 'Cheerful bastard, aren't you?'

The room seemed even smaller than usual. Outside the window the sky was dark and tempestuous. Heavy clouds hid the horizon above and beyond the white-tipped sea, while the gale bent the treetops, combing the streets of stray paper and battering buildings. Rain spat on the window. Soon the lights in the ward would have to be switched on, otherwise they wouldn't be able to see the Scrabble pieces. No, they were called tiles, not pieces. Trevor was very particular about that.

The door opened and Gregory turned around. It was a nurse, young and pretty. There was something familiar about her, although he didn't recognise her as one of the usual ward staff. She nodded and smiled at him and began to make Trevor comfortable, adjusting the pillows and smoothing the covers. He didn't wake. The window rattled and shook and Gregory looked out in time to see lightning flash on the grey hillside. The crack of the thunder followed almost at once. The gloom had become semi-darkness.

Gregory turned to ask the nurse about the lights but she was gone. The door was slightly ajar. Trevor lay still, sheets pulled up neatly over his head, arms tidily by his side under the blankets. The white stone of his bedhead shone briefly in the glare of another lightning flash. The thunder's explosion was deafening and immediate. Gregory only just made out the words, 'In Loving Memory...', before the room was dark again.

He ran to the door and out into the ward. It was empty. The noise of the storm retreated. Moonlight reflected on the polished rows of eternally silent beds. There was no sign of Nurse Mattie Hume. The sound of his feet echoed in front and behind him as Gregory began to run after her.

CHAPTER THIRTY-THREE

THE ROSE AND THE BRIAR

'So...why?' Faye stood with her back to Gregory. He sat at the other side of her kitchen table, an empty bottle of Bulgarian red wine, a bottle newly opened, and a half-full glass in front him.

'Why what?'

'Are you trying to be dense?' Faye slipped the plate which she had been half-heartedly rubbing with a dish cloth back into the foamy water in the sink and turned round. 'Why are you visiting him? And every day? Not so long ago you were treating that poor man as if he had the sodding plague. Don't tell me you're in love.' She dried her hands, lifted her glass from the work top and came back to the table.

Gregory was contemplating the rain, rolling like Lord Byron's Assyrian down the hillside at the back of the bungalow. The early evening was unseasonably gloomy. It was the second of August and the weather had been dank and dull for nearly a week. He did not turn around as Faye sat down.

'Don't be so silly.'

'Don't be so silly? Greg, it's not me that's being silly...'

'Yes it is.'

Faye looked at him in amazement. 'Why? Why am I being silly? All I want is a simple answer to a simple question. It's not as if...'

'There's nothing simple about it. If there was a simple answer I'd give it to you. But there isn't. I don't know.'

'You must have some idea.' She stood up again, in search of her cigarettes. They were on top of the fridge. Gregory waited until she sat down again before he answered.

'Not really. I think it all started because I was so angry with Philip. God, you should've heard him. Such a fucking hypocrite.'

'A what hypocrite? Look who's talking. You've been telling me off for saying the F-word for years. No...for fucking years.'

Now he turned round, squaring his chair to the table to face her. 'Sorry. I know. You're quite right.'

'About what?'

'I don't know. Everything.'

'Jesus wept. What's the matter with you? You're...'

'I'm not anything. And I don't think there's anything the matter with me either. Probably quite the reverse.'

They sat in silence. Gregory emptied his glass. Faye poured them both fresh drinks.

'It's just...' He swirled the wine round in the glass and then drank it. 'It's just, well, what else could I do? He's got no-one else. Not really. There's his sister, and there's a couple of other people. It's not just me. But he's so lonely. And, well, I suddenly thought, what if it was me? I might be glad enough to see Trev then.'

'Another one?' She refilled his glass before getting up once again, this time to fetch an ashtray.

Gregory went on. 'And in another way it is just me. I mean, this is about me as much as anything else, isn't it? I'm visiting him because I want to, not because I think I ought to... And in a sense that's all that matters. Why I want to probably doesn't...sometimes I think I've spent my whole life doing things I thought I ought to. Or, if I'm going to be honest, that someone else thought I ought to...it's like when I was with Philip, if you can call it that... Well I was thinking about it the other day, driving down in the car. You were asleep. Well that was, I suppose in a funny way that was something I thought I ought to do in the end. On his part, I think it was just some kind of challenge, but for me... Looking back on it, I don't think that I really wanted to...not really. That's probably why I can't just let it drop, even now. I feel a bit of a fool. Trying to be something I wasn't, something I'm not. And that was the problem in the end. No wonder he...' He paused for a minute. Faye stood watching him, silent too. 'Still, never mind. Too late to change that now... Anyway, visiting Trev is just something I want to do. That's all.'

Faye moved over and switched on a side light. It was growing dark inside as the rain washed down the window in waves and eddies, pushing and pulling the reflections this way and that, in and out of focus on the glass.

'That's better. Shed a little light on the matter...that's all very well you know, but you can't just ignore other people's – '

'No...but you can try having a few of your own as well.'

It was a moment before Faye spoke again.

'What's the outlook for him? I mean, what...'

'None. No chance at all. Barring a bloody miracle. Poor bugger. I went and looked it up, the leukaemia. There are different kinds, but the one he's got is about the worst. He'd have a better outlook if he was HIV bloody positive. It's only a matter of time, and probably not much of that. That's all.' Gregory's eyes shone wet in the small light shed by the bulbs in the hood above the cooker. 'And then...for some reason I started thinking about my mother. All those years she wouldn't let anyone close to her, the loneliness of it all. Dying with no-one by her. I know, there was Charlie, but you know what I mean. She might as well have been on her own, the way she kept everybody shut out. I could see myself going the same way, I suppose.'

'Does he know?'

'What?'

'How bad it is?'

'Aye. He knows. I don't know how he does it, I would just want to lie with my face to the wall. You know, we were playing Scrabble the other day – you should see him playing Scrabble, unbelievable – and what does he do? Only wins by making "cancer" out of "can". With a silly big grin on his face. Amazing.'

'He's got guts.' This time it was her own glass that Faye refilled. 'And how about your mother?'

'My mother?'

'Still popping in every now and then for a visit?'

'Sort of.'

'Sort of what? Have I got to bloody well drag everything out of you like the Spanish Inquisition? Don't forget ve haf vays of making you talk. Sort of what?'

'That's not the Spanish Inquisition either...' He laughed gently. 'Sort of...sort of different. Promise you won't laugh?'

Faye was lighting a cigarette and she nodded over the flame.

'Well, it's like she comes to see both of us now. Trev too. Maybe just him, I don't know. It's always in the hospital now, in the dream that is, and she's dressed as a nurse. In an old-fashioned nurse's uniform. It's weird.'

'You're telling me.'

'But he's dead.'

'Dead?'

'Yes, lying in the bed with the covers over his head. And it's not really the hospital, more like a cemetery really. Every time I have it I can't wait to get down there. To make sure that he's still alive.'

Faye shivered. 'Christ, that sounds even worse than the other one.' Across the table she took his hand.

'It's horrible. It really is.' Now there were quiet tears on his cheeks. 'I've got to do something.'

'Like what?'

'You tell me. I don't know."

Wasn't it sweet of Charlie to say hello. And Mrs Knox...who'd have thought it?' Faye looked at the photographs again. 'They're all very simple. But the one you chose is nice and plain.'

'They don't go in for anything too fancy up there. It was as much Charlie's choice as mine.'

'He's got good taste.'

'Speaking of which, there's something else. Here.' He took a couple of pieces of paper out of a manila file that lay on the table. 'What do you think of this?' It was another letter from Charlie, this time neatly word-processed.

24 Finlay's Terrace
Glenvie

28th July 1992

Dear Gregory,

It was good to talk to you on the phone last night. I think that you are right, the plain black stone is the best, and no fancy designs on it. It was the one I had picked out myself. I agree that "In Loving Memory", with your mother's name and the dates on it is just about right. I'll get it done.

I thought about something else too. I was reading a collection of old ballads I got out of the Library the other day, and I came across one that I thought was very apt. Very sad. It is very long, so I have just taken a wee bit and made a few changes here and there to make it fit. I have written it out separately. What do you think?

Yours sincerely,
Uncle Charlie

P.S. Say hello to Faye.

P.P.S. As you can see, I've bought a wee computer. Not bad eh? Maybe I'll look into this Internet business next!

On the other sheet of paper, Charlie had typed the following.

Fair Donald died at dead of night,
Sweet Mattie on the morrow;
Fair Donald died for pure, pure love,
Sweet Mattie died for sorrow.

She set her foot unto a stane,
And her back unto a tree;
She sat her foot unto a stane,
And her heart did break in three.

Fair Donald was buried without kirk wa',
Sweet Mattie in the quier;
On Donald's grave there grew a rose,
On Mattie's a bonny briar.

And aye they grew, and aye they threw,
As they would fane be near;
So all the world may plainly see
They loved each other dear.

They grew up to the church's top,
Up to the highest spire;
And grew into a true lover's knot
When they could grow no higher.

Faye read it through twice before she looked up. 'That's wonderful, really something.' She sniffed and her eyes were moist. 'Really. I don't know what to say... God, there's a lot more to that man than meets the eye. And there's a helluva lot that meets the eye... Can I have a copy of this?'

'Aye, I'll do you one, sure. I was thinking of having it framed or something...I don't know. Maybe not. It's not the easiest thing to read.' Gregory drummed his fingers lightly on the table top. With his other hand he gently rotated the wine glass between his thumb and forefinger. 'He's a funny one, though...Internet, indeed. What next?...anyway, I thought I ought maybe to go up and see him. You know, when it's all ready, the headstone, see what he's done... Thanks.' He busied himself replacing the prints and the papers in the file.

'He'd like that, I'm sure. And there's no reason why not.'

'No, I suppose not.'

'If I wasn't so busy I'd fancy the trip myself. I think you should.'

'Maybe I will then. Trevor said he didn't mind.'

'What? For crying out loud, you asked him? What's it got to do with him whether you go and visit your mother's grave? Bloody hell, Greg...'

'That's just what said, more or less.'

'Thank God he's got more sense than you have. I mean...apart from anything else, it's not very fair to him, is it? He's got enough on his plate without...'

'He said that too. Told me not to be such a twat, I believe his actual words were. No, I tell a lie, selfish twat, those were his very words.'

'I'm warming more and more to this man all the time.'

'You'd get on very well.' Gregory stared out into the kitchen interior, reflected in the window. The night beyond was dark and quiet. It had stopped raining. 'But what if...

what would happen if, you know, while I was away, if...'

'Nothing would happen. Don't be so stupid. Yes, stupid. Don't look at me like that, you are being stupid. You can't live your life like that. It's, it's not healthy. Bloody morbid is what it is.'

'Morbid? Stupid? Anything else while you're at it?'

There were lots of things, but Faye didn't say them.

Gregory returned from the toilet where he had taken temporary refuge, waving his hands in the air to dry them. Although he was more than a little drunk, he had the sense to see that it was not the best moment to mention the absence of a hand towel. Faye was still pissed off with him, and not attempting to hide the fact, so he tried another topic. Something on which they might agree.

'Meant to tell you...Ellie was in College the other day. She's starting to show now. Quite big.'

'Good luck to her, if it's what she wants.'

'D'you never think about it? Having a baby, I mean?'

'Yes. Course I think about it.' Faye lit a cigarette. 'But thinking about it's not enough, is it? Takes two, and I've yet to meet number two. But anyway, what's she doing still in work? Shouldn't she be taking it easy, feet up, Art waiting on her hand and foot?'

'That'll be the day. She was with Philip, so I didn't stop to chat. You should've seen the pair of them. Talk about full of your own bloody importance.'

'I'd rather not...talk about it. Change the subject.'

'So what d'you fancy? The weather? Wine? How about soft furnishings? That's always a good one. Or the post-modern American novel?'

'Oh shut up.' Faye went off in search of more to drink.

CHAPTER THIRTY-FOUR

IN LOVING MEMORY

Gregory turned right, between the Flower of Scotland Hotel on one corner and the chemist's shop on the other, just as the man who had given him directions further down the street had said. Up the hill for about a quarter of a mile 'til you come to the playground on the left, then another right turn and you can't miss it.

And he was right, you couldn't miss it. St Benedict's was a small but striking cement and glass construction, white with a bright red-tiled roof. A Mediterranean fantasy upon a theme borrowed from Coventry Cathedral. There it was at the end of the lane into which he had turned, behind a low hedge and a car park. Off to the left, surrounded by tall evergreen shrubs, Gregory could see the head and shoulders of a statue of Mary in pale blue and white.

But it wasn't what he had expected. Too new, 'sixties at the earliest. Gregory parked and got out of the car. He didn't bother to lock the door before walking over to the gate. In plain and simple white letters on black a wooden board identified the building as 'St Benedict's Parish Church, Aught. Re-consecrated 1965', before going on to list the services and name the parish priest. The grounds were clean and tidy, but the car park was small and the hinges on the gate didn't look much used. On the other side of the laurel hedge he could see no sign of a graveyard on either side of the path that led up to the church door. He looked around in the other direction. No sign of anything there which might have been a cemetery either: no headstones, nothing. All this way, and nothing.

The drive up from Glenvie had been long and uncertain. It was now nearly two o'clock and Gregory had left Charlie's house before seven. All the way he had been unsure about where he was going or how to get there. Once off the main road beyond Oban, his road atlas was too large scale to be much help, and he had to rely on some rough sketch maps drawn from an O.S. map which he'd borrowed from Hugh, the cartography technician in the Geography Department. Stupid sod, he should just have bought one.

He wasn't even sure he was heading towards the right Aught. In the Map Room, Hugh had managed to locate three. This was the closest to Glenvie, and Gregory had managed to convince himself that, being on the west, it was the one most likely to have enough Catholics for a church. If he drew a blank at the first stop, he faced the prospect of driving all the way up to the other side of Inverness. That was certainly a lot closer to Forres, the address on Andrew MacLeod's letter, and, realistically, he thought it was the more likely. His heart sank at the thought.

So, all this way, and no graveyard. And no point in dragging it out any longer either. Reversing to head back out the way he had come, Gregory was stopped by a movement which he noticed out of the corner of his eye. Leaving the car where it was, blocking both lane and car park, he walked back towards the church. A small man with a shiny bald head, wearing a dog collar and a black jacket, was carefully closing the gate. From behind gold-framed spectacles, Gregory was regarded by two still and unblinking grey eyes. The priest greeted his visitor in a soft Irish voice.

'Good afternoon my son.' He offered his hand. 'Father Collins. Can I be of any assistance?'

Gregory shook hands. 'I don't know, um...Father. Excuse me, I'm not...I'm not a Catholic, you see, and I'm not sure...what the proper mode of address is.'

'Well, Father will do very nicely, Mister..?'

'Oh yes, sorry. Of course. Alexander, Gregory Alexander.' Gregory managed to resist the impulse to shake hands again.

'Well, now we've got all that out of the way, what can I do for you Gregory?' The priest was smiling, clearly amused.

'Probably nothing at all, I'm afraid. I was looking for a grave, but the church looks too modern for the date I had in mind. And there doesn't seem to be a graveyard anyway.'

'A grave you say? How old would this grave be?'

'Late 'forties.' He had to think for a moment. '1947.'

'Well, you might be in luck. For a moment I thought you meant really old.' Father Collins had begun to move, almost imperceptibly, and Gregory was drawn along beside him. 'The church, do you see, is new. Well, new as the Church sees things.' He laughed quietly. 'Thirty years old now, sure that's no time at all. But what I should say that is that it's the building that's new. Because there's been a St Benedict's on this spot for many hundreds of years.' They passed by the Madonna and walked towards the back of the building. A narrow passage ran between the hedge and the high stone wall which formed one side of the car park. 'The old chapel fell into decay and ruin a long time ago, so it did. Sometime about the end of the eighteenth century, I think, maybe a little later, I'm not exactly sure. I keep telling myself that I should find out more about the history of the place, but, well, I'm not long here myself, and I find that the joys and the troubles of the living have a more immediate call on my time. Anyway, it's an old story. All the people went away, forced off the land, there was nothing here, nobody to worship. And those that would, couldn't. The Clearances, you know. Terrible times. I used to think it was only the Irish had a quarrel with the English, but...I'm not offending you, I hope?' Gregory shook his head. 'Good, good. But you never know, do you? I'm afraid I'm not very good at keeping my trap shut.' Another laugh. 'But where was I? Oh yes. There aren't that many people now, but there are some, not nearly enough, but... Well, I don't want to be bothering you with that. Have you come far Gregory?'

'From near Dumfries, a wee place called Glenvie. I've been on the road since seven.'

'Well then, you'll not be wanting to listen to an old blether like me, so you'll not.' There was a door set in to the wall at the end of the passage, dark brown wood and a heavy iron ring for a handle. 'The old graveyard's in through there. I'm afraid there's precious little of the old church left, just a bit of tumbledown wall, and most of the really old headstones were long since cleared away, but there were still burials up until the 'fifties. Everyone uses the new municipal cemetery these days, of course. It was getting a wee bit crowded in there.' He stopped in front of the door. 'What was the name?'

'Sorry?'

'The grave. Who is it you're looking for?'

'Oh yes, MacKillion. A friend of my mother's.'

'MacKillion is it? Well, ye'll find one or two MacKillions in there right enough.' He looked at his watch. 'Still, I can't be standing round here all day. Hospital visit, you know, and I'm late already.' He held out his hand again and Gregory took it. 'I hope you find the one you're looking for Gregory.' He nodded back the way they had come. 'The parish house is back at the end of the lane, on the left. You can't miss it. If there's anything else I can do for you, I'll be back in an hour or so. Not much longer. And the church is open, if you want a wee bit of peace and quiet.'

'Thanks...thank you, Father. It was a real stroke of luck. I'd have gone away again if I hadn't seen you.'

'Well, you know what they say, don't you my son, about God moving in mysterious ways? Sure who knows? Anyway, always a pleasure to see a new face.'

'It's been my pleasure. I'll just walk back with you and move the car. It'll be in the way otherwise.'

Gregory still wasn't sure exactly why he'd come. Yesterday, with Charlie, he had gone to see his mother's headstone. It was fine. More than fine, it was just right. A plain black slab of polished black stone. In simple letters it read:

IN LOVING MEMORY
MARTHA HUME ALEXANDER
1926-1992

Around the plot was a simple matching stone curb, inside which Charlie had turfed over the naked earth. At the opposite end to the stone was a small stone vase, half buried in the ground. Gregory was well pleased.

Although he had gone to the bother of discovering where Aught was – or where the Aughts were, at least – yesterday he still had no plan to go there. His visit to the Geography Department had been weeks before, and the sketch maps which he'd made then had been lying in the glove compartment of the car, unlooked at, ever since.

But standing by his mother's grave, the black stone and silvery lettering shining under the eaves of the kirk, the idea took form and shape. Not much form and shape, true, but enough. Then it was only really a question of whether it would be the following day or the day after that again.

The decisive thing had been the flowers. They were a mystery to Charlie. 'It's a wee bit strange. This is the third time somebody has left them,' he said. 'There's no card or nothing. Just the flowers. And always roses. The only one I can think of is, well...I don't know if it could be, but, funny enough, Maggie Knox was up here the other afternoon. Said she was visiting the doctor's grave. It's over there...' He nodded in the other direction. 'But I dinna ken...she was coming frae over here when I seen her.'

Gregory knew at once, Charlie's half guess was right. The vase on his mother's grave was full of freshly cut roses: yellow, white, red. Maggie Knox. It couldn't be anyone else.

And so he opened the door in the wall. The graveyard was small, a good bit less than an acre, made even smaller by the jumbled press on every side of stones and shrubs and overgrowth. It had the musty air of a place that didn't catch much of the wind or the sun. Directly in front of the entrance, a low uneven line of rubble masonry with a wrinkled and bent elder tree growing out of it was the old church. That someone persisted in an attempt to keep the place tidy was obvious. Around some of the gravestones – new-looking by comparison with those which were just visible in the surrounding long grass – an area had been cleared, and paths of mowed grass lead here and there among them.

He began with the more accessible plots. They were, indeed, relatively recent: 1946, 1951, 1957. He almost missed what he was looking for. He saw the headstone next to it first: a husband and wife, Oliver Martin MacKillion, died 1946, and Marion Esmée, died 1954. His eye had been peeled for the name Donald and it was only at the second look that he recognised the surname. There, beside his parents, was Donald.

Gregory didn't know what to feel. Didn't know what he did feel. Nothing. Everything at once. The world slowed down and speeded up, all at the same time. Words failed him then, and they would always fail him later on the few occasions when he tried to talk about it.

He hunkered down, resting first on his heels and then on the stone border of Donald's parents' grave. For what seemed like hours he sat completely still. When he finally did stand up, he remained there motionless for a while longer, staring at the inscription on the simple polished black stone:

IN LOVING MEMORY
DONALD GREGORY MacKILLION
1925-1947

Eventually he moved, wiping his eyes as if waking from a deep sleep. Reached into an inner pocket, he took out something, carefully wrapped in tissue. Gently separating it from the paper, Gregory bent down and placed on the grave the single red rose which he had brought from Glenvie. No longer as fresh as it had been yesterday, it was still startlingly vivid against the grass. He stood up again and stepped back, his head down. Then he turned and left.

CHAPTER THIRTY-FIVE

THREE KISSES

The light seemed to come from everywhere. Gregory blinked as he opened his eyes. The blanket was coarse and rough against his chin, the sheets so tight that he could only move his head. There was a noise beside him, on the left-hand side. He could just see Trevor in the next bed, asleep, snoring gently and rhythmically as the nurse who leaned over him gently lifted a hand that hung down and replaced it on the bed.

Gregory closed his eyes just in time as the nurse turned round. He felt her hands, expert and assured, adjusting his bed clothes, loosening and tucking them in again.

'There you are now, not so tight. You'll sleep a wee bit better now.' His eyes were still shut but he felt the warmth of her breath and the weight of her breast on his as she leant over him. Softly she kissed him on the forehead. Then twice more, once on each cheek. 'God bless.' Then she was gone. The light went out.

Gregory eased the bedroom curtains up on one side. It was still raining. More of the same was forecast for the next two days. After that there was a promise of high pressure moving up from the south. It was five o'clock but it was still quite dark. He went back to bed.

Trevor's face was blotched, creased and wrinkled and shiny and smooth all at the same time. What little hair had survived the chemotherapy lay thin and bedraggled across the top of his head. His hands, pink and swollen like grotesque imitations of rubber gloves, were too tender to do much more than rest in his lap. Day after day, when he could find the strength to reach the chair by the window, he searched the horizon, looking for a silver lining which did not immediately turn into a cloud, a mirage which might turn out to be something less cruel than the leaps and bounds of his own wishful thinking. This was where he sat now.

Trevor didn't move or speak when Gregory came in. His visitor was reflected in the glass, a light in the corridor behind him. Outside the clouds were breaking up sooner than expected and the sun was beginning to move shadows across the hospital car park below. When Trevor turned round he was smiling.

'I thought it would be you.'

'Well I said I'd be in to see you today.'

'When did you get back?'

'Last night, late. How are you anyway?'

'So so. Life in the old dog yet...shit, I'd better stop saying that, I sound like a broken bloody record. Good time?'

'Not bad, not bad. The drive home wasn't much fun though. Poured all the way. Apart from that it was fine.'

'No...It's been piss poor here too. Nothing but rain, rain, rain. And then more bloody rain. Tell you what, heard a great joke while you were away.' Gregory did not respond. His eyes were full, his hands and his mouth were empty. Trevor carried on anyway. 'It's one of those things you hear and, you know, it strikes a chord. Rings a bell, like. I suppose it sort of reminded me of my situation for some reason. You've probably heard it.' He looked at his visitor. 'What's the last thing that goes through a fly's mind when it hits a car windscreen?'

Gregory didn't know. He shrugged.

'Its arse...' Trevor started to laugh but never got past the blank incomprehension on Gregory's face. 'You know...God, you're a dull bugger and no mistake. Its arse? Splat.' He smacked the flat of one of his hands gently and gingerly onto the heel of the other. 'Splat!'

It took a few seconds before Gregory got the joke. He started to laugh. The more he laughed, the better it got. Tears began to overflow from his eyes.

Trevor looked at him wearily.

"S'not that fucking funny...'

The tears were running down Gregory's cheeks now. Patients further down the ward looked away from the television to see what the noise was. Gregory didn't care. It was the funniest fucking thing he'd ever heard.